# Edge of the Wilderness

## STEPHANIE GRACE WHITSON

**THOMAS NELSON PUBLISHERS®**

Nashville

Published in Nashville, Tennessee, by Thomas Nelson, Inc.

Unless otherwise noted, Scripture quotations are from The Holy Bible, KING JAMES VERSION.

Scripture quotations noted NASB are from the NEW AMERICAN STANDARD BIBLE®, © Copyright The Lockman Foundation 1960, 1962, 1963, 1968, 1971, 1972, 1973, 1975, 1977. Used by permission. (www.lockman.org)

Whitson, Stephanie Grace.
    Edge of the wilderness / Stephanie Grace Whitson.
      p.  cm.
    ISBN 0-7852-6823-5
    1. Women missionaries—Fiction. 2. Dakota Indians—Fiction. 3. Minnesota—Fiction. I. Title
    PS3573.H555 E28 2001
    813'.54—dc21                      2001030395
                                                CIP

*Printed in the United States of America*

3 4 5 6 7 - 07 06 05 04 03 02 01

2б3P

For Robert Thomas Whitson
1946–2001

my only one

". . . above reproach, the husband of one wife, temperate,
prudent, respectable, hospitable, able to teach, not addicted to
wine or pugnacious, but gentle, uncontentious, free from the
love of money . . . one who manages his own household well,
keeping his children under control with all dignity . . . and
not a new convert . . . and he must have a good
reputation with those outside the church."
—1 TIMOTHY 3:1–7 (NASB)

"This is my beloved, and this is my friend."
—SONG OF SONGS 5:16

Other books by Stephanie Grace Whitson

Prairie Winds Series
*Walks the Fire*
*Soaring Eagle*
*Red Bird*

Keepsake Legacies Series
*Sarah's Patchwork*
*Karyn's Memory Box*
*Nora's Ribbon of Memories*

Dakota Moons Series
*Valley of the Shadow*
*Edge of the Wilderness*

# Acknowledgments

THANK YOU, CHI LIBRANS, FOR CARING ABOUT MY personal universe.

Thank you, Cindy, for keeping me on track professionally with great kindness.

Thank you, IHCC family, for walking through the valley beside us.

Thank you, Whitsons and Irvins, for still being there.

Thank you, dear reader, for allowing me into your life.

Sometimes fiction mirrors life. I wrote the first book in this series, *Valley of the Shadow*, while my husband and I walked through our own valley of shadows as he underwent a bone marrow transplant. When the transplant failed, my beloved and I went to the edge of the wilderness together. And now, we are apart for a few years. Bob is in heaven while I am learning single parenting, widowhood, and full-time writing.

The fact that I was enabled to write two books in the last year has very little to do with any talent of mine and everything to do with the faithfulness of God, who is strong when we are weak, and who loves us enough to fashion trials that teach us to depend on Him. And so I acknowledge the eternal goodness of my heavenly Father and the everlasting rightness of all that He does and that He allows.

> "Although the fig tree shall not blossom,
> neither shall fruit be in the vines;
> the labour of the olive shall fail,
> and the fields shall yield no meat;
> the flock shall be cut off from the fold,
> and there shall be no herd in the stalls:
> Yet, I will rejoices in the LORD,
> I will joy in the God of my salvation."
> —HABAKKUK 3:17–18

# Prologue

"My soul is weary of my life."
—JOB 10:1

MANKATO, MINNESOTA, FEBRUARY 1863

He had bent his back against the winter wind and slumped over his pony's neck, trusting the animal to take him to safety in the midst of a blizzard. He had huddled in a muddy niche high above an iced-over creek while sleet pelted the countryside. But never, in his almost twenty winters of life, could Daniel Two Stars remember cold like this. It seeped through his blanket, penetrated his skin, and left him stiff like the ancient man he had begun to hope he would never live long enough to become. The only good thing in it was that when he was awake, the cold numbed even his thoughts. The effort to survive kept him from roaming through the past collecting bitter memories.

The man shackled to him was his friend. Both in body and mind he was the strongest man Daniel Two Stars had ever known. But since the beginning of the new year the whites called 1863, even Robert Lawrence, formerly known as the merciless warrior Little Buffalo, had given up encouraging those around him. He had become like the rest of the prisoners, crowding around pathetic fires every morning until their day's supply of wood was gone, shivering through the afternoons and evenings. The only relief came when the guards passed out bug-ridden bread and gruel made with half-rotten meat declared unfit for soldiers. But the half-starved Dakota shoved it into their mouths with trembling fingers, hoping it would stay down, not really surprised if it didn't.

They were in prison because of something begun by a half-dozen braves six moons ago. An argument over a few stolen eggs ended in war, with hundreds of Dakota taking vengeance against the whites encroaching on their traditional way of life. No one knew how many had died, but everyone knew stories of atrocities. No one cared if all the stories were true or not. Everyone in power wanted the Indians gone from Minnesota. Many wanted them all dead.

Daniel Two Stars was among the dozens of Dakota men who had refused to fight. A recent convert to Christianity, he did what he could to protect his family and his missionary friends. He managed to avoid disaster—until he made the mistake of trusting the army. Leaving the girl he loved and the children she cared for safe at Fort Ridgely, Daniel had returned north to the Dakota camp planning to interpret for his Dakota friends who did not speak English and the army commission conducting trials. What he did not know was that the army of the Great Father in Washington had redefined justice. Those in power had decided that every Indian was guilty—unless proven innocent.

The irony of his rescue still made Daniel smile a little. While everyone expressed their outrage at the way captive women had been treated, one of those captive women—a spinster missionary—strode up and defended him. "Captain," Miss Jane Williams had said, putting her hand on Daniel's shoulder, "if you harm this man I will shoot you myself!"

Thanks to Miss Jane's testimony, Daniel was declared innocent of any crimes. Again, he stayed to help his friends. But then the missionaries all left to untangle their own devastated lives. Daniel Two Stars's identity was confused with another man named Rising Star. Based on eyewitness reports about Rising Star's crimes, Daniel was forced into prison along with the guilty. Initially he protested. "I know Rising Star. I saw him ride out of camp with Little Crow and the rest of his warriors. He is gone from here." He gave up protesting when an irate soldier named Brady Jensen nearly broke his jaw with the butt of his rifle.

After the trials concluded, the Dakota were divided into two groups. Hundreds of women and children and old men were sent upriver to Fort Snelling. Guilty of nothing, they were still sentenced to life inside a stockade until the powerful could decide what to do with them. Three hundred "guilty" Dakota men were driven like cattle through the streets of New Ulm, a town twice attacked by Little Crow and his hostile warriors during the uprising. White people came out to meet them, raising clenched fists in the air as they screamed for vengeance. Daniel kept his eyes on the road, trying not to hear the words as the throng raged, "Exterminate them!" "Savages!" "Murderers!" He was nearly knocked unconscious when a woman screaming, "They killed my family, they killed my family!" hurled a brick at him.

And yet, as hopeless as things seemed, Daniel found reason to hope. When he was hit by the brick, the man who helped him up was Robert Lawrence—Robert, who had been wounded at the very beginning of the outbreak, whom Daniel had rescued from one of the burning agency buildings and sent north along with his family to Standing Buffalo's peaceful people. Daniel had wondered if his friend had survived or died of the gaping wound in his belly. Robert Lawrence was a true Christian and a leader among the peaceful Dakota. His sudden reappearance in Daniel's life buoyed both men's hopes.

And so, when they finally arrived at Mankato and were crowded into a hastily built prison just west of the city, Daniel joined Robert in praying for deliverance. They were among 303 men sentenced to die by the military court. But the Great Father in Washington had mercy. He delayed the impending execution and demanded evidence to review the cases. Throughout the fall of 1862 Daniel and his fellow prisoners waited while President Lincoln reviewed each case. When he was finished, the Great Emancipator reduced the number to be executed to forty. Daniel and Robert prayed for patience. They prayed for endurance. They prayed for their missionaries to come back to them.

On December 4 of 1862, four months after the uprising, a mob from Mankato threatened to overrun the camp and take justice into their own hands. The prisoners were moved out of tents to a more secure setting inside a low log building positioned on a huge vacant lot that sat between two houses in town. Unable to stand upright along the walls, the men huddled around fires or crouched shivering against the walls under the constant vigilance of three or sometimes four soldiers stationed through the middle of the building. Sickened by the smell of rotten food, unwashed bodies, and illness, the men began to lose heart.

The week before Christmas Daniel and Robert said little. A gallows was being constructed within eyesight of the prison. The pounding of hammers and nails and the scent of fresh-sawn wood filled the air. The forty condemned men were taken away to spend time with missionaries from various denominations. Daniel heard the guards say all but two accepted Christian baptism.

"All I can say," Brady Jensen said when another soldier told him, "is if I see one of them strolling down them golden streets, there's going to be murder in heaven."

On the day of the executions, Daniel and Robert stood shoulder to shoulder, peering through a crevice in the log walls at the gallows. When the military drums pounded out the impending order to cut the rope holding the trapdoors shut beneath the men's feet, Daniel looked away. He leaned his forehead against the rough log wall, wishing he could not hear the crash as those floors dropped away, the odd sigh that went up from the crowd of onlookers. Inside the prison it was deathly quiet for a long while.

Finally Daniel whispered hoarsely, "Do you think they really believed in Jesus? Or were they just agreeing that the white man's God was more powerful than theirs?"

Robert sighed and shook his head. He looked at his young friend. "We will know when we get to that next place and see who is there."

They learned how to accommodate the shackles that joined them together at the ankles so they could slide down the log wall of the prison building and sit without causing cramps in their legs. They did so now. Feeling suddenly cold, both men pulled their worn blankets over their heads. Clouds of moisture rose from the opening in his blanket when Daniel asked, "Now that they have had their revenge, do you think they will let the rest of us go?"

Robert grunted. "We can only pray so, my friend."

Daniel closed his eyes to squeeze back the tears that welled up. He fought the lump rising in his throat. Robert was beginning to doubt. So was he. He was beginning to think they would never be free again.

He wasn't ready. She was walking toward him down the path, and he almost panicked. He shouldn't be here. Not now. Not yet. He glanced down at the greasy spots dribbling down the front of his shirt, the filth splashed across his thighs. He brushed his hand through his matted black hair. It had grown long these past few months. He couldn't remember the last time he'd been near enough water to think about washing it. He looked horrible. He smelled worse. He had to get away. She must not see him like this. But he couldn't move.

How, he wondered, had she managed to find him? Did she know that just the sight of her made him catch his breath? He thought the white antelope-skin dress she wore had been ruined in a fire long ago. She must have found a way to repair it. The fringe down the sides and around the hem of the simple dress swayed when she walked, brushing against her soft skin. He knew the feel of that skin. Just thinking about it made his whole body grow taut with emotion. She hadn't braided her hair. Did she know how he loved it when she let it hang down her back that way, a gleaming, flowing stream of dark silk?

She couldn't see him. Not like this. Not when he looked and smelled like some wild animal. He couldn't let her see him until he could take her in his arms and tell her that the time they'd been apart meant nothing . . . that, just as he had told her on the day he said good-bye, her blue eyes had followed him everywhere, given him hope to live another day.

Why was it so difficult to move? He needed to get away—to get ready—but it was too late. She saw him. He grabbed a hank of matted hair and tried to push it behind his shoulders in a vain attempt to look more acceptable. She stood still for a moment, and then those eyes—those blue eyes that had been with him since the only time he had kissed her long ago—blinked and widened with recognition. The full mouth parted in a smile so beautiful it made him ache with longing. Her eyes filled with tears and she ran to him, threw herself at him, oblivious to all the things that had made him want to run away.

He wanted to bury his face in the river of her dark hair and whisper what he had learned in all the months they had been apart. But something was wrong. He clenched his jaws in an effort to make his arms wrap themselves around her. But he could not move. The words he had practiced for months died before reaching his lips. He heard something—something odd. His head filled with words, pounding against his temples, wanting to get out. The pressure inside his head was infuriating. She was murmuring words of love, touching his face, her gentle fingers stroking his hairline.

Something cold pressed against the place Blue Eyes had just touched.

Two Stars woke to the sound of someone cocking a pistol very near his head. He could feel the cold end of the barrel pressing against his temple. He opened his eyes. He was lying on his back staring up at the sod-covered roof of the prison building.

"Someone wants to talk to you," the soldier grunted. He waved his gun at Robert Lawrence. "And you. Let's go." Two Stars sat up, blinking stupidly as a shaft of bright light streamed in through the doorway. Next to him Robert Lawrence sat up. They looked at each other, frowning.

From where they sat, Daniel and Robert could see the soldier waiting at the door. He wore knee-high brown leather boots with metal tacked over the toes. Dirty blond hair spilled out of his felt hat and over the collar of his blue jacket. *Private Brady Jensen.* He had been one of the guards assigned to the Dakota prison since its creation, and he made no attempt to hide his feelings about Indians. Jensen used his steel-toed boots to stomp rats and to kick Dakota prisoners out of his way with equal relish. Waking a slumbering Dakota warrior by pressing a gun barrel to his temple would give Jensen a new anecdote for the mess hall tonight. Daniel was glad he hadn't shown any sign of fear. He hadn't really been afraid for a long time now. He almost wished Jensen would have pulled the trigger and sent him back to the dream where he could hold Blue Eyes in an eternal embrace.

Fresh snow had added a layer of pristine white atop the frozen sludge surrounding the prison building. Two Stars and Robert struggled for a few feet before adopting the strange hobbling gait that enabled them to follow Jensen through the snow in spite of the irons holding their ankles together. Each man bent down and scooped up a handful of snow. After taking a mouthful, Daniel swiped his face with the rest of it in an attempt to shake off the last vestiges of his dream about Blue Eyes. Snow was filling his moccasins, numbing his ankles and feet.

To the men's surprise, Jensen was leading them to the gate. Two Stars had not spoken English in weeks, and he made little effort now to understand what was being said when Jensen talked to the guard at the gate. Whatever was happening probably meant nothing good for either he or Robert. He glanced behind him at the fenced compound, squinting his eyes and trying to imagine winter camp. The wind shifted and blew the smell of the place at him. He looked down and saw the snow blow away from the faces of two more bodies stacked next to the gate. Any imaginings about winter camp disappeared.

Jensen shoved him ahead, pointing to a two-story stone building just across the street from the prison lot. The men were welcomed inside by a blast of warm air. Someone had fired up a small stove in the center of the large, nearly bare room. Whatever happened, Daniel hoped he would be here long enough to get next to the stove. He had almost forgotten what it was like to be warm.

Three other Dakota men were sitting on the floor near the stove. Jensen stepped back outside without a word. Daniel and

Robert hobbled over and sat next to a half-starved brave about Daniel's age. To the question in Daniel's eyes, the brave only shrugged.

Voices sounded at the door. Jensen swore loudly. "You can't be serious! Who's idea was *that?!*"

When he saw who Jensen was yelling at, Daniel nudged Robert. "I thought he died up at Fort Snelling."

"Rumors," Robert whispered back. "We know nothing except rumors." His voice trembled with emotion as he looked toward Sacred Lodge.

Sacred Lodge crossed the room towards them. He paused and put his hand on Robert's shoulder. "It is good to see my old friend is well," he said, shaking Robert's hand. He nodded at Daniel. "I was glad to know you were not hanged. They had your name on the list." Daniel felt a chill go through him as Sacred Lodge turned away without waiting for his reply.

Walking to the center of the half-circle where the men sat waiting, the brave began to speak. He was middle-aged, lean but powerfully built, and he spoke with the quiet confidence of a man accustomed to leading, accustomed to being followed. Every man in the room knew the history of this half-breed raised by his full-blooded stepfather. Sacred Lodge could have escaped to the north and avoided all the trouble when the uprising began. Instead, he remained, unifying the peaceful Dakota by organizing a soldiers' lodge for peace, gathering and protecting white captives in his camp. Because of his extraordinary actions, General Sibley had offered to let Sacred Lodge return to his farm near the now destroyed Lower Agency. But Sacred Lodge would not leave his Dakota brothers. Instead of returning home, he had gone to Fort Snelling, willingly suffering with them. The prisoners at Mankato had been told Sacred Lodge died there. But here he was, dressed in a soldier's jacket adorned with extra brass buttons, sporting a black hat decorated with feathers.

To Daniel's surprise, Brady Jensen remained by the door, his arms folded across his chest while Sacred Lodge took charge of the meeting.

Everyone present had heard Sacred Lodge's voice ring with the proud authority of a Dakota chief, but today his tone was gentle and persuasive. "In the end of the Deer Rutting Moon," he began, "I went to General Sibley. I had heard that when the weather is warm again, the army will go after the hostiles who have escaped to the north. I was concerned for my peaceful brothers who are still wandering around the country. I told General Sibley that if he would let me, I would choose worthy Dakota men to go out as scouts and convince these friendly Dakota to come in where they will be safe."

Big Amos tried to say something, but Sacred Lodge motioned for him to be silent as he continued. "I said we would also help the army chase down any hostiles still in this territory. And I told the general that when the warm moons come these scouts could lead him to the camps of the warring Sioux." He paused, taking time to look into each man's eyes before continuing. "This seemed good to the general. But he said he must write the Great Father in Washington and ask him about it." Sacred Lodge smiled. "The Great Father thought it might be all right."

Daniel felt a surge of emotion. Did Sacred Lodge mean they would be leaving this awful place? He tried not to let the hope rise too high. He glanced at Jensen who had uncrossed his arms and was standing, his fists clenched, his face a mask of disgust.

"The five men I chose pleased General Sibley." Sacred Lodge paused and looked down at the four men seated around the stove. "But when I learned that you five were here at Mankato, I said that I wished also to take Daniel Two Stars, Robert Lawrence, Big Amos, Spirit Buffalo, and Good Voice Hail with me."

Jensen snorted loudly and rubbed his nose.

Sacred Lodge continued. "The General asked, 'Do you think

it is a wise thing to take full-blooded Dakota Indians out of prison and turn them loose as scouts so soon after what happened?'"

Daniel bent his legs and hid his face by leaning his forehead onto his knees. Robert shifted his position to accommodate Daniel's movement, although he chose to look Sacred Lodge in the face.

Big Amos interjected, "The General is such a *wise* man. He understands that *all* mixed-bloods are good Indians and *all* full-bloods are bad." It was an attempt at humor, but no one laughed.

"When they doubted me," Sacred Lodge continued quietly, "I told him he should not think of all full-bloods as hostile or all mixed-bloods as good. I said you five men are more steadfast and more to be depended upon than many of the mixed-bloods in the peace camp."

Daniel looked up at Sacred Lodge as he concluded, "General Sibley listened to me. We have permission to go."

Big Amos snorted in disbelief. He waved a broad hand in the air. "The general speaks and suddenly Dakota prisoners may take horses and guns and ride away?" Looking at the other four men, he said, "You know what I think? I think they want us to go outside Mankato so they will have an excuse to kill us."

Sacred Lodge sat down before them. "They aren't giving us horses or guns here in Mankato. We will ride in wagons that glide over the snow—with soldiers as a guard. Once we have made camp at Rice Creek they will leave us with horses and guns. Then we will be free men, my brothers."

Daniel heard Jensen swear under his breath. He stomped out the door and shouted for someone to take over guard duty while he went to talk to the commanding officer.

Sacred Lodge repeated, "We will have horses and guns, freedom to hunt—"

"—freedom to hunt our friends," Big Amos said bluntly.

Good Voice interrupted Big Amos. Nodding toward the log

prison barely visible through the filthy windows, he said, "Part of what Sacred Lodge says sounds good to me." He looked up at Sacred Lodge. "I want to be a free man. But I could never bring my peaceful brothers to a place like this." His voice lowered. "Better they die than come here."

Sacred Lodge argued gently. "Any peaceful Dakota we find will camp with us until spring. Then all Dakota will be going to a new reservation. Even the ones at Fort Snelling." He stood up and began to walk slowly around the little circle of men as he spoke. "Our frightened brothers who are still wandering around the country need to hear this good news. There is a place where they will be safe both from soldiers and from the hostile Sioux who hate them for not fighting."

Good Voice reasoned, "If we help Sibley find the hostiles, perhaps the Great Father in Washington will let us have a home again."

"You will be able to keep any horses you capture," Sacred Lodge said quickly. "And guns. And they are sending a cook with us."

"You mean we won't have to *kill* our bread before we eat it?" Big Amos joked.

"You must promise the army to stay for six moons," Sacred Lodge explained. "They will give you uniforms now. Horses and guns once we reach camp. They will pay seven U.S. dollars a month in wages. And," he looked at Robert and Big Amos, "the scouts' families will join them in camp."

Daniel jerked his head up and looked at Robert. He saw the emotion flashing in his friend's eyes, and spoke up immediately. "Robert and I will go."

Good Voice joked, "Daniel and I have no wives. Will they bring us one?"

"When do these come off?" Daniel asked, rattling the chain that joined him and Robert together.

The guard who had replaced Jensen didn't speak Dakota. Still, he knew what Daniel was asking. Holding up a small brass key he said in English, "If you swear allegiance to the United States, those come off now. Scouts leave at dawn tomorrow."

Daniel looked up at him, studying the young face, wondering if what sounded like kindness in the yellow-haired man's voice was real. The soldier met his gaze honestly and pressed his thin lips together in a faint smile. When Daniel and Robert slid their feet across the floor toward him, he knelt, quickly unlocking the shackles. When the other new scouts followed suit, he worked quickly, tossing the shackles in the far corner of the room with obvious relish. He inspected the spot where Good Voice's ankle had been rubbed raw. "I'll get the doctor over to look at that before we leave in the morning," he promised. He smiled at Good Voice. "Can't have a lame scout."

"Wait here until I come back," Sacred Lodge said. The men waited, moving as close to the stove as possible, rubbing their ankles, grunting with satisfaction as they walked about the room, free of chains for the first time in months. Big Amos leaped off the rough board floor and stomped around the room in an exaggerated dance that made the other men laugh under their breath.

Daniel wrinkled his nose as the five men's unwashed bodies began to warm up and sweat. He looked down at his filthy hands and ran his hand over his matted hair. Glancing toward the blond-haired soldier who was standing near the door sucking in fresh air, he felt ashamed.

Sacred Lodge returned followed by a dozen soldiers carrying stacks of blankets and clothing. They brought in buckets of snow and set them around the stove to melt.

Brady Jensen dropped a half-used bar of lye soap at Daniel's feet. "See you don't *eat* it. It'll gnaw a hole in your gut." He stomped off, commenting to the blond-haired soldier about the stupidity of wasting soap on filthy savages. Once the men had washed and donned their outdated army uniforms, their clothing was burned in a bonfire just outside the front door.

That night they ate army rations for supper, stuffing themselves with fresh boiled beef and potatoes and corn bread until their bellies swelled. One by one they staggered away from the stove and fell on their bedrolls with satisfied sighs.

Late in the night, Daniel woke thirsty. He took an empty pail and stepped to the door, asking permission to get more snow. Once back inside he set the bucket on the stove and crouched down, waiting for it to melt. His first taste of the ice-cold water reminded him of a spring bubbling out of the earth near one of his family's favorite campgrounds. He remembered following the stream of water from its source all the way to a lake they called Singing Waters, then alongside the lake and across the prairie to another creek and thence to Broken Pipe's trading post. He had visited the trading post often with his friends Otter and Red Thunder, who enjoyed flirting with Genevieve LaCroix, the trader's beautiful daughter.

The fire was dying again. Daniel looked outside. Snow was falling thicker and faster. Someone inside the log prison across the street was wailing a death song. It had become a familiar sound. Daniel looked toward the door. The guard stationed there was sitting on an upturned barrel, half asleep. Beyond him was the town of Mankato, and beyond Mankato, Fort Ridgely, and beyond that, far to the north, he imagined his friend Otter still living the old way, hunting buffalo, making war against his enemies. Somewhere out there, beyond Mankato and Fort Ridgely, was a beautiful half-Dakota, half-French girl named Genevieve LaCroix, whose dazzling blue eyes had once promised him everything a man could want.

After swallowing another mouthful of icy water, Daniel lay down. Pulling a buffalo robe around his shoulders, he stared into the darkness, wondering if the scouts would eventually revisit the agency and the nearby mission where he had once attended school. Someone had told him all the old mission buildings were gone now, burned to the ground along with the agency that had stood only a few miles from the mission. He wondered if the cabin had been burned down, and smiled at the memory of the strong-willed Miss Jane Williams. He thought about the vine that nearly hid the front of her cabin and the little bird that flitted around the flowers hanging on that vine. They were the color of the setting sun, beautiful against the plain wooden cottage. He remembered standing beneath that vine in the moonlight, with Blue Eyes staring up at him, breathless with emotion.

Try as he would, Daniel could not completely conquer the sense of hope threatening to overtake him. For a long time now, God had not seemed to hear the prayers he and Robert Lawrence prayed daily. But just when he had determined to stop praying, Sacred Lodge had arrived to take them out of prison. Perhaps it was a new beginning. Perhaps, Daniel thought, he would find peace wandering the places that, like him, had once been filled with life, but were now ruined and empty.

## One

"For he saith to the snow, Be thou on the earth."

—JOB 37:6

"YOU SURE IT'S THERE?" ROBERT LAWRENCE LEANED toward Daniel, screaming above the wind.

"It's there." Daniel hunkered down in the saddle, dipping his nose beneath his upturned collar, trying to protect his frost-bitten ears.

They were half ashamed, this handful of Dakota scouts sent out earlier that day to reconnoiter from the camp down by Rice Creek. They had grown up in this land, knew it as well as any-one. Should have known when the wind shifted. Should have seen the wall of dark clouds and headed back to camp. But Brady Jensen thought he had picked up a fresh trail. He cursed their cowardice. Said he wouldn't quit because of a little snow. So they followed him past the old mission and around the edge of the lake.

When the wall of snow first slammed into them they weren't all that concerned. Late spring snows weren't anything unusual in Minnesota. No one wanted to give up on the first good trail they had located since being sent up here a few weeks ago. They wanted prisoners to hand over to General Sibley in the spring. And no one had proof that Little Crow had actually left the area. It might be Little Crow himself they were trailing. And so they had kept on until the wind began to freeze their noses and their horses floundered in blizzard-deep drifts.

Once Jensen relented, once they realized they needed to find shelter, someone mentioned old Fort LaCroix. The trader had been dead a while. No one knew if it was even still standing. Hostiles might have burned it on their way north. But if even one of the buildings still stood, it might save their toes—maybe even their lives.

Their leader, a man named Daniel Two Stars who spoke in grunts and stayed to himself, said he had been to Fort LaCroix more than once in the old days before the war. He said they were close. They all knew he was the best tracker among them. They had grown to trust him. So they followed him blindly through the snow.

Dumb luck or answered prayer. Take your pick. Either way Daniel slid off his bay gelding and, after feeling his way a moment, shouted for help. He and Robert worked feverishly, clearing away a drift and then pulling a rickety gate toward them. The men stumbled into a deserted compound that had once been the best-stocked trading post in Minnesota. Presently they were shaking the snow off inside a barn with stalls enough for each of the six horses and even a few piles of old hay in the loft above. By nightfall, with the storm still raging, they had knocked apart old

LaCroix's table and started a fire in the stone fireplace inside the trader's own cabin.

Empty tin cans scattered across the floor told them others had taken shelter inside the compound in the past. When they heard something skitter across the ceiling, one of them charged up the stairs to the loft and returned with a huge raccoon, which they promptly killed, skinned, gutted, and roasted over the fire.

As night fell they stretched out atop their bedrolls around the fire. It had been known to snow for days when one of these storms stalled over Lac Qui Parle. There would be plenty of time to see what else old trader LaCroix might have left behind.

After everyone else was asleep, Daniel crept away from the fire. When none of the other men moved, he crouched low and made his way to the room at the back of the cabin. He sat down on the straw cot eschewed by the men as the probable residence of a few thousand fleas. Glancing behind him to make sure no one was watching, he leaned toward the wall and pulled the mattress up, disturbing a field mouse. As the mouse scampered across the floor, Daniel withdrew the book he had left there in the ancient past. He stroked the smooth leather cover, remembering the day he and Otter had come here seeking Etienne LaCroix to give him news of his daughter down at the mission school. They had found him dead and buried him on the hillside outside the stockade next to his Dakota wife, Good Song Woman. And then they had returned south to the mission school where Daniel told the young woman with the huge blue eyes that her father was dead. It was the first time he had held her in his arms. Even now he could remember how right it had felt.

He opened the book and turned the pages, finally concentrating on one illustration, a sketch of Blue Eyes as a girl. Her father had drawn a tangle of dark brown hair falling across one shoulder. His sketch captured the slight dimple in her chin, the featherlight eyebrows arching over those unforgettable eyes. Her expression in the drawing was defiant. Daniel had seen that look more than once. He knew just how she looked when she was afraid too.

A cold draft blew through the room, and he reached up and rubbed his left shoulder. It always seemed to ache worse when the weather changed. He looked down at the scar running from his elbow to his wrist, remembering when, half-crazed with pain from a gunshot wound to his shoulder and the ensuing fever, he had awakened in a missionary's barn. When a girl came in to milk a cow, he had grabbed her ankle in a desperate, wordless plea for help. That was when the missionary's white dog slashed his arm open. He remembered little else of that day until he woke beneath a warm blanket beside the fireplace in the missionary's cabin. Drifting in and out of consciousness, he had begun to call the girl Blue Eyes. He had continued to do so even when he realized she was Genevieve LaCroix, the daughter of the trader up north.

As he sat on the edge of the now dead trader's cot staring down at Genevieve LaCroix's face, Daniel closed his eyes, relishing the emotion that welled up inside him. The longing was so intense it was almost physically painful, and yet it was the first thing that had sliced through the dullness that had overtaken him in the recent weeks. Perhaps, he thought, he could come alive again, after all.

Looking down at the drawing he reminded himself, *You are dead to her now.* Sacred Lodge had told him his name was on the list of the men to be hanged. Blue Eyes would probably have heard that. She would think him dead. It was probably for the best, he told himself. The children they had protected during the uprising would give her life new meaning. The missionary Simon Dane would want her. His wife was dead. His children loved Blue Eyes.

Daniel turned his thoughts away from the idea of a union between Reverend Dane and his Blue Eyes. He thought about the white baby they had rescued from a deserted cabin during the uprising. If no one claimed the child, her presence would provide a link between them that would transcend everything that kept them apart. Even if Blue Eyes thought him dead, she would look at the child and remember him. That would have to be enough.

*She has friends and children who love her. She is safe somewhere far away from all this trouble. You have no home and no future beyond tomorrow. You are dead to her . . . and that is good.*

Still, when he got up to return to his pallet by the fire, Daniel tucked the book that held her image into the wide blue sash wrapped around his waist.

# Two

"Lord, make me to know mine end,
and the measure of my days, what it is."
—PSALM 39:4

"MA-MA-MA-MA-MA." THE BLONDE-HAIRED CHILD THEY
had come to call Hope pulled herself up to the kitchen chair
where Genevieve LaCroix sat shelling peas.

"Ma-ma-ma-ma," Hope said a little louder, rocking back and
forth on her bare feet and patting Gen's yellow calico skirt with
one dimpled hand.

Miss Jane Williams swiped a bit of dried food off the canning
jar she was washing and winked at Gen.

"Ma-ma-ma-ma!" Hope shouted gleefully.

Miss Jane blew her frizzy red bangs out of her eyes. "Bossy
little miss wants her mama to pick her up."

Gen swallowed, surprised at the lump in her throat, the tears filling her eyes at Miss Jane's use of the word *mama*. She ignored Hope's hand drumming on her skirt just long enough to strip the last five pea pods of their treasure. Then she swept Hope up and sat her on the edge of the table before her, leaning forward to rub noses and kiss the toddler on her cheek.

"I'm not your 'ma-ma-ma,' little doll," Gen said softly, pulling Hope into her lap.

"Closest thing to a mama she'll ever have," Miss Jane interjected. She continued scrubbing jars as she added, "And I imagine her first mama is looking on from glory and thanking the dear Lord for sending you and Daniel Two Stars up to that cabin."

Gen smiled sadly. She lowered Hope to the floor, then extended one finger of each hand for the child to grasp. Hope pulled herself up immediately and began to march across the spotless board floor. As she followed Hope, Gen murmured, "Sometimes I wonder if Hope's mother would be all that happy to have *me* raising her child—after what happened."

"You don't have any more relation to the Indians who killed that baby's mama than I have to President Lincoln," Miss Jane said firmly. "And if you and Two Stars, God rest his soul, hadn't wandered up to that homestead a few days after the murders were committed, Hope wouldn't even be alive. And look how she adores you. Can't anyone argue with that. I'd say the good Lord provided Hope a mother . . . and," she said with conviction, "I'd say He did a good job choosing."

Gen had reached the screened back door of the kitchen, following Hope's baby steps across the kitchen. "I'd say the good Lord did a similarly good job when He led Rebecca and Timothy to you, Miss Jane." She guided Hope back toward the table and sat down again.

Miss Jane snatched a linen towel down from the shelf above the sink and began to dry the clean canning jars. She sighed.

"Thank you. I have to keep reminding myself that Rebecca and Timothy are only mine temporarily." She shook her head. "I just don't understand why someone in St. Louis hasn't responded to any of Reverend Dane's letters to the newspapers." She paused for a moment, absentmindedly putting one hand in her apron pocket. "You'd think anyone with relatives in this part of the country would be desperate to know about them—and thrilled to hear about children who survived."

"I don't understand it either," Gen agreed, handing Hope a wooden spoon and bowl to play with. "Simon has written so many letters about the Suttons—and Hope." When Hope began to beat on the upturned bowl, Gen grinned at Miss Jane. "It would be just *awful* if we had to keep them, wouldn't it?" She bent down and tapped on the bowl, creating her own rhythm along with Hope.

Hope dropped the spoon and, placing her little hands on either side of Gen's head, grabbed two hands full of thick dark hair and pulled. Gen protested, "Ouch! That hurts!" and scooped the toddler off the floor and back onto her lap, whereupon the child reached into the bowl before her, grabbed a handful of raw peas and shoved them into her mouth. Gen laughed. "If only Two Stars could see what a scamp he rescued!" She ducked her head and swiped unexpected tears away with the back of one hand.

"It's perfectly natural to grieve, Gen. You needn't be embarrassed with me," Miss Jane said gently.

Gen sighed. "I *have* grieved. I was very nearly a complete idiot for two whole months." She caressed the back of Hope's pudgy hand and said quietly, "Simon shouldn't have to put up with any more of this."

"Reverend Dane doesn't consider himself to be 'putting up' with you, Genevieve," Miss Jane said gently.

Gen blushed and led Hope in a rendition of patty-cake before setting her back down on the floor. "Can you watch her while I pick more peas?" she asked. "We have at least four more rows ready. With the weather turning so warm, they won't last much longer."

Miss Jane nodded and set a pot of water on the stove to boil. "I'll get these blanched and put up while you're outside."

But Gen paused at the doorway. Turning around, she asked abruptly, "Does God—does He ever ask His children to do things they really don't want to do?"

"Constantly," came the abrupt reply. Miss Jane looked over her glasses again. "Does that surprise you?"

Gen shook her head. "Not really. At the mission school we memorized all kinds of verses about giving one's life to save it, and sacrificing yourself." She sighed. "But I'm new at really wanting to *live* what the Scriptures teach. Sometimes I think I'll never learn it all." She bit her lower lip.

"What is it, dear?" Miss Jane prodded. "You know you can ask me anything."

"What about the promise that He will give us the desires of our heart? Doesn't He *ever* give us what we want?"

Miss Jane dried her hands and leaned against the sink while she talked. "I don't think that promise means God gives us what we want. At least not in the way you mean. I think it means He shapes our desires. And He does give us everything we *need*. We need to be loved. God gives us His perfect love. We need someone to share our lives with. God promises to never leave us. We need to know who we are, why we are here, where we are going. God tells us."

"I know all that," Gen said impatiently. "I was talking about more practical things. Everyday things."

Miss Jane bent down and picked Hope up. "When God says *no* to something His children *want*, it is because He has something better for them. It's not just a cliché, Gen. He does what is best. Always."

"Did you feel God was doing what was best for you when your fiancé died?" Gen asked abruptly.

Miss Jane shook her head. "No. I didn't."

"But you feel that way now?"

Miss Jane didn't hesitate. "Yes. Absolutely." She kissed Hope on the cheeks, gave the baby a cracker, and set her back on the floor. "If I had married Andrew, I would never have become a teacher." She looked at Gen with a mischievous smile. "And I am a *much* better teacher than I would ever have been a wife." She sighed, picking up a fresh dish towel. "Don't misunderstand me. It took a while before I stopped longing for the leeks of Egypt. Even after twenty years, there are still times when I don't especially *like* being a spinster. But this I know: in a hundred million years, it will not matter if I was Mrs. Andrew Ganesborough. It *will* matter if I stepped through the open doors God gave me after He called Andrew home to heaven." She smiled at Gen. "God was patient and He brought me through. He will do the same for you."

Gen leaned against the screen door, her hands behind her back. "Simon wants me to marry him."

"Of course he does," Miss Jane answered matter-of-factly. Her blue-gray eyes sparkled with amusement.

Gen looked at her, startled. "You aren't surprised."

"Not in the least," Miss Jane said. "Everyone has expected it."

Gen sighed. "He asked me weeks ago." She walked back to the kitchen table and sat down. "Nina Whitney once told me a marriage doesn't have to be based on romance to be right."

Miss Jane nodded. "I've seen many good marriages that began as friendships. So have you."

Reaching up to touch the frill of lace at her throat, Gen said quietly, "Last week, after we went down and saw the prisoners from Fort Snelling leave for the new reservation, I came back here and took that beaded necklace—the one Two Stars gave me—I took it off. Hearing the Dakota singing after all they'd been through—I told you how it affected me. I felt a new determination to have my life count for something. I even pictured myself putting my future in my hands and tossing it up to God—the way Mrs. Riggs said she used to do with her burden for her Indian students at the mission." Gen continued to fumble with the lace on her collar. "I thought the thing I could do to count for God was to marry Simon and be a mother for the children. I even waited up for him to come home from a meeting one night. I was going to tell him. To say yes." Gen's voice quavered. "But when I heard his steps come up the walk, I . . . I just couldn't go through with it." She looked at Miss Jane and drew her dark eyebrows together in a little frown. Then she blurted out, "I'm very fond of Simon. We could have a good marriage. A very good friendship. But—" Her face grew red with embarrassment.

"Go on, dear," Miss Jane said gently. "Get it out."

Gen sighed. "I want more than just a *good* relationship with my husband. I want what my parents had. They were—" She dropped her hand away from her collar and reached up to tuck a strand of dark hair behind one ear. "One night when I was little I heard an odd noise. When I realized Papa wasn't getting up to check on it, I crept down the ladder to get him. But when I got to the doorway to Papa and Mother's room—" She grinned sheepishly at Miss Jane, then shrugged. "The next day, I began to see things I had never noticed before—Papa winking at Mama in the morning; the way his hand lingered on her waist; the way she smiled at him after supper some evenings." She shook her head and brushed her hand across her forehead as if to erase the thoughts. "Tell me what to do, Miss Jane. Tell me what *you* think."

Miss Jane gestured toward a kitchen chair. "Sit down, dear," she said, taking Gen's hand as soon as the girl obeyed. She waited a moment before speaking. "You have been through a great deal in the past two years of your young life. First your father virtually forced you to leave home and go to school, and then he died before you ever got to see him again. Then you traveled back to New York with the Danes, and Mrs. Dane died. You arrived back in Minnesota only to be taken captive by your own people. And then you lost your first love when they mistakenly hanged Daniel Two Stars. As if that weren't enough, everything in *all* our lives is a muddle right now. Our missions are destroyed. We are living in temporary quarters with Samuel and Nina Whitney and we have three orphaned children to care for." She patted Gen's hand. "It's no wonder you can't decide what to do. Give it time, dear." She asked, "Is Reverend Dane pressuring you?"

Gen shook her head, clutching her hands in her lap. "No. He's just"—she took a deep breath—"he's just *there*." She shivered slightly. "I feel him watching me."

"Like your papa watched your mother?" Miss Jane asked with a smile. Without waiting for Gen to answer, Miss Jane said, "You can't expect him not to *look* at you, Gen. You didn't refuse his proposal. And you are a beautiful young woman—all that dark hair, and those eyes." She continued, "And as if it weren't enough for you to be so attractive physically, you are by far the best person to satisfy his fatherly concern for his children." Miss Jane smiled. "You must remember that he's caught up in the same uncertainties as the rest of us. No congregation to preach to. No students to teach. No real schedule to keep. About the only thing the poor man can see clearly is that you love Meg and Aaron and they love you. You can't blame him for wanting to settle his personal life."

"But—" Gen protested quietly.

Miss Jane held up her hand. "Let me finish. I'm certain Reverend Dane's love for you will make him want what is best for *you*. He'll wait while you sort things out." When Gen didn't budge, Miss Jane added, "I'm sorry I don't have anything more earth-shattering to advise, Genevieve. God has placed you here, for this moment, among children who need loving in a house that needs keeping—" At the sound of children's voices just outside, Miss Jane finished, "—and peas that need picking." She picked up the empty pot and handed it to Gen. "Very often I've found that in simply *doing the next thing* God has given me to do, His will is revealed." Miss Jane patted Gen's shoulder. "Give it time, Gen. While you wait, just do the next thing. Harvest the peas. God will eventually show you what must be done about Reverend Dane. If He can turn the heart of kings, He can turn the heart of one slightly defiant Dakota-French nanny." She winked as four children clattered up the back stairs and into the kitchen.

Dark-haired Timothy Sutton threw his arms around Miss Jane. "I can write my *name*, Auntie Jane. My whole entire name, first and last and everything!"

Timothy's older sister Rebecca, bronze-haired and dark-eyed, corrected her brother. "In *cursive*, Timothy. That's even more special." She looked at Miss Jane soberly. Witnessing the murder of her parents by Dakota warriors had settled the mantle of parenthood over Rebecca's thin shoulders only a few months ago. She would never return to innocent girlhood. "Was there any mail?" she asked.

Miss Jane shook her head. "Not yet, dear."

Twelve-year-old Aaron Dane interjected wisely, "It takes a good while for letters to come from St. Louis, Rebecca."

Rebecca shifted her gaze to the ceiling, then to Timothy. "Yes, but it only takes a few *minutes* for a telegraph message. And the reverend said he requested a prompt reply. Those were his exact words. Anyone would know he meant to telegraph." Her voice wavered. "Anyone who really *cared* about lost relatives would—" She stopped abruptly. "Are there more peas in the garden?" she asked Miss Jane in a perfectly calm voice. "Timothy and I can pick them."

"Me, too!" Meg Dane said quickly. She slammed her books down on the table. "I'll help!"

"Not before you all have some milk and cookies," Miss Jane said. She walked across the room into the pantry. Reappearing with her arm wrapped around a large gray-and-blue crock, she removed the lid and frowned. She bent her head and peered fiercely at the children over her gold-rimmed glasses. "Now *who* do you suppose ate the last one?"

Timothy giggled. Two brown curls on either side of his head bounced as he pointed to the taller boy next to him. "Aaron did it!" When Aaron nudged him, Timothy added, "But I helped."

Miss Jane sighed. "The guilty must be punished." She set the crock on the table and pointed to Aaron and Timothy. "You'll have to make more."

Grinning, Aaron began to roll up his sleeves. Timothy headed for the pantry to get flour and sugar.

"Cook-eeeeee!" Hope shouted suddenly, pointing at the crock.

Everyone's eyes grew wide as they stared, disbelieving, at Hope.

"Cook-eeee," Hope repeated firmly.

"The cookies are all gone, Hope," Rebecca said, showing the baby the empty crock.

Hope thrust her lower lip out. She looked up at Gen mournfully. "No cook-eee, ma-ma."

The four children clustered around Hope.

"Say Aa-ron, Hope." Aaron leaned down and peered into the baby's face.

"No—" Meg shouldered Aaron out of the way. "*Meg*. Say *Meg*."

Aaron picked up Hope and headed outside. "I'm teaching her to say my name first!" he taunted the other three, just as Reverend Dane came up the back steps.

"Hope can talk!" the children shouted gleefully. "She called Gen *Mama*. She said *cookie*."

Simon took off his hat and grinned at the baby, who poked his cheek with a chubby finger.

From where she sat at the table, Gen watched Simon smiling at Hope. Suddenly the children grew quiet. Simon blinked in surprise.

Aaron spun around. "Gen! You won't believe it. She called Father *Pa*."

# Three

"If any man come to me, and hate not his father, and mother, and wife, and children, and brethren, and sisters, yea, and his own life also, he cannot be my disciple."

—LUKE 14:26

"I'LL BE ALONG IN A WHILE, SAMUEL." SIMON STOOD at the open church door, bidding his fellow missions committee member good night. "I need some time alone to think about what we discussed tonight."

From where he stood on the church steps, Samuel looked up at the full moon just visible through a break in the thick clouds hovering over St. Anthony. He adjusted his oversized hat. "I know you are hesitant to venture off without your children, Simon. But even if they went down to Davenport with you, they wouldn't see much of their father. You'll be spending nearly every waking hour with the prisoners. The board is right to urge you to leave the children here and to go alone—at least initially. Once we know the fate of the prisoners, you'll have a better idea about where to settle your family. For right now, St. Anthony is the best place for them. Nina and I are delighted to have them stay." He reached out to put his hand on his friend's bony shoulder. "You know we all look on your children with great affection. What with Miss LaCroix and Miss Williams's attentions, I daresay your main worry will be how to abide them after they've been spoiled within an inch of their lives."

Simon nodded. "But I still want to pray on it." He stepped back into the church.

With a sigh, Samuel handed a ring of keys to his friend. "You'll lock up then?"

Simon nodded again, closing the door firmly before Samuel could say anything more. With his back against the door, he stared across the entryway and into the dimly lit sanctuary. *Why was it,* he wondered, *that empty churches always seemed to give him such comfort?* He entered the sanctuary, pausing beside the last pew to look up the aisle toward the pulpit. It was a simple church. No stained-glass windows soared heavenward. But tonight the clear six-paned windows gracing the west wall were bright with moonlight. And just enough light shone to illuminate the simple cross hanging above the baptismal to the left. His eyes on the cross, Simon made his way to the first pew and sat down. Before he had a chance to pray, a verse of Scripture came to mind: *All things work together for good to them that love God, to them who are the called according to his purpose.*

Simon leaned back against the hard pew rubbing his hands together.

All *things. Not just the things you understand, Simon.*

Not certain whether he was talking to himself or hearing some inner voice of God, Simon thought, *But they want me to leave my children, Lord. And Genevieve.*

*You've been praying about returning to the Dakota people for months. They need you now.*

Simon knew it was true. He *was* needed down at Camp McClellan. At the meeting tonight, there had been great concern for Reverend Masters. All the long months while the Dakota men were imprisoned in Mankato, Reverend Masters had faithfully walked the fourteen miles from his home in St. Peter to Mankato in all kinds of weather, arriving in Mankato on Wednesday and staying through the weekend, conducting meetings and teaching before walking back home for a rest the following Monday. He had kept the grueling schedule from December until April when the men were moved to Camp McClellan above Davenport, Iowa. He was exhausted. It was time for someone to relieve him. Would Simon go and help? the board had asked at tonight's meeting. No one knew how long he would be needed, but they hoped he could leave for Davenport before the end of May.

*This is the way, Simon. Walk ye in it. I cause all things to work together for good.*

Simon ran his hand over the gray stubble sticking up out of his nearly bald pate and sighed. He had much to be thankful for. No one knew that more than he. Patient, loving, kind Ellen Leighton had married him without knowing she was getting a self-righteous, noisy gong of a pastor for a husband—a man who was cold and indifferent to emotional need. Not until Ellen died early in 1862 did Simon realize how much he had depended on her. But by shattering the world Ellen had created around Simon and their two children, God began transforming him.

Six months after Ellen's death, Simon thought he might finally have changed enough to be of some real use among the Dakota people. But then that world was shattered too. It was August of 1862 and Simon had just begun a promising work in a new Dakota village when the Minnesota Sioux uprising occurred and everything about the Dakota Mission was thrown into utter chaos—chaos that was not yet resolved, even nine months later.

*All things work together for good to those who love Me, Simon.*

Simon looked up at the cross. *Yes, Father.* He began to think over the good that had come from the uprising. He was separated from his children at the outset, but God protected Meg and Aaron. They were with Genevieve and Miss Jane through the entire ordeal. And just when things seemed their worst, Daniel Two Stars appeared in camp and helped them escape to the safety of Fort Ridgely.

Unable to find Meg and Aaron, Simon had become involved in events that continued to mold him into a better man. After he helped a group of mission workers escape to safety, somehow God had given him the idea of attaching himself to the troops as a chaplain and going with them after the hostile Dakota. Simon knew it was God working in his life, because nothing could have been more unlike him. He had always been a man of books— never a man of action. But the outbreak changed that. Once physically weak and indecisive, Simon became lean and muscular. Living among profane military men forced him to learn a new kind of leadership. And while he was changing he learned to trust God in ways he would never have thought possible. He prayed day and night for his children and Genevieve LaCroix, *Lord, I believe . . . help Thou my unbelief.* He knew he shouldn't doubt, but it had always been his nature to be a little suspicious of God, wont to confine Him to the attributes of righteousness and justice, tempted to forget His love and mercy. After all, he reasoned, he had prayed desperately for Ellen, and she died. At the time of the outbreak he was still a little suspicious of God, wondering if negative answers to prayer might be his lot in life. But when Simon prayed for his children, God answered with a resounding *YES!* Eleven-year-old Aaron and five-year-old Meg returned to him physically whole and remarkably unscathed emotionally.

Leaning back in the church pew, Simon smiled and counted God's blessings off on his calloused fingers. Neither son nor daughter hurt physically. Neither one damaged emotionally. His prayer life renewed. Self-righteousness nearly conquered. Usefulness enhanced. Simon listed blessing after blessing, good after good, praising and thanking God for it all. But still, even after he spent time thanking God, there was the dread at the center of his being, the awful reluctance to leave St. Anthony.

He leaned forward and rested his elbows on his knees, putting his head in his hands. *I've just gotten a family again, Lord. After all the weeks of separation and fear, after all the grieving for Ellen. You have given me a family again. Surely You cannot mean that I should leave them. Not now.* He finally whispered aloud, "I know I shouldn't ask, Father, but I can't seem to conquer these feelings. Please, God. Give me time to win Genevieve's heart. Just let me stay a while. After she says she'll marry me, then I'll go. Is it too much to ask?"

The phrase *feed my sheep* rang in his mind.

*I have fed Your sheep, Lord. I've been doing it ever since we came to St. Anthony.*

It was true. Together with the Whitneys, Simon had given relief to many of the white victims of the uprising. He and Aaron had driven literally hundreds of miles to deliver supplies and relief funds from sympathetic eastern churches. It was good work. He did it heartily and was blessed to learn that his son had a remarkable gift of mercy. The boy might be only twelve years old, but he had lived through things that either matured or destroyed children. In Aaron's case, they matured him. In many ways Aaron Dane was already a young man.

*I sent you to the Dakota Mission, Simon. FEED MY SHEEP.*

Before the native prisoners were moved, revival had come to the camps at Fort Snelling and Mankato. Men who had never been open to the gospel message were asking to be baptized.

Praying. Taking communion. It was a miracle. Workers were needed. They were barely able to keep up with the demand for books, for Bibles, for teachers. Mission teachers Miss Huggins and Miss Stanford had already left to work with the women at Fort Snelling and had been with them when they transferred to steamships to be taken to Dakota Territory just two weeks ago. Miss Jane would be going, too, as soon as Rebecca and Timothy Sutton's situation was resolved. In many ways it was one of the most exciting times in the mission's life. How like God, Simon thought, to do His best work when everything was in a shambles from a human perspective. *I know that's often how God works. I shouldn't wait for things with Gen to be resolved. I just need to trust Him and get on with it.*

But when he thought of Camp McClellan, he couldn't help shuddering with dread. Two hundred Dakota men had been transferred there from Mankato. In Mankato they had been shackled to one another and fenced in like cattle. Treated worse. Falling victim to disease and dying—a few every week. There was no reason to think Camp McClellan would be any different. But they needed him. For the first time in a quarter-century of Dakota mission work, the Indians actually *wanted* missionaries. And if it were not for his children, for Gen—

*If any man come to me, and hate not his father, and mother, and wife, and children, and brethren, and sisters, yea, and his own life also, he cannot be my disciple. And whosoever doth not bear his cross, and come after me, cannot be my disciple. All things work together for good to those who are called. And I am calling you to Mankato.*

Sighing, Simon stood up. He stared for a few more moments at the cross. Then he made his way down the aisle and out into the foyer. Shrugging into his worn coat he stepped out onto the front stoop and pulled the church door closed behind him and locked it. It had begun to rain. He turned his coat collar up against the light wind and headed up the street, past neat brick homes as far removed from the log cabins he had inhabited over the past few years as the moon above was from the earth. If it stopped raining, he would take the children fishing tomorrow. Perhaps Gen would go along. They could picnic beside St. Anthony Falls.

Simon shoved his hands in his pockets and headed up the street toward the Whitneys'. When he arrived, he paused to look up at the rambling two-story frame house. It was another example of God's blessing. Samuel and Nina had been sent west from Illinois to help with the relief effort for white refugees from the southwest corner of the state. They agreed to rent the house almost on a whim, simply because it was offered so cheaply they could not resist. But once they were ensconced in the small quarters at the rear of the first floor with their two small children, they began to wonder about the wisdom of taking on such a vast property. God verified their choice by proceeding to fill the rest of the house. Two displaced Dakota Mission teachers, Lizzie Huggins and Belle Stanford, arrived first. Next came Miss Jane Williams with young Rebecca and Timothy Sutton in tow. And, finally, Simon and company.

Simon walked slowly up the steps and opened the door as quietly as possible, pausing in the entryway just long enough to hang up his coat and hat. At the bottom of the soaring staircase he removed his worn-out shoes. He looked around him, thanking God that his children lay safe in warm beds just upstairs. Then he felt ashamed, knowing that at this very moment Dakota children were dying of disease and neglect while their fathers and brothers were held at Camp McClellan. While they were still in Minnesota, the men had engaged in a lively correspondence with their families in Fort Snelling. Dr. Riggs said he once transported two hundred letters back to Fort Snelling in one week. Simon wondered how the two groups would communicate now that they were so far away from each other.

At the doorway to what he had come to think of as "his girls'" room, Simon paused. He turned the doorknob slowly. Careful to stay mostly out in the hall, he peeked around the door and toward where his precious Meg lay asleep, her red curls spilling over her pillow. It had stopped raining. Moonlight poured through the one tall window in the far wall. Perhaps a picnic would be possible, after all.

To his right, baby Hope lay asleep in the crib they had managed to cram between the doorjamb and the corner of the small room. A soft, rhythmic gurgling accompanied her thumb-sucking. Simon smiled to himself and started to back out of the room. But then he allowed himself one look back to where, next to Meg, lay the real reason he did not want to leave St. Anthony.

She had come to Simon and his wife nearly three years ago, the autumn before the uprising. She boasted the flowing dark hair and rich brown skin of her Dakota mother. But Genevieve LaCroix had none of her mother's placid nature. She had been forced to stay with the Danes by her determined French father and she did not hide her reluctance. Love for her father and loyalty to her dead mother's wishes made her stay with Simon and Ellen Dane, made her study and learn, but love and loyalty could not keep the emotions raging inside her from shining in her brilliant blue eyes. Simon smiled to himself, remembering Genevieve's defiance in the face of what she considered to be his willful ignorance of the Dakota people. *You think everything Dakota is bad,* she had yelled at him one night long ago. She had been so furious she had stomped her foot as she accused him, *You think everything Dakota should be forgotten.*

He hadn't appreciated hearing it one bit. Mostly because he had realized she was right. He had spent ten years among the Dakota and managed to learn very little. Only Ellen's death had ripped him out of himself and down to earth where he could forge a real relationship with his orphaned children and a new life as a true shepherd among the Dakota. And that, he owed to Genevieve. He longed to cross the room, to reach out and run his hand through the torrent of dark hair. He loved the two narrow streaks of white that had appeared at her temples during the weeks of her captivity. She had earned them protecting his children. Every time he saw them, his heart swelled with gratitude and love.

He closed his eyes for a moment, remembering the emotion that had overwhelmed him when, after weeks of uncertainty, he saw her, unhurt and healthy, safe at Fort Ridgely with Meg and Aaron, holding a blonde baby in her arms that she and Daniel Two Stars had found, miraculously alive in a ruined cabin. They had named the baby Hope and to Simon she had become almost a symbol of the future family he hoped to create with Gen.

*This will not do,* Simon said to himself sternly. He jerked his head out of the room and closed the girls' door firmly, standing with his head bowed for a moment while he tortured himself with memories. After being reunited at Fort Ridgely, Simon had taken his family to St. Peter for a few weeks. Aaron read the paper the day after Christmas and saw Daniel Two Stars's name on the list of the condemned. Screaming "No!" Gen leaped on Simon's horse and tore across the country to try to stop it. But she arrived too late. He found her, pale and trembling, seated on a board-walk, her head in her hands.

Simon had never seen grief like that before. It nearly killed her. In the weeks that followed she grew so thin her clothes hung on her. She trembled with weakness and fear at every loud noise. Once, he found her hiding between the bed and the wall, her hands over her ears, her face streaming with tears.

And then . . . and then they had come to St. Anthony, been reunited with the other teachers, and slowly, over the past few weeks, Gen had come back to him. She began to smile again. She began to eat. Her slim figure filled out. Her blue eyes shone with health and a newfound peace. She laughed as she worked with the children.

Sighing, Simon ran his hands over his face and headed down the hall to the room he and Aaron shared. *Genevieve.* He whispered it aloud, listening to the beauty of the French name as it floated into the night air. She had been there when Ellen died. Had loved his children and waited patiently for him to recover. And when, instead, he sank deeper into self-pity and grief, she had pulled him out. She had set him straight and pushed him toward his children. How he loved her for it. Loved her for crying in his arms when overwhelmed by her own grief, loved her for listening as he read the Psalms to her in a desperate attempt to help her.

Simon crept into his room. Disrobing in the dark, he once again made the case for why Gen should marry him. They shared so much. And yet, Simon thought as he laid his head on his pillow and turned his face to the wall, he knew that Genevieve LaCroix had never once looked at him the way she had looked at Daniel Two Stars. Perhaps she never would. He punched his pillow and closed his eyes. He would not pressure her. He would give her time. By God's grace, he would be patient.

But dear God in heaven, he prayed, how he loved her. How he longed to—*This will not do.*

Just before he fell asleep, Simon decided. He would go to Davenport.

*Four*

"The way of a fool is right in his own eyes."
—PROVERBS 12:15

"ARE YOU OUT OF YOUR MIND?!" MAJOR ELLIOT LEIGHTON nearly jumped out of the seat he occupied in his mother's opulent New York dining room.

Margaret Leighton glared at her son and glanced meaningfully toward the massive cherry-wood sideboard where the kitchen maid was preparing their after-breakfast coffee.

Elliot grabbed the gold damask napkin off his lap and dabbed at his mouth. He smoothed his black mustache around the sides of his mouth. "Aren't you finished with that coffee yet, Betsy?" Elliot watched with satisfaction as a blush spread across Betsy's cheeks. She quickly picked up the sterling-silver coffeepot and filled the two waiting cups. As the aroma of fresh coffee filled the room, Elliot smiled to himself. He had been right, of course. The little busybody was lingering to hear the rest of his disagreement with his mother.

Neither Elliot nor his mother spoke until Betsy had set a steaming cup of black coffee at their places and, with a nervous little curtsy, backed through the door into the butler's pantry. Adding two lumps of sugar to his coffee, Elliot said, "You cannot be serious, Mother. It is absolutely out of the question for my sister's children to be raised in the howling wilderness of Dakota Territory by a half-breed savage."

Margaret sputtered, "Genevieve LaCroix is *not* a half-breed savage! Why won't you believe me, Elliot?" She reached up to brush a wisp of white hair out of her eyes. "I won't deny that last year when Ellen wrote that she and Simon would be bringing one of their students here, I had my doubts about housing an Indian. But, Elliot, Genevieve was nothing like what we have read in the papers. Everyone here was impressed with her."

Elliot harrumphed and stabbed the meat on his plate. Stuffing it in his mouth, he chewed, staring defiantly at his mother.

Seeing that her pleas were having little effect on her eldest child, Margaret pressed on. "She *is* half French, you know. And Miss Bartlett had only praise for her as a student." She pleaded, "You weren't here, Elliot. You didn't see. Simon was completely undone when Ellen died. If it hadn't been for Genevieve, I honestly do not know what would have become of Meg and Aaron. She brought Simon back to his children." Margaret's deep brown eyes filled with tears. "It was so touching, Elliot. Truly. Simon became a *father* after Ellen died. And Genevieve made it happen."

Sarcasm dripped from every word as Elliot enjoined, "You mean the great, the all-righteous, the holy Reverend Dane came down from his throne?"

"If only you had seen it, Elliot, you wouldn't be so disbelieving. God worked a miracle in Simon. And He used Genevieve to do it. The children adore her. She was practically their mother already by the time they left for Minnesota last August." Defiance shone in her eyes as she said, "I think Simon *should* marry her." While her son snorted his disapproval, Margaret withdrew a rumpled envelope from a pocket. She laid it on the table and pushed it across toward Elliot. "Read for yourself, son. You'll see how the children feel about her."

"Children haven't the slightest idea what's best for them," Elliot said crisply. He ignored the envelope, reaching for a biscuit instead. Cutting it in half, he slathered it with butter. Taking a huge bite, he spoke as he chewed. "At least that's what my mother told me when she packed me off to a military academy against my wishes." He swallowed and stared across the table at his mother with icy gray-blue eyes.

Margaret paled and bowed her head. She fumbled with her napkin and blinked back tears.

Taking a boiled egg from a silver bowl to his right, Elliot laid it on his plate and began to tap the shell with the back of his spoon. "It's all right, Mother," he said. "I'm not chastising you." He sliced the egg in half and removed the shell from each half with one hand. "In the end, you were vindicated. Military life suits me. Or should I say *suited* me." His mouth turned down at the edges. "What a pity I won't be able to continue the family legacy of stellar military careers." He ran his hand through his long white hair.

The gesture sent a pang of grief through Margaret Leighton. She had given a healthy, raven-haired son to the Union. The Union had taken him first to Bull Run, then on to Shiloh. And on Bloody Monday, down at Antietam, the Union had taken his left forearm and hand, turned his hair white, awarded him a medal, and then handed him his discharge papers.

"You have served the cause well, Elliot," Margaret said gently. She ran a finger absentmindedly around the rim of her coffee cup as she said, "I'm very proud of you, son. As is the entire village. As would be your father and your grandfather if they were still alive." Margaret looked up. Her voice trembled as she said, "What you gave to preserve the Union can never be repaid."

Elliot shrugged and took a swig of coffee. He looked down at his empty left sleeve and pulled the end of it across his lap before picking up his fork and stabbing a piece of boiled egg.

The simple gesture brought tears back to Margaret's eyes. She looked away for a moment. When she could speak again without emotion clouding her voice, she said, "You gained a reputation for levelheadedness and compassion as an officer, son. Please don't allow what you have read about the West—about Indians— to cloud your reason."

Elliot set down his fork and ran a finger down a column of the newspaper that lay open on the table beside him. "Listen to this, Mother. It's an eyewitness account of the recent release of a few white captives who were separated from the main group and kept all winter:

The poor creatures wept for joy at their escape. They had watched for our coming for many a weary day, with constant apprehensions of death at the hands of their savage captors, and had almost despaired of seeing us. The woe written in the faces of the half-starved and nearly naked women and children would have melted the hardest heart.

He continued, "This article speaks of wide, universal, and uncontrollable panic all across the southeastern corner of Minnesota. It says more than five hundred people were murdered, and it describes every mode of death that horrible ingenuity could possibly devise." His eyes flickered with rage when he looked up at his mother. "When I think of my sister's children, my own niece and nephew being subjected to that—" He shook his head.

"There are other stories, Elliot," Margaret argued. "Stories of heroism and bravery—"

"Oh yes, I know. I know. The noble savages who protected the helpless whites."

"Don't be sarcastic!" Margaret snapped. "Simon wrote that one of them saved the children. At great risk to himself."

"It doesn't matter," Elliot said firmly. He took another swig of coffee before continuing. "I was too young when Ellen married to do anything about her foolish choices. I was away fighting for the Union when she died. Then I was in that godforsaken military hospital for an eternity. But I am well now, and I will *not* sit idly by while her children wander along the edge of the wilderness with their weakling father and his half-breed concubine."

"Elliot!" Margaret's voice trembled with anger. "Stop it. Simon may have had his weaknesses in the past, but he has done nothing to deserve such contempt. He is a good father and a sincere minister of the gospel. Genevieve LaCroix is a woman of impeccable character."

Elliot smirked. "Excuse me if I prefer to believe the obvious about the self-righteous reverend's true reasons for keeping Miss LaCroix close by."

Margaret frowned. "What do you mean?"

"I mean that after a conspicuously proper period of mourning, the reverend has conveniently found it to be God's will that he warm his bed with a beautiful young woman."

Margaret inhaled sharply. Two circles of bright red color appeared on her already rouged cheeks. Removing the napkin from her lap she slapped it down on the table and stood up. "That will do, Elliot. You may be thirty-five years old, but you are still my little boy, and I'll thank you to keep such improper thoughts to yourself."

Elliot mumbled a halfhearted apology.

Margaret sat back down. She pushed her plate away before saying, "You seem to think that I am a complete idiot, swayed by romantic notions about noble savages and superhuman missionaries. I'm not a fool. I had months to observe both these people. And I'm telling you that your evaluation of them is wrong." She took a deep breath and leaned forward.

Elliot got up and poured himself another cup of coffee. Leaning against the sideboard he said, "You are happy, then, for the Reverend to be hauling Aaron and Meg off to Dakota Territory to be raised in the wilds? You think that is a proper fate for your grandchildren?"

Margaret hesitated. She shook her head. "I've never been *happy* about Aaron and Meg being so far away. That's why I prevailed upon Simon to send them to me for their higher education."

Elliot nodded with satisfaction. "Good. Our reasons may differ, but in the end we agree on what must be done. Aaron must certainly be ready for more schooling than they can provide in Dakota. And I can probably convince Meg to come at least for a visit." He walked to the end of the table and put a hand on his mother's shoulder. "I've booked passage west, Mother. I'm bringing Ellen's children home where they belong."

"You—you've *what?*" Margaret looked up in disbelief.

"Booked passage west." Elliot patted his empty sleeve. "As soon as I get fitted for my hook, I'm headed west. I've been rattling around home long enough." He strode to the door and paused. "If the Reverend Dane has changed as much as you say, he'll do what's best for the children. He can't possibly believe it's best for Ellen's children to grow up among savages. Once I'm there, he'll listen to reason." He smiled at his mother. "And however civilized the reverend's dusky maiden may be, I doubt she really wants to raise two white children she didn't know existed until last year." Elliot picked up the newspaper and tucked it beneath his arm. "Trust me, Mother. Everything will be fine."

*Five*

"Lying lips are abomination to the Lord:
but they that deal truly are his delight."
—PROVERBS 12:22

"AND SO YA' SEE, REVERAN', WE JUS' HAD TO COME AND
see if the baby is our little Charlotte Marie." The unkempt man
who had appeared at the door introducing himself as Harlan
Potts of Dayton, Ohio, leaned forward. Resting his dirty shirt
cuff on one knee he reached into his frayed pocket and withdrew
a strip of rolled-up tobacco.

Just as he opened his mouth to take a bite, Simon interrupted
him. "If you don't mind, Mr. Potts, we don't allow tobacco of any
kind in the house."

Mr. Potts bit thin air. His Adam's apple bobbed up and down
as he swallowed, then nodded vigorously. "Oh. Sure. 'Scuse me,

Reveran'. Shoulda known that." He shoved the plug of tobacco back into his pocket.

Simon settled back in his chair, trying to hide his nervousness. He looked out the window, praying that their outing with a group of church friends would keep Gen and the children away until—well, until he could think what to do. He cast a prayer for wisdom and patience heavenward. *The very thing we've feared has come upon us, Lord. Help. Please help.* At least, he thought, the Pottses had arrived before he left for Iowa. At least Gen didn't have to deal with them.

The birdlike woman with the dark circles under her eyes sitting next to Mr. Potts coughed none too daintily into a gray handkerchief. She leaned against her husband to catch her breath. Potts shifted uncomfortably in his chair. When he felt Simon's gaze on him, he put one arm around his wife. "There, there, Sally, darlin'." He looked up at Simon. "She's been feelin' poorly for some time. Seems like ever since we read the awful news of the uprising. She took it hard, thinkin' on her own sister out in the West, right there in the center of things. We woulda come sooner, but we had to save up money for passage upriver."

"Where exactly did you say your sister and her husband located their homestead?" Simon asked.

"Don't know as we can say 'zactly," Potts said, scratching his chin. "Somewheres near the agency."

"The Yellow Medicine or the Redwood?" Simon asked. When Potts responded with a blank stare, Simon said, "There were two agencies a few miles apart. Which one were your relatives near—the northern or the southern agency?"

"Well now," Potts said, twirling his stained felt hat in his hands, "Sally's kin didn't write regular, you know. There was only the one letter tellin' us how they was settled and the baby was a little girl."

"When can we see her?" the woman intoned abruptly, her

eyes pleading. "I'll know soon as I see that baby if she's my sister's. Blood tells."

Simon cleared his throat. "She's on an outing with the rest of the children." He looked down at the floor, his heart beating. *And dear Lord, please keep them there.* "We've become very fond of Hope. My own children think of her as a sister."

Footsteps sounded in the hall and Gen peeked in, Hope in her arms.

Hope pointed at Simon. "Pa!" she shouted happily.

With a glance toward the Pottses, Simon stood up. "Excuse me. I'll just—"

But before Simon could wave Gen and the baby out into the hall, Potts jumped up and whirled around. "That's her, ain't it, Reveran'?"

Instinct made Gen put a protective hand on Hope's shoulder.

"Come in, Genevieve," Simon said, crossing the room to cup his hand under Gen's elbow.

Her heart pounding, Gen walked across the room and perched on the edge of an empty chair with Hope on her lap. She looked at Simon uncertainly.

Simon cleared his throat. "The Pottses saw my notice in the Dayton newspaper. Apparently Mrs. Potts's sister and her husband were settled somewhere across the river from one of the agencies. They had a child—a girl. Mr. and Mrs. Potts are hoping—"

Potts leaned forward, tilting his head and inspecting Hope carefully. He looked back at the woman seated next to him. "That's her, ain't it, Ma?" he said, grinning and nodding. "The spittin' image of your own sister, ain't she?" Potts reached out to touch the baby's cheek.

Hope frowned at him and leaned away. "No!" She clutched Gen's shoulder tightly and hid her face against Gen's neck.

Gen stared at the Pottses and then at Simon. She swallowed hard. "I was—I was j-just putting Hope down for a nap."

"Oh," Mrs. Potts crooned, "don't take her away so fast. Can't we jus' hold her for a minute?" She held out her hands, imploring.

Gen looked at Simon. When he nodded encouragement, she struggled to unleash Hope's death grip on her dress. "It's all right, Hope. Say hello." In spite of Hope's protests, Gen handed the child over to Sally. Hope strained to get away, reaching for Gen and screeching, "Ma! Ma!"

Finally, Mrs. Potts set Hope down on the floor. Immediately, the baby crawled to Gen and pulled herself up, demanding to be held.

"It'll take her a while to know us, I 'spect," Harlan said. He shook his head. "We hardly slept these past nine months, worryin' over our own kin." He turned to Gen. "You the one that saved Charlotte Marie?"

Gen shook her head and opened her mouth to speak, but Simon interrupted her. "Actually it was a Dakota Indian named Two Stars. He stole a canoe and took Genevieve and my children out of the captives' camp under cover of darkness. They traveled downriver toward Fort Ridgely by night and hid during the day. One morning, they found they had spent the night just below a deserted cabin. It was growing colder, and Two Stars went up to the cabin hoping to find some blankets. He found the man dead out by the barn. The woman was in the house, curled around her child. She'd been scalped. Of course Two Stars thought the child was dead, too. But Hope was only asleep." He continued, "Two Stars and Genevieve buried the couple beside their house. They couldn't find anything that identified the family." Simon asked abruptly, "Do you have children, Mr. Potts?"

"Sally and me ain't been blessed."

"Where do you work?"

"Wherever," Potts said. He began to twist his hat in his hands. "Unloading at the railway station. Hauling for one or t' other."

He swallowed hard. "They's plenty of jobs about, what with all the young fools goin' off to fight."

"It has been a terrible time for our country," Simon said carefully. "My late wife's brother lost a hand and part of his arm at Antietam."

Potts reacted quickly. "Well, the fact is I woulda volunteered by now, if it weren't for my Sally here bein' so poorly." He rushed to add, "But then I wouldn't have been at home to read your notice, Reveran'."

Simon nodded. "You know, Mr. Potts, my son and I have made more than one trip back to the cabin looking for the surveyor's stakes. We never did find them. We advertised in the Dayton newspaper based on a neighboring tract of land." Simon paused. "It's not uncommon for settlers to come in groups. I hoped that might be the case with this situation. I've been writing letters to the Dayton newspaper for months. I had just decided we could give up the search in good conscience—we'd done all we could to locate Hope's relatives. It's a wonder—since you were so worried about your wife's family—it's a wonder you didn't see my notice before now."

Potts cleared his throat. "Well, now. Fact is I don't read the newspaper all that often."

"Now Harlan," Mrs. Potts blurted out, nudging him. "You know you cain't read a-tall." When her husband glared at her, Mrs. Potts blushed and averted her eyes.

Harlan cleared his throat. "Sally and me was upriver all winter with my kin. We got back t' Dayton last month and I heard someone talkin' about all the orphans in Minnesota. Then I heard 'em talkin' 'bout your notice," he said quickly. "And I rushed right down to the newspaper office to have them read it to me."

Simon nodded. He stood up abruptly. "Why don't you see to Hope's nap, Genevieve? And I'll—I'll make us all some tea." He looked at Mr. Potts. "Or coffee?"

"Coffee," Potts answered gruffly.

"Coffee, then," Simon said quickly. He helped Gen up and turned to the Pottses. "If you'll excuse us for just a moment—"

He could feel Gen trembling when he cupped his hand under her elbow and guided her to the door. Hope had snuggled into Gen's shoulder and was nearly asleep.

"Simon," Gen whispered brokenly the moment they were outside.

"I know." Simon nodded.

Gen blinked back tears.

"Take Hope upstairs to bed. Then meet me in the kitchen." He made his way down the long hall.

Gen went upstairs and laid Hope in her crib. Covering her with the new quilt she and Miss Jane had just finished, she prayed desperately, *God—dear God—you can't mean for those people to have her. You can't.* She slipped out of the room and down the back stairs leading directly to the kitchen.

Simon had stirred up the fire in the stove and set a pot of water on to boil. As soon as Gen came into the kitchen he asked, "Are the rest of the children—"

"Having a wonderful time. They won't be back any time soon. I only came home because Hope was exhausted and she was so fussy she was ruining everyone's fun." Gen inhaled sharply, trying to smother a sob.

Simon set the coffee grinder on the table before her. Gently taking her hand, he motioned for her to grind the coffee. "Don't cry, my dear."

Gen closed her eyes, inhaling the aroma of fresh ground coffee beans. Presently she retreated to the pantry to get four cups and saucers, sugar, a tray. When a cup hit the floor and shattered, she slumped in a chair. "I can't," she croaked. "I can't be hostess to people who are determined to break my heart."

Simon knelt before her and picked up a piece of the broken

cup. "No one is going to break your heart, Genevieve." He reached up and laid one finger on her chin, forcing her to look at him. "Something isn't right here. The Pottses claim to have been desperate to have news of their relatives. And yet they didn't see my notice in the newspaper. Don't they have *friends?* Wouldn't someone have told them about it before now? And they don't even know which agency the homestead was near." He stood up and began to pace back and forth. "Did you watch Mrs. Potts when I described the scene Two Stars found? The woman bawled like a calf when you handed her a baby she'd never seen. But when she learns that her own, supposedly very beloved, sister has been scalped and left to decompose—she doesn't flinch." Simon shook his head. "Something isn't right. I can sense it."

"What—what can we do?" Gen asked nervously.

"I'll think of something. For now let's serve the coffee." When Gen went to pick up the tray, Simon intervened. "Let me get it." He smiled down at her. "*One* broken cup is quite enough to have to explain to Mrs. Whitney."

When Gen and Simon reentered the parlor, Mrs. Potts squeezed a tear out of one eye and dabbed at her face while she made a strange mewing sound. "Poor orphaned baby," she muttered. "Poor Charlotte Mary."

"I thought you said your sister named her child Charlotte *Marie*," Simon said while Gen poured coffee.

With a fearful glance at her husband, Sally Potts nodded. "That's right. Charlotte Marie. My sister's name was Charlotte Mary."

"Mr. Potts," Simon said as he handed Potts a cup of coffee, "I must tell you that it has been a shock to both of us having you suddenly appear at our door expecting us to give Hope up."

Simon sat down. "Do you happen to have any family records with you? Anything that might help us verify Hope's parents' names so we can check the land office records more carefully?"

Potts squinted at Simon. "What kind of family records?"

"A Bible. Church baptismal records. Something like that." Simon looked down momentarily and then smiled. "You say your sister wrote about the baby. Perhaps you have the letter?"

Mrs. Potts rolled her eyes toward her husband.

He cleared his throat nervously. "We didn't keep the letter. But that's Charlotte Marie or my name isn't Harlan Potts."

"Please don't take offense, Mr. Potts," Simon said. "It's just that we must be careful—for the child's sake."

Potts seemed to relax a little. Sitting back in his chair, he rubbed his chin with the back of his hand.

"You wouldn't want us to just hand your niece over to anyone who came knocking," Simon continued.

"'Course not," Potts agreed.

"Well, then, please don't take offense when I say I am somewhat disturbed by a few things." Simon stared at Potts as he enumerated, "You don't seem to know the exact location of the homestead. And you didn't keep the one letter your beloved sister-in-law wrote."

"Now look here," Potts said, shifting nervously on the couch.

Simon pressed on, "You must understand, Mr. Potts, that we love Hope as if she were our own child. The fact is," he said firmly, "we really aren't prepared to give her up at all. Not without some very convincing proof that we must."

Potts glared at Simon for a moment. He stared across the room at Gen and then back. Anger flickered in his deep-set eyes. Mrs. Potts swallowed hard and stared down at her hands.

"The news that your brother-in-law was murdered, your sister-in-law scalped, left you strangely unmoved."

"I was tryin' not to embarrass *her*," Potts protested, nodding toward Gen. "Anyone can see she's part Injun'." He looked back to Simon. "And anyone can see you two ain't even married, so don't be talkin' to me about lovin' my Charlotte Mary—uh, Marie—like she was your own. You got no claim to bein' anybody's *parents*, unless the church has changed its rules about sich things since I was a boy in Sunday school."

Simon got up and stood behind his chair. His pale eyes flickered angrily as he asked, "Let's get to the business at hand, Mr. Potts. Exactly how much were you expecting us to pay you to take the next steamship back to Dayton *without* Hope?"

"A child oughter be with her kin," Mrs. Potts whined. She raised the handkerchief to her face and began to cry. "Oh, my poor dead sister . . ."

"Will you hush up?" Potts said, elbowing her. Instantly, she quieted. Potts studied Simon, whose gaze didn't waver. Finally, he looked at Sally. "We ain't here to do harm by the child, are we, Mother?"

"'Course not," Sally said.

Potts sighed. He leaned back on the sofa and contemplated the ceiling. After a moment he said, "It don't take a genius to see that Charlotte Marie's attached to ya both." He ran one hand through his greasy hair, then licked his lips before continuing. "Fact is, Reveran', now that we come all this way and we see what a fine house little Charlotte Marie has and all—" He cleared his throat.

"How much, Mr. Potts?" Simon said. He added, "You have no documentation of who you are. You have no proof of anything. But in the interest of settling this peaceably, I'd like to hear the figure you had in mind when you headed our way."

"Five hundred dollars," Potts said abruptly. The woman next to him gasped and stared at him wide-eyed, but she did not protest the idea of losing the opportunity to take "precious Charlotte Marie" back to Dayton.

Simon didn't hesitate. "Done. I'll have legal papers drawn up to reassure us that you won't rethink that figure when you get halfway to Dayton. Can you meet with me at my attorney's this evening?"

Potts ignored Simon's insult and nodded.

"Then I'll show you out." Simon gestured toward the door.

Gen closed her eyes and leaned back in her chair, willing herself to be still when all she wanted to do was throw her arms around Simon Dane and—the front door closed, and she waited for Simon to reappear. When he didn't, she went out into the entryway. She called his name, but the house was obviously empty except for her and the sleeping baby upstairs. Simon's hat was missing from its hook by the door.

"Ma-ma-ma-ma-ma."

The sound of Hope's voice echoed down the broad upstairs hall. With a last glance at the empty hook by the door, Gen headed upstairs.

Six

"For the wrath of man worketh not the righteousness of God."

—JAMES 1:20

EDWARD POPE WAS TERRIFIED OF "THE HOS-TILES." He was a miserable horseman and a worse shot. But Edward could cook. It wasn't long after their arrival in the scouts' camp north of Fort Ridgely that Edward had earned a Dakota name. Little by little, the scouts added to Pope's combined sleeping quarters and kitchen until he occupied a shelter that would have arguably survived a hundred-year blizzard. Edward Pope became the universal favorite in camp, and the scouts made certain he— and Brady Jensen—knew it. Those who could speak English talked to Pope—unless Jensen was within earshot.

"You don't worry about bad Indians, Good Soup," Big Amos

was heard to say. "We not taking you to scout. You be safe here in camp. You make good food when we come back with bad Indians."

As the weeks went by, Edward began to think that "his boys" were exceptions to everything he had been taught about Indians. They were clean, honest, and, in Pope's mind, exceptionally brave. They handled horses better than any cavalry officer Pope had ever seen. More than once he watched in openmouthed amazement as they performed their version of a cavalry drill, clinging to their horses' sides as the animals charged across the landscape at full speed.

Pope's admiration for the scouts came full circle one evening when he was ladling stew into Big Amos's bowl and asked shyly, "You think I could learn to talk Injun?" He hesitated. "I ain't never been too smart, but I'd like to be able to talk to the boys what don't know English."

Big Amos's eyes widened with surprise. Instead of answering, he looked down at Daniel Two Stars, next to him in line. "*Wicaste kin waste*," Big Amos said, nodding at Pope. *He is a good man.* Not knowing what Big Amos had said about him, Pope blushed furiously and busied himself with cleaning a rabbit one of the scouts had brought in earlier in the day.

It wasn't until after the rabbit stew had been consumed and most of the Dakota scouts had rolled into their blankets and gone to sleep that Daniel and Big Amos approached Pope's shelter. Seating themselves beside his cooking fire, they motioned for Pope to join them. Daniel held up his left hand and raised his thumb. "*Wanca,*" he said. When Pope just stared at him, Daniel motioned for the man to raise his hand and extend his thumb. Nodding when Pope did it, Daniel extended his index finger and said, "*Nonpa.*"

"Oh, I get it," Pope said, grinning. "You're teachin' me to count Injun'!"

"*Dakota,*" Daniel said gruffly. He continued counting, waiting for Pope to repeat each word, "*Yamni, topa, zaptan . . .*"

After a few minutes of practice, Daniel grinned at Pope. Mimicking the boy's accent, he said in English, "For someone who 'ain't never been none too smart,' you learn Dakota fast."

❦

West Point-trained Brady Jensen had relived the infamous cornfield scene from the Battle of Antietam a thousand times. What if he *had* run away in the face of the onslaught of rebels. Hadn't dozens of other men done the same thing? They called it Bloody Monday. Twelve thousand men had died. Jensen was sorry his commanding officer had lost a hand in the melee begun by his premature retreat, but the man had lived, which was more than he deserved in Jensen's opinion. Being reassigned to the equivalent of military hell baby-sitting a bunch of savages in Minnesota was more than a man should have to endure—even one who had had a momentary lapse of judgment in battle.

Initially, Jensen had expected to bunk with the only other American in the bunch. But Edward Pope was made of different stuff than Jensen's West Point comrades. He didn't seem to mind when warm weather arrived and the Dakota made a mess of cavalry drills and charged around the camp like mindless idiots, hanging off their mounts and screaming. Pope was even trying to learn to speak their dissonant language—if one could call it a language. It rankled Jensen that apart from Sacred Lodge, the scouts made almost no attempt to speak English. Since all the native peoples on the continent would be exterminated before the millennium dawned, Jensen saw no reason to learn Dakota—a language he considered to be beneath him. He kept himself apart from the scouts, trusting Sacred Lodge to interpret his orders and waiting for the army to come to its senses and send him on to more important assignments.

"You oughter talk to them," Pope urged Jensen. "What you gonna do when Sacred Lodge heads out and leaves us here?"

"They aren't leaving camp without me," Jensen asserted. "I didn't come out here to be a cook." He glared at Edward Pope.

Pope shrugged off the insult. "Which is better for the army," he asked, "a good cook or an officer who won't talk to his men?"

One spring night Jensen stalked off after arguing with Sacred Lodge about an upcoming foray to the north, Daniel said, "Let him go. He doesn't trust us. He thinks because we don't line up and march like white men waiting to be shot at, we make bad soldiers. He doesn't think the Great Father's army needs help from savages." Smiling bitterly, Daniel tucked his nose down into his collar and crouched beside the fire.

"Exactly what do you find amusing about me?" Jensen called from where he had been watching the exchange between Daniel and Sacred Lodge. He marched toward the fire and stared across the amber tongues of golden light to where Daniel sat, his dark eyes glittering as they reflected the flames. Daniel lifted his eyes from the fire to Brady's long-jawed face, but he made no move to answer. The other scouts sitting around Daniel shifted slightly, but stayed put.

How many weeks had it been, Jensen thought, he'd been treated like so much baggage. They all treated him like he was some blubbering idiot. Or, what was worse, like he wasn't even *there*. Especially this Daniel Two Stars and his friend Robert Lawrence. Someone had told him Robert Lawrence had a reputation as being a merciless killer before he got religion. He and Two Stars were good friends. But Lawrence was gone to take messages to Sibley and wouldn't be back for a couple of days. It might be a good time to settle the score with Two Stars.

He'd done plenty to "make nice" with these savages, Brady thought. Only yesterday when he heard Two Stars's stomach rumble with hunger, he'd offered a piece of jerky. The savage had taken it too. And now he sat there, looking into the fire, laughing with his friends at a West Point graduate! Kicking at a piece of kindling sticking out from the fire, Brady sent a shower of sparks upward and watched with satisfaction when Two Stars and the other scouts sitting near him startled and moved back from the fire.

"I asked you a question!" Jensen growled, planting his feet and folding his arms. "What'd I say that you think is so funny?"

Daniel looked up at him briefly, shrugged, and stared back into the fire.

Jensen leaned over and thrust his chin out. "I know about you. You speak English as well as any white man. You read well enough to have picked your own name out of the Good Book. I don't appreciate being laughed at. So speak up, Two Stars." Jensen made a fist and pounded the open palm of his opposite hand. "Speak up, or be prepared to be shut up once and for all."

Daniel sighed. Holding his hands out to the fire for a moment to warm them, he got up and headed toward where they had picketed the horses for the night.

When the Indian turned his broad back to Jensen, something tightly wound inside the soldier came undone. He sprang on Two Stars, pummeling him with his fists, yelling at the top of his lungs.

The surprise attack caught Daniel off-balance. He tumbled to the earth, Jensen atop him, flailing madly at his back. The scouts formed a circle around the two men and began placing bets on who would win.

When Jensen finally landed a solid punch near Daniel's left shoulder, the Dakota brave yelped with pain. Rolling onto his side, Daniel unseated Jensen and scrambled to his feet. But Jensen wasn't finished. Lowering his head he charged Daniel, wrapping his arms around the brave's midsection and driving him backward. The wiry soldier's strength surprised Daniel, who found himself lying on his back holding his hands in front of his face to fend off the man's blows.

When Jensen showed no signs of letting up, Daniel lurched to one side and with all his strength managed to unseat him again. The instant the soldier landed in the dirt beside him, Daniel put one hand on his assailant's throat, gripping hard enough to cut off Jensen's air supply. His face red, his eyes bulging, Jensen grabbed desperately at Two Stars's hand. When he was satisfied that most of Jensen's fury had been spent, Daniel let go, only to receive a well-placed punch to his left eye that made him roar with pain. He released Jensen and leaped up. Meaning to land a kick to the soldier's rib cage, he once again found himself on the ground as Jensen grabbed his raised foot in midair, threw Daniel to the ground, and was atop him again.

Over and over the two men rolled, until Jensen let out a yelp and, pushing himself away, grabbed his left wrist with his right hand and ran for the nearby creek where he plunged his singed hand into the water. The sensation in his backside told Daniel he, too, had rolled too close to the campfire. Smiling ruefully, he stood up and pounded the seat of his pants.

Two Stars followed Jensen to the creek, but at his approach Jensen took his gun from his holster. Waving it in the air he said, "Hold it right there. Don't come any closer." He winced and shook his hand. "I may have a singed paw, but I'm still man enough to fight you off."

Daniel backed away and headed for Pope's shelter. Emerging in a moment with a bucket in hand he headed for where Jensen still knelt by the creek. "Good fight," Daniel muttered in English. When Jensen looked up at him in surprise, Daniel grabbed his hand and plunged it into the pail of animal fat he had retrieved from Pope.

"Let me see," Daniel said.

Jensen complied, withdrawing his hand from the pail of fat to reveal bright red skin, which Daniel inspected closely.

"Not bad," Daniel muttered. He looked at Jensen. "Finished fighting?"

Jensen squinted up at him. "You finished giving me the silent treatment?"

"What means *silent treatment?*" Daniel said.

"Not talking. Silent." He grimaced and looked away. "I know what you think. You think I'm some kind of idiot just because I can't track like you. Well I'm not."

Daniel stood up. "I touched the fire once when I was young. My mother taught me how to care for it. Keep your hand in the pail for now. Before you sleep, have Pope wrap your hand with more fat inside the rabbit skin. By tomorrow morning, your hand will be fine." He headed back to camp, then stopped and turned around. "Jensen," he said abruptly.

Jensen looked up.

"You don't know what I think," Daniel said. "About anything." He raised one corner of his mouth in a half-smile. "Except for one thing."

"What's that?" Jensen asked.

"I think you fight pretty good," Daniel said.

With the arrival of warm weather, Daniel began to feel restless. They had come out of Mankato in February and traveled nearly seventy miles to the northwest, camping on Rice Creek, just south of the Minnesota River and almost exactly between what had been the Upper and Lower Sioux Agencies. Other scouts were added to the original five until ten were in camp. They spent the next few weeks going on expeditions, either up the Minnesota River or westward. Only once did they think they saw tracks indicating hostile Indians, but nothing came of it and they headed back south to camp.

Scouting proved to be little more than a new kind of prison. Wherever the scouts went, they were confronted with brokenness.

Burned-out cabins and destroyed agency buildings served as constant reminders that the deserted landscape had once been home to hundreds of peaceful Dakota Indians. While the scouts weren't confined behind a guarded fence anymore, they were still under the watchful eye of Private Brady Jensen. Daniel had hoped their fight would have put them on better terms, but nothing changed. Jensen still watched everyone suspiciously, still considered himself above "fraternizing with a bunch of savages," still despised Edward Pope for getting along.

There were days when Robert Lawrence's persistent faith made Daniel angry. The man quoted Scripture he had memorized and even hummed—albeit off key—Dakota hymns when they rode together. He reminded Daniel they were better off here than back in prison in Mankato. He listed things he was thankful for.

"Remember Daniel in the Bible," Robert said one night by the campfire. "He was a captive in a strange land, but he did not forget his God. We must be like that. God knows where we are, and when He is finished teaching us here, He will take us somewhere else. As long as we have Him, we can be at peace."

But Daniel felt no peace.

One May morning when the sky was a brilliant blue, Daniel saddled up his bay gelding and rode out of camp alone. He followed the river, up and down rolling hills and greening valleys, past where Sacred Heart and Hawk Creeks flowed into the Minnesota River, across the Yellow Medicine River, past the Upper Agency until he came up over a rise and looked down on the charred remains of what had been the Hazelwood Mission. He took in a sharp breath and let it out slowly, surprised at his physical reaction to the ruined site. He urged his horse past what had been missionaries Mary and Stephen Riggs's two-story home, picking his way through the remnants of Mrs. Riggs's white garden fence and heading across the open space to where the sawmill had stood. It was there, after a serious talk with Robert Lawrence about the merits of life at the mission, Daniel had caught his friend Otter drinking whiskey behind a woodpile. Daniel looked away from the blackened rubble and glanced toward the north. He hoped Otter was up there across the border, still living the old life, still hunting buffalo, still free.

A half-burned book lay on the ground near the school. The winter had nearly obliterated the print, but Daniel could tell it was a Dakota grammar book. For the first time, he wondered how the missionaries felt about what had happened. Their lives, too, had been destroyed.

Robert Lawrence had been talking about trying to have church services at the scouts' camp. Big Amos and the army cook Edward Pope expressed interest. Daniel's gaze lingered on what was left of the mission church. Dr. Riggs would be pleased to know that some of his converts had not forgotten Christ, Daniel thought. Perhaps they should try to have services. Perhaps it would help.

Dismounting, Daniel walked toward the place where a wild vine was sending green tendrils up over the blackened remains of the teachers' cottage. He bent down and touched a green shoot, remembering how, by the end of last summer, the mature vine had nearly swallowed up the entire porch. He wondered what had become of the brilliantly colored little bird that used to flit around the orange blossoms, totally impervious to the presence of Miss Jane and Blue Eyes as they sat on the porch drinking tea.

Sitting down on the earth beside the vine, Daniel pulled Etienne LaCroix's journal out of the blue sash at his waist. He leafed through it, watching Blue Eyes grow up in the sketches. Presently he closed the book and, standing up, tucked it back in his sash. He looked around at the mission and frowned. He should never have come here. Now he was in a darker mood than ever.

He looked down at the journal. He should throw it away, he told himself. Stop thinking about her. Both Robert and Big Amos had wives. Robert had children. Sacred Lodge had said they would be brought to the scouts' camp. It had not yet happened, but neither Robert nor Big Amos brooded or complained. They simply went on with their duties. They seemed to be able to ignore Brady Jensen.

Daniel mounted his horse and trotted away from the mission. Following a line of trees along a ridge and down into a valley, he dismounted at the lowest part of a dry creekbed. Taking the sash from around his waist, he wound it around the journal. In a few moments he had found a crevice deep enough to hide the bundle. He piled several rocks across the hiding place, climbed back up the bank, and prepared to ride away. But then he stopped and looked behind him. If rain swelled the creek as it had in the past, the book would be swept away and ruined. Daniel sat for a moment arguing with himself. It put him in a dark mood to linger over the past. What did it matter if the book was ruined? Both it and the sash were part of a life that no longer existed.

His horse was growing restless, dancing nervously and pawing the earth. Finally, Daniel let him lower his head and graze. While the bay snatched up huge mouthfuls of the rich prairie grass, Daniel scrambled down the creekbank and retrieved the bundle.

# Seven

"He healeth the broken in heart, and bindeth up their wounds."
—PSALM 147:3

SIMON HAD LIT THE GAS LAMP IN THE KITCHEN JUST long enough to make coffee, then turned it back off. He sat alone in the darkened room, sipping from his cup and thinking back over the previous day's events. His closed Bible lay before him. As soon as he finished his coffee he would walk up to the church. By then it would be light enough for him to be able to reread the first chapter of Philippians. The idea that Paul had written the letter from prison had struck him a few days before, and now he was reading it over and over again, with a new appreciation for Paul's ability to look upon his imprisonment as a kind of blessing. Simon especially liked the passage that read, "But I would ye should understand, brethren, that the things which happened unto me have fallen out rather unto the furtherance of the gospel." Simon hoped to use Philippians to encourage the prisoners at Davenport.

A commentator had mentioned the Roman guards who heard the gospel because of being assigned to the apostle Paul. Simon hadn't thought of it before, but now he wondered how many U.S. soldiers had heard the gospel because of their assignment in Mankato, where the prisoners held prayer meetings twice daily and heard preaching at least once a day. It was interesting food for thought, and it resulted in Simon's looking forward to his ministry in the prison camp at Davenport. Perhaps God would do something through him down there, after all.

For the moment, though, Simon was content to sit alone in the dark thinking back over the previous day's events. He had done his best to "walk in a manner worthy to his calling," and he felt strangely content with whatever reaction Genevieve LaCroix displayed when she learned what he had done. He had already cross-examined himself innumerable times in that regard. As much as he could tell, he had taken action as much for himself as for her. No, he thought with a new sense of joy, he wasn't trying to manipulate her feelings at all. He had simply done what he thought best for everyone concerned. He certainly had no doubt that he had accomplished what was best for Hope.

Footsteps sounded on the narrow staircase that connected the kitchen with the back upstairs hall. Snatching up his Bible, Simon made for the back porch, but before he could get there Gen called his name. He turned back into the room just as she lit the gaslight over the table. She apparently had dressed in haste, for her hair hung in one thick braid across her shoulder. She pulled the note he had slid under her door the night before out of her pocket. Looking down at it she stuttered, "I— How—" She sat down at the table and pushed the note across the table toward him. "How can this be true?" She reached up trying to smooth a dozen tendrils of dark hair back from her face.

Simon smiled. "It's true. Samuel Whitney witnessed the signing of the papers yesterday evening in the offices of Marshall & Dodd. The Pottses were booked passage on the *Abigail* and settled into their room last night in preparation for the trip back downriver." He tucked his Bible under his arm.

"And Hope stays with us?" Gen asked.

He nodded. "All the Pottses wanted was five hundred dollars."

"But Simon," Gen asked, frowning slightly, "where did you get five hundred dollars?"

He winked. "You didn't know I was independently wealthy, did you?" He turned to go. "It's been taken care of. That's the important thing. I'll be back in time for breakfast."

Gen called out, "I'll only ask Samuel if you won't tell me. But I'd rather hear it from you."

He turned back around and leaned against the door frame. "I had some money saved," he said vaguely.

"Just last week we were wondering how to pay for Aaron's schoolbooks," Gen said in disbelief.

Simon walked to where she sat and patted her hand. "The only thing you need to know is that Hope is securely with *us*. The Pottses agreed to appoint me her legal guardian and they gave up all rights to her, which, according to the attorney, means if we ever so desire we can adopt her." He turned to go. "I hope you don't mind that I gave her my last name. I thought it would be easier for her in the future if she shared Meg and Aaron's family name."

Gen snatched his hand up. "Your wedding ring—" She touched the white band of exposed flesh where the ring had been, then looked up at him, her eyes filling with tears. "Oh, Simon— you sold your *wedding* ring?"

He pulled his hand away and shoved it in his pocket.

She moved his coat open a little and peeked at his vest pocket. "And your gold watch—and that gorgeous fob Mrs. Leighton sent out for Christmas—" She stood up, clutching his coat lapel. "What else? What else did you sell, Simon?" When he looked away nervously, her eyes widened and she half whispered, "Not Ellen's wedding ring? Not the diamond—oh, Simon—that was her *grandmother's*—it was for Meg—"

"Both Ellen and Meg would have granted permission had they known the situation," he said firmly. "What *is* important is that Hope is secure in a new life where she is loved far more than gold or diamonds."

Beginning to cry, Gen wrapped her arms around him, sobbing out thank-yous. He held her for a moment, fearful of the emotions that rose in him at the feel of her body against his. He patted her head awkwardly, murmuring, "Don't cry, my dear."

They stood together for a moment until Gen backed away and gestured toward the table. "Let me make you some breakfast."

"You don't have to do that," Simon said. "I was just going out the back door to head for the church. I'll be back in time to eat with the family."

"Please, Simon," Gen begged. "We never have time alone." She had already reached for the rolling pin and biscuit cutter.

"All right," he said uncertainly. Putting his Bible back on the table, he sat down. Gen's back was to him, and for the first time in a long time he could admire her profile without the threat of someone else noticing. When she spun around to pour him a second cup of coffee he looked away quickly and felt his cheeks growing warm.

"Read to me," she said, quietly nodding at the Bible.

He opened the book and began to read: "'I thank my God upon every remembrance of you, always in every prayer of mine for you all making request with joy, for your fellowship in the gospel from the first day until now; being confident of this very thing, that he which hath begun a good work in you will perform it until the day of Jesus Christ: Even as it is meet for me to think this of you all, because I have you in my heart . . .'"

Gen asked over her shoulder, "Where is that?"

"Philippians," Simon answered quickly. "Paul wrote it from prison. I've been studying it, thinking it might encourage the men at Davenport."

She nodded. "I like the idea of God beginning a work . . . and then sticking with it—bringing it to its logical end someday. It's comforting, thinking that He cares enough to be involved in our lives that way." While they talked, Gen made fresh biscuits, scrambled eggs, and dished up applesauce. She set the meal on the table half apologetically. "I know we usually have potatoes, too, but we—"

"I'm not really that fond of potatoes for breakfast," Simon said quickly.

"Oh—I—I didn't know that." She sat down beside him.

The simple fact that she chose to sit *beside* rather than *across* from him did not go unnoticed. Nor did the way her dark hair glistened against her crisp yellow gingham dress. He managed to mumble a juvenile blessing, but afterward an awkward silence reigned over them both until Meg appeared on the stairs, scooting down on her bottom, Hope in her arms.

"We smelled breakfast," Meg said, yawning.

The instant Meg's feet touched the floor, Hope strained to get out of her arms. When Meg put her down, Hope crawled toward Simon, who scooted back from the table and welcomed her with outstretched arms.

"Good morning," Simon said, looking over Hope's head to Meg. "How are my two girls this morning?"

"Hungry!" Meg said, and sat next to Gen at the table.

"Pa-pa-pa-pa!" Hope said, and patted Simon's cheek.

Gen and Simon exchanged glances, and for the first time

neither one felt compelled to look away, lest they reveal too much to the other.

❧

Only one week later, Simon stood alone again in the predawn dark. This time, he was in the parlor, looking out toward the street. He had packed last evening and spent a restless night waiting for morning and the time to go. Everything pointed to it being God's will that he go to Camp McClellan. And every emotion in him still cried out against his leaving. He would miss Hope's next new words. He would miss her learning to walk on her own. He would miss hearing Meg read aloud every evening and discussing theology with Aaron, who had recently developed a precocious interest in Bible doctrines.

Added to the burden of loneliness he would feel apart from his children, Simon dreaded separation from Genevieve. Still, he knew it was right to go. He had not heard God's voice audibly, but phrases from Scripture still rang in his heart, confirming that he was to feed the sheep. If he didn't obey the inner voice, how could he call himself a Christian? If he did not distance himself from Genevieve, how would he avoid behaving like a love-struck fool? He had seen Miss Jane Williams watching him closely over the last few days. He assumed Gen had mentioned their private breakfast the previous week. It was time he put some distance between himself and the situation.

"There's a storm brewing to the northwest," Genevieve said from the doorway. She walked toward him and stood at his side, pointing to the west where clouds were just becoming visible on the horizon.

His heart pounding at her proximity, Simon answered, "I'll be on my way long before that reaches us. As dry as it has been this spring, I'd welcome a thorough drenching if it breaks the drought."

"I made coffee," Gen said. "And there's a small lunch tucked into your saddlebags by the door."

"Thank you, my dear," he said. "I appreciate your thoughtfulness."

"I wish you wouldn't do that," Gen said quickly.

"What?"

She mimicked his tone as she said aloud, "*my dear*." She continued looking out the window while she talked. "Yesterday when Aaron was so angry about your not letting him go along, you told him you needed him to 'look after the girls.' And you looked right across the table at *me*." She glanced up at him. "I'm not one of 'your girls.'"

"I didn't mean it to sound that way," Simon said carefully. "I'm sorry if I offended."

Gen backed away. "I'll be in the kitchen," she said and left.

Simon followed her down the hall toward the oblique slant of light coming from the open kitchen door. Gen worked quickly to serve up breakfast for the two of them and then placed the plates opposite one another at the kitchen table.

They ate in silence until Simon said, "I don't mean anything by calling you 'my dear', or one of 'my girls.' It's just—" He hesitated. "I suppose it's meant as an affectionate way of addressing you without trying to overstep—"

"Overstep?" Gen said abruptly. She set her coffee cup down. "Do I remember correctly? Did you not propose marriage earlier this month?"

He nodded. "I did. But you said—"

"I asked if you would wait," she interrupted him. "I never intended for you to go into hibernation." She watched him carefully, waiting for him to respond. When he didn't, she stood up and took the two empty plates to the sink. Without turning around she said, "This isn't working the way it should, Simon. And I don't know how to repair it. I've asked Miss Jane for advice.

I've asked Nina Whitney for advice. And I've asked God. But nothing changes. What should I do?" She turned to face him.

"You needn't do anything," Simon said carefully. "You owe me nothing." Distracted by the silhouette of her slim figure outlined against the white sink behind her, he got up and retreated to the door. Taking his saddlebags off the hook, he slung them over his shoulder. He started to go, then turned back. He couldn't keep the tension from his voice when he said, "I will ask after Daniel Two Stars at the prison camp. Someone may know something." He turned to go.

"Wait!" Gen said, rushing to him. When he stopped, she raised both hands and laid her palms on his chest. Drawing them back toward herself she pressed her palms together and rested her chin on the tips of her fingers. She looked like a woman at prayer as she said softly, "Daniel Two Stars was hanged in Mankato, Minnesota, on December 26, 1862. It was a mistake. He was innocent. But he died." She looked up at Simon again and slowly waved her hands across the space that separated them. "And it is time that he stopped standing in this space between you and me." Her eyes filled with tears. "I thought you wanted that, too, Simon. But you've been so remote lately—and you've taken to using that imperial *my dear*, like you used to do with Ellen." She shivered. "I hate it. It puts up a barrier between us—"

"A barrier that must exist," Simon said abruptly.

"But why?" she asked.

"Because, *my dear*, I promised you I would keep my distance. And if I don't put up a few barriers, I'm not going to be able to do that." He shook his head and swiped one hand across his forehead. Imperceptibly he shifted his weight so that he was almost leaning away from her. He gripped the door frame behind him. "I'm not good at this sort of thing, Genevieve. You should know that."

He looked down at her. Taking a deep breath he said, "When I look at you I think I must have been truly insane to suggest even such a ridiculous thing as marriage." He swallowed hard and plunged ahead, "You are the most beautiful woman I have ever seen. How could I have thought—" He stopped abruptly and brushed his open hand across his head. "I've lost nearly all of what little hair I ever had. The remains are turning gray, so that I look older than I feel. My nose is too big. My eyes are too small. I've failed more than once in various aspects of life, and have little to show for my thirty-some years of life other than my children and Hope." He gripped the leather strap connecting his saddlebags so tightly his knuckles turned white as he rushed to say what had been on his heart for weeks. He sighed and shook his head, "I keep my distance because I promised you I would. Because it would be ridiculous for me to expect a woman like you to feel anything for this—" He hit his chest once and looked away again. He laughed sadly. "I'm not the kind of man women like you fall in love with, Genevieve." He blinked and then looked back at her, smiling kindly. "But I am grateful to you for making an attempt at friendship."

Gen clenched her fist and gently pounded on his chest. "I do want to be your friend, Simon. But—" but friendship isn't enough. I don't want a marriage of convenience. I don't want us to marry simply because it's the right thing to do for the children. It *is* the right thing for the children. But I want it to be right for *us* as well." She looked up at him. "I want passion in my life, Simon. We are going to be man and wife long after Aaron and Meg and Hope grow up and leave us to each other. I don't want to look across the breakfast table the morning after Hope's wedding and wonder who that stranger is. I don't want either of us to think the reason for our marriage has expired once the children have lives of their own."

Her voice gentled as she continued. "What if you aren't the most handsome man in the state? So what? When you take Hope or Meg on your lap and snuggle with them, it's completely charming. Your voice has taken on a depth—a tone that I love. You aren't *scrawny,* as you put it when you proposed to me. You're—*wiry.*" She caught one of his hands in hers. "And I like your hands. They used to be soft and almost feminine. But after your time with the army and driving relief wagons all over the countryside, they've become callused and rough—and I like it." She didn't let go of his hand when she looked up at him. "And women don't mind bald heads nearly as much as most men think."

She reached up and turned his face back toward her. Searching his eyes, she finally saw the feelings he had tried so carefully to hide.

He surprised her by bending down and touching his lips to hers. She closed her eyes. As quickly as it had begun, the moment dissolved. Simon pulled away.

"I'm sorry, my dear—I didn't mean—"

But Gen reached up and, wrapping her arms around his neck, pulled him toward her. She kissed him again and still didn't release him, but instead laid her head on his chest. "You proposed marriage and then it seemed you moved away. I needed to know—"

"Well now you know. I love the way your hair glistens in the firelight when you sit in the parlor reading to the children. I love the sound of your laughter." Simon chuckled and held her close. "You are, all in all, a terrible distraction for this old missionary."

Gen looked up at him. "Miss Jane said I should wait and pray. I've been praying. Obviously I'm not so very good at waiting."

"And this trapping me into a blatant display of my carefully concealed emotions," he asked, "whose advice was that?"

"If you're talking about one-and-a-half kisses, Reverend Dane," she answered, "I came up with that on my own."

He smiled at her and cupped his hands around her face. "If that's the case, my dear Miss LaCroix, I'd say you should take your own advice more often." He sighed. "And now I don't want to go to Camp McClellan."

"Nina said that hers and Mr. Whitney's courtship was conducted almost entirely through the mail."

Simon cleared his throat nervously. "I'm not very good at courting, Genevieve."

Gen raised one eyebrow and looked up at him. "I suspect you could learn, though, Simon."

"Yes," he replied, smiling, "I suspect I could."

# Eight

"There be three things which are too wonderful for me,
yea, four which I know not: The way of an eagle in the air;
the way of a serpent upon a rock; the way of a ship in the
midst of the sea; and the way of a man with a maid."
—PROVERBS 30:18–19

*JULY 4, 1863*

*My Dear,*
*    I begin this letter with a term not meant to patronize,*
*but rather to remind you my heart holds you dear . . .*

Simon read the words he had just written, exhaled sharply,
crumpled the piece of paper, and sent it the way of its predecessors
into the small stove in the corner of his room. He struck a match
and dropped it in the midst of several wads of paper. Closing the
stove door, he crossed the room to stand looking out the window

as dawn illuminated the river town of Davenport, Iowa. He had been here several weeks but thus far had sent only one letter—a pitiful missive in what he had come to think of as *Old Simonese*—formal, distant, cold. It would not do to send Genevieve another like it—not when she had smiled up at him with those eyes and said she would like to be courted through the mail.

He sighed, oblivious to the city just outside his window. Life held so many unpredictable elements. When he had wanted to hold her close, she remained distant. Now that she was willing to cross the distance between them, had even invited it, he could not find the words to realize the goal. *Help me, Lord. I feel she is Your gift to me, but I don't quite know how to claim her. You know me, Father. I'm from the old school. Ellen and I didn't show our true feelings often, even in the private moments. Genevieve won't put up with that. She's completely different. Wonderful. Show me how to court her. Show me how to love her.* Simon's eyes strayed to the table beside his bed where his Bible lay, yet unopened that morning. *Please look down on this poor old preacher and help me, God.* Simon went to his Bible, opened it to the Song of Solomon, and began to read.

The thunder of horses' hooves in the distance announced Camp McClellan's morning cavalry parade through town as the men took the first of their two daily treks to the river. It seemed to Simon that a cloud of dust had hung in the still air since his arrival. Already this morning he could feel grit collecting beneath his shirt collar. Unbuttoning the starched collar, he laid aside his Bible, rolled up his sleeves, and returned to the small desk near the window. Casting a plea to heaven for help, he wrote:

*My Dear,*

*If all I meant to accomplish in this letter was to tell you about the city of Davenport, to describe the condition of the Dakota prisoners and the status of our work here, I would not have destroyed several earlier versions of my writing.*

*Have you any idea how awkward I feel convincing my old self to move aside so that you can get a clear view of the man who loves you? The old Simon Dane would never have engaged in anything like a courtship by mail. But then that Simon Dane was a fool blessed by the love of a woman he did not deserve. I am amazed, dear Genevieve, at how history has repeated itself, for even as I attempt to cast aside my formal, distant self, I am once again blessed by the interest of a woman I do not deserve. How is it that God has chosen to bless me in such a manner not once, but twice in a lifetime?*

*I pause to reread the above paragraph as I sit at my desk looking out on the city of Davenport, and I realize that this is hardly a letter suitable for the ears of my children. I entrust to you the task of interpreting this letter for their ears in a manner that protects our privacy and yet conveys my love to them. How I miss them! Just last evening when I was walking back to my little room from the prison, I glanced in at one of the hotel windows to see a family dining, and the long amber-colored curls of a little girl about Meg's age made my heart ache to see her.*

As Simon bent to the task of writing Gen, sweat collected on his forehead. He rose and lifted the window in a vain attempt to catch any errant breeze that might drift up from the river. The morning's traffic to the river below had begun, and the noise of commerce competed with Simon's attempts to concentrate.

*If you were with me this moment we would be hurrying to escape the sweltering heat which penetrates the walls of this little room. We would descend to partake of Mrs. Smith's boardinghouse breakfast where I imagine you would disdain her rather nondescript biscuits and long for a huge dollop of Miss Jane's blackberry jam to increase their palatability.*

*However, once we exited the boardinghouse you would be treated to the sights of a rather substantial river city which, although it has existed only a little longer than you have been alive, boasts many imposing brick buildings and fine residences. We would stroll along one of the boardwalks erected to protect the fair citizens from disappearing into the endless mud that accompanies any rain. I would offer you my arm lest you stumble on one of the many loose boards that rise without warning to trip unsuspecting pedestrians. You would no doubt comment on the hogs roaming the streets at will, rooting up grass, fences, and seedling trees planted by the more hopeful citizens of this city.*

*Twice daily, the cavalry from Camp McClellan rides through the city in order to water its horses down at the river. The resulting cloud of dust deposits a gritty film over everything. Miss Jane and Mrs. Whitney would be driven to distraction trying to keep the furniture dusted!*

*The city has seen several hundreds of recruits arrive, train, and depart for the battlefields in the East. Now they are adjusting to the presence of the Dakota prisoners. The camp itself is situated on a high bluff overlooking the Mississippi River, the railroad bridge, and the city of Davenport. A fine belt of tall trees will help shield the prisoners from winter storms, and this will be needed as the barracks in which they are housed were hastily erected and are quite drafty.*

*The men are confined inside an enclosure about two hundred feet square inside of which are four buildings—former soldiers' barracks, albeit without the beds. Of these four buildings, two are occupied by prisoners, one is a combination hospital and women's quarters (about a dozen squaws have been brought down to do the cooking and laundry—two even assist the post doctor in the hospital). All is surrounded by a high* board fence, four feet from the top of which is a walkway constantly patrolled by sentries.

The average age of the Dakota men here is about thirty, although we have a few very old men whose health is in such a precarious state I do not expect they will survive the winter next.

I long to tell you more, but the sun shining in my little window reminds me that my duty is up the hill inside the board walls I have been describing.

I miss you terribly. My love to the children.

We hold religious meetings three times each day. God is doing a great work here and has certainly remembered His children in their affliction. Chaska, a new convert, speaks at many of these meetings. He is a gifted orator and dispenses the gospel in a very fluent and impressive manner. His audience listens with profound respect, and more than once I have seen a time of spontaneous encouragement break out as the men speak of the freedom they have found in Christ and what His promises mean to them.

When not in religious meetings the men write to their friends at Crow Creek, play games, sing, or make bows and arrows or other trinkets for which there has sprung up a lively market in Davenport. There is talk of allowing groups of the prisoners under guard to be employed by neighboring farmers for the fall harvest.

New recruits to Camp McClellan usually begin by being quite harsh with the prisoners. However, after a few days their opinions inevitably change and the treatment mitigates. I have observed nothing so harsh as to compare with what these poor souls endured at the hands of the citizens of Minnesota, *and thus I have concluded that the Lord has been gracious to bring them here where they can serve whatever term of imprisonment the government sees fit to impose. The men seem resigned to their lot. Yesterday one even said to me that for all the whites that were killed he supposed someone must pay a price, and that if being held in prison would be accepted as payment for his brother's crimes, he was willing to do it.*

*I am gaining more than I am giving while I serve among these men. Their resolute faith humbles me. I would wish that I could be so content as they. And yet I am not, because I am removed from the one my heart holds dearest of all. Please write every word Hope speaks, every lesson Meg recites, and tell Aaron that if he dares grow taller than his father during his absence, he will have some very serious explaining to do when I return.*

*I miss you terribly. And yet I am where the Lord wishes me to be. Tell me, Genevieve, does absence make the heart grow fonder?*

As time went on, Simon Dane grew more and more astute in the finer points of courting by mail. He began to take risks, sharing observations and feelings about life that he would have avoided in Gen's presence.

Gen faithfully responded to each letter with anecdotes about the children, news from St. Anthony, and nonjudgmental acceptance of Simon.

When the war chief Little Crow was killed while picking raspberries in a thicket north of Hutchinson, Minnesota, Gen expressed outrage that the chief's body was thrown on a heap of entrails at a slaughterhouse. *Whatever crimes he may have committed,* Gen scribbled angrily, *he deserved to be treated with the dignity owing any human created in the image of God.* Simon agreed.

A seventy-five-dollar bounty was offered any man in Minnesota who could prove he had killed a Sioux warrior. Gen wrote, *Do you not find it ironic that Dakota scouts—men who accept the duty of scouting for the white army and may find themselves forced to act against their former friends and brothers—are offered only twenty-five dollars for the same scalp! I shudder to think of it.*

Reports of General Sibley's campaign against the "savages" filled the newspapers. Amid the reports of battles at Stony Lake, Big Mound, and White Stone Hill, Gen and Simon kept up a lively correspondence in which they wondered about their Dakota friends and church members. *Samuel Whitney says that a church has been formed at the scouts' camp. I like to think of Nancy and Robert Lawrence being reunited there and having some semblance of a happy life.*

Small parties of hostile Sioux continued to participate in violent raids in isolated parts of Minnesota. A soldier of the Second Nebraska lost his entire family when they were massacred while he was away fighting with Sibley.

Gen and Simon discussed all these events in their letters, and as they discussed and shared their thoughts, little by little, their hearts began to come together. Simon began reaching out by asking her to pray for him. Eventually he shared his innermost thoughts in a way that might never have been possible except for the safety of physical distance. Little by little, Simon and Gen opened their inner selves to one another until one evening Gen wept as she read aloud Simon's account of the death of one of the older men. She replied, *As I reread your letter alone in my room, I weep with you at the loss of the dear old man. It is as if I can feel your heart breaking, even though you know he has entered the eternal kingdom where none can do him harm. How I wish that even now I could put the children to bed and come sit beside you and mourn with you and yes, hold you while we cry together.*

❧

"What is it?" Miss Jane asked, looking up from the half-knitted sock in her lap. "Is something wrong?"

"It's nothing," Gen said quickly, studying Simon's most recent letter carefully.

Miss Jane's knitting needles flew as she glanced over her glasses at Gen.

Gen shook her head. "Really. It's nothing."

Miss Jane nodded and got up. "Well, then, I'm retiring." From the door she said, "Timothy and Rebecca both need new shoes. I promised them we'd trek uptown tomorrow after school. Is it all right if we take Meg and Hope with us?"

No answer.

"Miss LaCroix?"

Gen started and looked up. "I'm sorry, what did you say?"

"I said it appears as if *nothing* is mighty distracting," Miss Jane said.

Gen blushed. "Do you remember Cloudman having a daughter about my age?" she asked abruptly.

Miss Jane shook her head. "No. Why?"

Gen read aloud, "'One of the women claims to be the daughter of Cloudman who she says died in battle against the troops in Minnesota. She is quite lovely and boasts finer blankets and ornaments than the other women. This has given her some power over the soldiers assigned to guard the prisoners, which would be opportunity for evil if she did not use it to benefit her fellow Dakota. Since she generously shares whatever favors she receives with the other women, I cannot fault her enjoyment of the attentions she receives. She speaks most graciously of her days at the Hazelwood Mission and remembers the new work I had just begun near her father's camp when the outbreak began. She expresses an interest in the gospel and sits in rapt attention when

I teach. It is quite encouraging to have a woman whose labors are many take time to attend to the preaching of God's Word.'"

Miss Jane chuckled and shook her head. "You are jealous, Miss LaCroix."

"Don't be ridiculous," Gen protested. "I'm just concerned for Simon's reputation. A missionary serving alone has to be careful." Gen traced down the letter until she located another passage. "Listen: 'Our Indian princess says that her name is Light of the Moon. She seems hurt that I do not recall meeting her in her father's camp. Tell me, my dear, do you recall Cloudman having a daughter? She would have been a bit older than you. Other than an aristocratic face the only thing I can think that you might recall is her hair, which is exceedingly long and reaches nearly to her ankles.'"

"Write the reverend and express concern for the princess," Miss Jane advised quickly. She looked at Gen over her glasses. "And sign it as affectionately as you dare." She smiled knowingly. "You are jealous."

Gen blushed. "I suppose I am. A little."

# Nine

> "This I recall to my mind, therefore have I hope.
> It is of the Lord's mercies that we are not consumed."
> —LAMENTATIONS 3:21–22

"WHAT YOU THINK YOU'RE DOIN' IN MY CORNFIELD?"

Daniel Two Stars stood as still as possible, trying to keep his voice from trembling as he explained, "I'm a scout for the army. See my uniform?"

The farmer's cold eyes showed surprise at being answered in English. He scanned Daniel's blue jacket. "I heard about Sibley using Dakota scouts. But all those troops left for Dakota Territory. For all I know you took that jacket off a dead soldier."

"I have a paper from General Sibley," Daniel said evenly. He looked down toward his left. "In that pocket. Can I show you?"

"Turn around." The farmer motioned with his rifle.

Daniel moved slowly until his back was to the farmer. He could feel sweat trickling down his back while the wiry little man stepped up and searched him, then carefully reached into his left pocket and withdrew the piece of paper.

"All right," the farmer said. "Turn back around." When Daniel once again faced him, the man balanced his rifle across one forearm while unfolding and reading the paper. It was dated June of 1863—just a few weeks ago. The farmer read,

*The Bearer, Daniel Two Stars, is a civilized Sioux Indian who deserves the gratitude of the American people for having been prominently involved in saving the lives of white women and children during the late Indian war. He is employed as an Indian scout and assigned to Fort Ridgely for the purpose of reconnoitering the area to apprehend any Sioux Indians, be they hostile or friendly, and returning them to Fort Ridgely from whence they will be removed to the Sioux Reserve in Dakota Territory or imprisoned after due process of the law of the United States of America.*

*I recommend Daniel Two Stars to the kind consideration and attention of all citizens of the United States.*

> *General H. H. Sibley*
> *United States Army*

"Says here you saved white women and children," the farmer said, squinting up from the paper.

Daniel nodded. "I did what I could."

The farmer folded the paper and put it in the breast pocket of his red plaid shirt. He motioned again with the rifle. "You can put your hands down. Just don't make any sudden movements."

Daniel lowered his arms, rubbing his numb hands and waiting for the farmer to speak.

The farmer patted his pocket. "It says you're a scout for the U.S. Army. But like I said before, Sibley took his scouts with him. So what are you doing in my cornfield?"

"Since Little Crow died there have been rumors hostiles might try to cross back into Minnesota."

The farmer took his hat off and swiped his forehead with his shirt sleeve. "I know all about that. What's that got to do with you?" He settled his hat back on his head.

"They decided to divide the scouts up into camps. They left three of us at Fort Ridgely to help protect the settlers coming back. Someone rode in yesterday and said they found a campsite down here. They said an Indian child was buried in the old way, high in a notch of a tree. Captain Willets sent us to check it out."

"*Us?*" The farmer looked around warily.

Daniel jerked his chin up, indicating the cornfield behind him. "My friend Robert Lawrence is in there hoping you don't kill me."

"Come on out of there, Robert Lawrence," the farmer called loudly. He took two steps backward and waited. At the opposite end of the cornfield a few stalks of corn moved. The farmer repeated, "Come on. I see where you are. I won't shoot."

When Robert finally appeared, the farmer motioned him to stand beside Daniel.

"How come your uniforms don't match?"

"They give us old uniforms," Robert said. "Whatever they have."

"I heard about that Indian campfire," he said. "It's on my neighbor's place. Down by the creek that runs through his south field." He shuddered. "Small child wrapped in a buffalo robe high up off the ground. It ain't Christian." The farmer nodded at Robert. "You got one of those papers that tells what a fine citizen you are?"

Robert nodded.

"Let's see it."

The farmer looked over Robert's paper carefully and added it to his pocket. "You two walk down here from Fort Ridgely?" he asked abruptly.

Robert answered, "We left our horses tethered to a bush just over that ridge. They aren't very well broke. We didn't want to trample down any of your crop."

At the farmer's look of surprise, Robert shrugged, "We were farmers before the trouble last fall." He added, "I wouldn't have wanted anyone riding half-wild horses through my cornfield. Not until after harvest, anyway."

"You find any trace of hostiles on my place?"

Robert nodded. "They passed by here maybe two days ago. Probably a small group of women. Maybe a young boy with them. That would explain how they got the dead one up so high in the tree. We'll follow them and take them to the fort."

The farmer frowned. "How can you be sure it was women?"

"Warriors ride stallions," Daniel said. "All this group had with them was one half-lame mare." When the farmer still looked doubtful, Daniel went on to explain how he could tell the sex of the horse he was tracking.

The farmer shook his head. "Well, I'll be." He studied the ground for a minute before clearing his throat and asking, "If that was a stallion and you'd found yourself a hostile Indian, what'd you do then?"

"Take him back to Fort Ridgely."

"What if he didn't want to go?"

"Then we shoot."

"You'd do that?" the farmer asked. "You'd shoot one of your own?"

"A warrior planning to murder families is not one of my own."

The farmer studied Daniel and Robert carefully, taking in the ill-fitting uniforms, the high-crowned felt hats, the long dark braids trailing down the men's shoulders. "You two hungry?" he asked abruptly.

Daniel started to say no when his stomach growled. He grinned sheepishly.

"Get your horses and come on up to the house," the farmer said. "My missus just made a raspberry pie."

The men hesitated.

The farmer waved at them. "Come on. My Marjorie ain't some fool woman that faints at the sight of an Indian." He curled up one side of his lip in a crooked smile. "My granddad was friends of Chief Paducah on the homestead in Kentucky. Indians never did us any harm, and we done what we could to make life easier for them." He turned to go, and it was then that Daniel and Robert noticed the man limped. "Johnny Reb burned us out so we come here." He turned back. "I never learned to be afraid of Indians. Hope it don't get me killed." He limped away.

Robert and Daniel retrieved their horses, then followed the farmer to his cabin. When they reached the farmyard, they found him bent over a bucket of cold water splashing his face and washing his hands. At their approach, he stood up. He ran his fingers through his brown hair, wiped them on the seat of his pants, and extended his hand. "Jeb Grant." When a plain, dark-haired woman appeared in the doorway to the cabin, he turned to introduce her. "My wife, Marjorie."

Marjorie blushed furiously when Daniel and Robert introduced themselves. "You men just set yourselves down there in the yard," she said, waving toward a rough-hewn bench alongside the house. "I'll be right out with that pie." She disappeared inside the cabin.

Jeb reached into his pocket and handed their papers to the two men. "Guess you better keep these," he said.

Marjorie emerged from the cabin with the pie in one hand

and plates in the other. Resting the pie on the edge of the Grants' new well, she dished up one-fourth of the pie to each of the men. Just as Daniel took the last bite of pie, she lumbered to the cabin and returned with a loaf of bread in an old sack. "You men take this, now," she insisted, then smiled at Robert. "And when your missus comes, you bring her down for a visit. It gets mighty lonely here."

Robert and Daniel picked up the trail of the unknown Indians just across an open piece of ground opposite Jeb's cornfield. They followed it up a hill and turned to look back toward the farm. "He put the well in a good place," Robert commented as they surveyed the valley.

Daniel nodded, looking across the valley to the ridge where his own farm had been. "I wonder if Mrs. Grant would have served us pie if she had known she baked it in Nancy's stove," he said.

Robert shrugged. Together they rode back to where the grieving Dakota had left a dead child. Daniel climbed the tree and lowered the body to Robert's waiting arms. Together, they dug a grave and laid the child to rest beneath the earth.

When he was first sent to guard Indian prisoners in Mankato, Minnesota, Brady Jensen had thought his military career was at an all-time low. He was wrong. Three weeks after he marched out of Minnesota with General Sibley's troops, he was ordered to Crow Creek Reservation where he was given a wagonload of squaws to deliver to various scouts' camps along the frontier. He would end up right where he had started his career in the West—Fort Ridgely.

Like many of his comrades in arms, Jensen had taken to referring to the Indians as "Mr. Lo." It was a bad joke on the sympathetic whites and their constantly calling attention to "Lo, the poor Indian." He could hardly believe his ears when he was called in and told that for as long as the Dakota scouts' services were needed, it had been decided to let their families join them as an incentive to encourage faithful service. Family ties were strong among the Dakota, Jensen's commander explained, and if the men had their wives with them, the army wouldn't have to worry about deserters. "There's another reason for sending the wives out. After the men hear about conditions at Crow Creek," the commander had said with a wry smile, "they'll be more than happy to do their best on behalf of the army just so they can stay in service and keep from having to go there."

Whatever the reasoning behind the plan to take the scouts' families to them, Jensen wanted no part of transporting "the poor Indian." He was sick of getting the worst assignments available because of one mistake in one battle over a year ago, and by the time he crossed the river at Redwood Ferry and climbed the hill past the sutler's house and a few stores, he didn't care who knew how he felt. When he pulled his team up in front of the U-shaped stone building that served as a combination surgeon's residence and headquarters at Fort Ridgely, he ignored the two ragged squaws sitting behind him in the wagon and headed immediately inside, leaving the squaws to themselves.

The women looked at each other nervously. They surveyed the fort. Nancy nodded toward the dozen or so new buildings. "Little Crow must have burned the old ones," she muttered under her breath to her companion. The two women were aware that their arrival had been noticed by several soldiers standing at the corner of the two-story barracks building on the opposite side of the parade ground. They hunkered down in the wagon, afraid to move.

But then two riders approached from the south. One of the squaws watched their approach. Her hand went to her throat. She nudged her companion. And then, as the two riders came closer, she leaped out of the wagon, threw her arms into the air, and ran straight for the approaching riders.

And so it was that Robert Lawrence was reunited with his wife, Nancy. She fell into his arms the moment he jumped down from his horse, wrapped her arms around his neck, and began to weep.

"Do not cry, little wife," Robert whispered huskily. He held her close and whispered her name over and over again until she had calmed down enough to hear him.

Daniel dismounted and stood at a respectful distance, holding the reins to both their horses. He looked toward the stone building where the captain lived and saw that Big Amos had also found his wife.

"Where are the children?" Robert asked.

Nancy could not look at him. She buried her face in his shirt and shook her head.

Robert swallowed hard.

After a moment, Nancy took a deep breath. Turning her head so he could hear her but still leaning against his chest, she said brokenly, "There was so much sickness. At first I tried to stay away from it. I made Clara stay in the tent and take care of the baby. I told her to stay away from the sick ones. It was so cold. And we never had enough firewood. The missionaries did what they could to help, but there were too many of the people—and too few who cared to help. Clara began to cough." Nancy broke off and began to sob.

"Shh, shh, shh," Robert soothed his wife wordlessly, in the rhythm of a Dakota lullaby.

Daniel stepped between the horses and began to rub his bay gelding's ears, blinking away the tears in his eyes. He looked over his saddle horn and saw Big Amos, who had had no children to lose at Fort Snelling, lifting his wife in the air. He could hear the giant man's booming laughter as he spun his wife around and around. And he wondered about the blue-eyed girl he had once loved.

Tears streamed down Nancy's cheeks as she looked up at her husband. "I lost them, my husband. I lost our children." Her voice broke as she half whispered in Dakota, "Forgive me."

Robert pulled her to him again. "Don't," he said softly. He closed his eyes. When Nancy's sobs quieted, Robert put one arm around her and together they walked to where Daniel waited. Robert took the reins of his horse and the three joined Big Amos and his wife beside the wagon.

Brady Jensen emerged from the post headquarters followed by Captain Willets.

"I've ordered another tent put up near your camp," Willets said to the men. "We'll arrange something more permanent if you're to stay the winter. For now, let me know what you need." Willets eyed Jensen and then looked back at Robert. "Take a while to get your women settled. Then I'd like to hear what you found down south."

# Ten

"A friend loveth at all times, and a brother is born for adversity."
—PROVERBS 17:17

THE SKY WAS JUST BLUSHING CORAL-PINK WHEN BIG
Amos roused Daniel early the next morning. "Private Jensen
turned his team and a few horses out last night to graze. They
wandered off somewhere. Captain wants us to find them."

Daniel got up slowly. He stretched and twisted from side to
side. Running his hands through his tangled, dark hair he
looked past Big Amos and grinned. Big Amos turned around to
see his wife peering out from the tent's opening. Motioning
toward the tent Daniel said, "You stay here."

"You sure?" Big Amos said hopefully.

Daniel pulled his boots on. "Just tell Rosalie to name the baby
Daniel."

From inside the tent, Rosalie laughed aloud. Big Amos grinned and cleared his throat. He opened his mouth to say something, but Daniel waved him toward the tent and headed across the road to the stables. He had just mounted a lanky mule named Hank when Brady Jensen appeared from the opposite end of the building. "I told the captain I'd take care of it," he said gruffly.

"Robert Lawrence and I scouted south of here yesterday," Daniel said. "We found signs of an Indian camp. As far as we could tell, it's just a small band of old women. But you shouldn't go out alone."

Jensen patted his holster. "Don't think I'll have any trouble I can't handle," he said and headed out toward the south.

Daniel urged Hank to a sloppy lope and caught up with Jensen at the top of the first rise. He nodded in the opposite direction. "Trail leads that way," he said. "One of them has a loose shoe. They shouldn't be too far away." He pulled Hank around and rode away without waiting to see if Jensen was following.

An hour passed with no signs of the team. Daniel had just turned back to get help when two Sioux rode up over a hill and headed for him and Jensen, whooping and yelling at the top of their lungs.

They were too far from the fort to expect any help. The only hope was to head for Jeb Grant's house to the south and hope that Jensen was a better shot than he was a soldier. Screaming for Jensen to follow him, Daniel kicked Hank and headed out, thankful he had at least chosen the biggest of the mules available in the stable that morning.

They had raced along for nearly half a mile, the Sioux steadily gaining in spite of Jensen's wild firing, when Daniel headed down into a valley and saw Jensen's team off to the right. One brave headed after the team. But the second warrior was obviously more intent on scalps than horses. Glancing behind him, Daniel saw why. Not a single horse at the fort could begin to compare with this warrior's mount, a sleek white stallion that glided over the rough terrain effortlessly and, Daniel noted grimly, tirelessly.

The lone Sioux was gaining with every stride. An arrow sailed past Daniel's left ear, so close he felt the feathered tip brush against his temple. His pursuer was quiet. Daniel leaned down over the mule's neck, willing the animal to go faster. Glancing behind him, he saw the warrior raise a long lance in the air and knock Jensen off his horse. He counted coup on Jensen, then raised his war lance and charged after Daniel, his mount easily eating up the distance between them.

Daniel slid to the side of the mule, but Hank was not accustomed to such maneuvers and the minute Daniel's weight shifted, the mule slowed up and began to bray loudly, sidestepping and crow-hopping until Daniel's grip around his scrawny neck was loosed and Daniel fell off with a thud. He rolled instinctively, simultaneously avoiding the warrior's lance and landing his head a glancing blow that left him lying on his back looking up half-dazed toward the sky.

Sensing victory, the warrior leaped off his mount and knelt beside Daniel. With his left hand, he grabbed a wad of thick black hair. He raised his knife just as Daniel's vision cleared. The two men's eyes met. The Sioux warrior frowned and grunted. Exhaling sharply, he slumped onto his backside in the dirt and began to laugh, revealing the space where two teeth had been knocked out long ago.

Daniel reached up to rub his scalp, pushing himself upright with his free hand.

"The only soldier I have had a chance to kill in over two moons," Otter grumbled as he got up and stood facing Daniel, "and he turns out to be my friend."

The two stood gasping for breath, staring wordlessly at each other. Daniel finally broke the silence. "I hoped you were far up north, free, living the old way."

Otter shrugged. "When the other chiefs would not unite with him, Little Crow said he would come back to the Big Woods. Some of us came with him." Otter pointed toward his horse. "Some got good horses." He shrugged. "Some got killed. I am glad you listened to me that night in camp. When we came back from fighting, Mother Friend told me you were gone." He smiled. "But she wouldn't say where."

"I took the missionary's children and Blue Eyes down the river in a canoe. I left them at Fort Ridgely and then I went back to the camp to help my friends." Daniel shook his head. "They put us all in prison for a while."

Otter poked at one of the brass buttons on Daniel's worn blue coat. "And yet you serve them?"

"We find our peaceful brothers and bring them to safety. We protect the supply lines taking food west." He looked at his friend. "And if we find hostile Indians, we are to take them to the fort."

"That will be hard to do, my friend," Otter said, smiling. "Since you have no gun."

"And since I have no gun," Daniel said quietly, "you will probably be able to escape unharmed and I will have to go back to Fort Ridgely and report that I chased you halfway to Dakota Territory but you had a fine war horse while I was riding only a mule and you will probably never be heard from again."

Otter sighed. "We have come a long road since we were two young braves with no problem bigger than getting Genevieve LaCroix to notice us when we visited her father's trading post." He shook his head. "These are bad times for a Dakota warrior. The white man's God gives His power to the white soldiers and they defeat us everywhere we go."

"He is not the 'white man's God,'" Daniel said quietly. "He is your God as well—even though you have not acknowledged Him."

Otter pondered what Daniel had said. "Tell me something," he asked abruptly. "Why do you care about this God? Has He given you anything you wanted? Has He protected you from danger? Has He made the white man give your farm back? Have you got the woman you wanted?" Otter spat on the ground. "What kind of God sees His children suffering and gives yet more power to evil men to make them suffer more?" He put his hand on Daniel's shoulder and shook his friend gently. "Answer one of those questions, my friend, and perhaps we will talk more of your God."

Daniel opened his mouth to say something but his words disappeared in the sound of gunfire. Otter's eyes opened wide as a spot of red appeared on his chest. He took one step backward and crumpled to the earth.

Daniel whirled around to see Jensen standing a few feet away, his smoking gun at his side. Screaming a protest, Daniel lowered his head and charged like a bull. He heard the air escape from Jensen's lungs, heard a crackling sound as two ribs gave way. He landed atop Jensen, meeting with no resistance as he grabbed the gun out of the man's hand and flung it as far away as he could. Making a fist he landed a crushing blow to Jensen's jaw. The soldier went limp.

Otter was trying to get up, but by the time Daniel knelt at his side, the red spot on his chest was spreading and Otter was coughing up blood. He put his hand on Daniel's forearm and stared into his friend's eyes.

Daniel gripped Otter's forearm and returned his gaze for what seemed like an eternity. When at last he let go and closed his friend's eyes, he sat back on the earth, covered his face with his hands, and wept.

❧

"Don't," Daniel growled. "Don't touch him." He had just come back from rounding up his mule and Otter's stallion to find Jensen standing over Otter's body.

Jensen whirled around. "You stay away from me!" he mumbled. Fear shone in his eyes as he coughed, grimacing in pain and clutching his side. "I heard what you said. That savage was a friend of yours. You were going to let him go. When Captain Willets hears—"

Daniel grabbed Jensen's shirt collar. "When Captain Willets hears *what?* That you wouldn't have gotten within five miles of those lost horses without the help of a *savage?* That you nearly fainted out of fear when you saw your first real Dakota warrior? That you shot an unarmed man?" He stared coldly into Jensen's eyes before letting go of his shirt collar. He shoved the mule's reins into Jensen's hand. "You're going to tell Captain Willets that a small war party stole the horses. You're going to tell him that I sent you back to get the other scouts and that we'll report back to him tomorrow about what we find. Then you're going to go to Robert and Big Amos and ask them to meet me at 'the farm'." He glared at Jensen. "Of course, if you prefer, you are welcome to come with me to get our horses back. My friend here mentioned only four or five other braves waiting just across the river."

Jensen blanched. He rubbed his jaw. With a grunt, he climbed up onto the mule's back and was gone.

Daniel hefted Otter's body over the stallion's back, then led the horse into the shade and let him drink noisily from a nearby creek while he thought. Finally, he leaped up behind Otter's body. He barely touched the stallion's sides with his boots and the animal moved into an easy, smooth lope.

❦

Jeb Grant called "whoa" to his team and shaded his eyes with his hand to watch the lone figure approach. His heart lurched when he realized the rider was probably Indian. He had some kind of blanket rolled up in front of him. Nice horse. Mopping his fore-head with a soiled kerchief, Jeb stepped away from his team. He tried to appear relaxed as he quickly stepped from row to row of the newly plowed field toward the house. He whistled sharply, relieved when Marjorie appeared in the doorway of the house, his rifle tucked under her arm.

When the rider came closer and Jeb recognized Daniel Two Stars, he relaxed momentarily. But then he realized the "blanket" draped in front of the scout was a dead Indian. "You all right?" Jeb asked abruptly.

Daniel nodded. "I wanted—" He choked up and sat staring down at the body. He sat for a long moment. Then, taking a deep breath he laid his hand on Otter's back and said, "This man was my friend. If I take him back to the fort, they will—"

"They'll likely scalp him like they did Little Crow," Jeb said quickly.

Daniel swallowed hard. He looked away as he said, "You said your family never hated Indians. I wondered—"

"Of course you can bury your friend here," Marjorie said abruptly. She looked at her husband. "Can't he, Jeb?"

Jeb looked surprised, but he hesitated only a moment before nodding toward the barn. "There's a big oak tree just up the rise there. Shades a big flat rock. There's a spring—"

"I know the place," Daniel said. He slid off the stallion and stood leaning against the animal's side for a moment.

Marjorie's eyes filled with tears. "I'll—I'll have supper wait-ing when you—when you come back down the hill," she said softly and disappeared back inside the house.

"There's a shovel just inside the barn door," Jeb said, nod-ding up the hill. "I'll be along directly."

Two Stars led the stallion to the barn door. Reaching inside, he retrieved the shovel and headed up the hill. Tears nearly blinded him as he began to dig. He had barely marred the earth when Jeb Grant led his team into the barn. It wasn't long before he climbed the hill, another shovel in hand, and took his place alongside Daniel.

Pointing at a small white cross a few feet away, Jeb said abruptly, "Our baby." He stabbed the earth and turned another shovel full before adding, "It was a boy. He lived half a day." He inhaled sharply and blinked back tears.

Before Daniel could say anything Marjorie appeared around the corner of the barn, a tattered quilt folded over her arm. "I don't know what the right customs are," she said shyly. "But if you wanted to wrap him—" She held out the quilt.

Jeb stood his shovel up in the mound of earth beside the open grave. Putting his arm around his wife, he said to Daniel, "You come have supper when you're done. We'll wait." They walked down the hill and disappeared inside the cabin.

When Daniel had shoveled the last bit of earth over his friend's body, he knelt beside the grave. He held his hands open and sat quietly for a few minutes before getting up and walking down the hill.

He found Jeb inside the barn, forking fresh hay into a stall where the stallion stood, eyeing him suspiciously.

"I thought if anybody came looking for you," Jeb explained, "they maybe oughtn't to see your friend's horse. At least not until you know what you're going to do."

"I sent the soldier who was with me back to the fort to get Big Amos and Richard Lawrence," Daniel said woodenly. The stallion stepped close, nuzzling at one of Daniel's hands. Daniel stroked the white velvet muzzle and the horse pressed its forehead against his chest, demanding to have his ears rubbed.

"The soldier killed your friend?"

Daniel nodded. "Otter knocked him off his horse. Counted coup and came after me. Then he recognized me. We were just talking when Jensen shot him."

"This Jensen sounds like a fine example of manhood," Jeb said sarcastically.

Daniel shrugged. "He hates Indians." He rubbed the back of his neck. "Otter shouldn't have been in this part of the country."

Together the men went to the house. Jeb sat down at the head of the table. Marjorie ladled up stew and then handed Jeb a Bible. Jeb took her hand and read,

> *Lord, make me to know mine end,*
> *    and the measure of my days, what it is;*
> *    that I may know how frail I am.*
> *Behold, thou hast make my days as a hand breadth;*
> *    and mine age is as nothing before thee:*
> *    verily every man at his best state is altogether vanity.*
> *Surely every man walketh in a vain show;*
> *    surely they are disquieted in vain:*
> *    he heapeth up riches and knoweth not who shall gather them.*
> *And now, Lord, what wait I for?*
> *    My hope is in thee.*

Jeb said a hasty "amen" and closed the book.

"I've never heard anyone pray that way," Two Stars said quietly.

Jeb shrugged. "Sometimes I don't know what to say. Fact is, I've been kind of holding out on God since our baby boy died last year." He swallowed. "He was our third child. God took each one before they was a year old."

Marjorie got up quickly. She turned her back, but Two Stars could see her swipe tears from her face as she bent to open the oven and toss fresh biscuits into a basket.

Jeb continued, "Marjorie says we aren't going to be like heathens and not talk to God. So I got this idea of just reading the Psalms." He took a swig of coffee before adding, "It gives me words to say when I don't have my own."

Daniel nodded. He finished his meal quickly and then went outside to wait for Robert Lawrence and Big Amos. It had been a long time since he had had anything to say to God. He thought that if he could get hold of a Bible again, maybe he would look at those Psalms Jeb Grant was using.

# Eleven

"Devise not evil against thy neighbour,
seeing he dwelleth securely by thee."
—Proverbs 3:29

"Crow Creek?"

The stranger at the door pursed his lips and looked away for a moment. His wide mouth turned down, whether in anger or disappointment, Miss Jane could not quite tell. When he removed his hat with a metal hook instead of a hand, she felt herself withdraw.

"I apologize, madam," he said in a beautifully resonant, deep voice. "It's just that I was caught off guard. I was hoping to speak with Reverend Dane personally."

"I'm truly sorry. The reverend has been away in Iowa. He was back for a short visit, but then he left again only a few days ago for the west." Miss Jane looked up at him. "Is there anything I can do?"

The man sighed and shook his head. "I imagine not. Unless—" He hesitated before saying, "I've actually come more about the Dane children than anything else."

"And you are?" Miss Jane asked, looking up into the stranger's gray-blue eyes.

"Elliot Leighton. Their uncle. Their mother's brother."

"Well," Miss Jane blustered, "why didn't you *say* so? Goodness, come in, come in!" She waved Leighton into the entryway of the great house. "Hang your hat right there and follow me into the parlor. Aaron went west with his father, but Meg will be home from school directly, and of course you will have met Miss LaCroix already when she was back east with the reverend and Mrs. Dane."

Elliot obeyed Miss Jane, hanging his hat on a hook beside the door. "I—uh—didn't have the pleasure of meeting Miss LaCroix," he said quickly. He glanced down at his hook. "I was with my regiment when they arrived. And then regrettably detained in the hospital. Word of Ellen's death didn't reach me until long after Simon and the children had already come back west."

"I'm so sorry," Miss Jane said. "Please come in and sit down. If you'll just make yourself comfortable—" She indicated a wing chair beside an open window. "As I said, Meg should be home any minute. And Miss LaCroix and the other children are just doing some marketing—"

"The other children?" Leighton asked, frowning.

"Why, yes," Miss Jane said, smiling. "We've quite a little family here. The Whitneys—they own the house—have two of their own, and then there is Hope, an orphan the reverend has adopted, and we have Rebecca and Timothy Sutton, who were orphaned in the outbreak. We are of course trying to contact their family, but there's been little success in that regard." Miss Jane stopped abruptly. "Excuse me for rattling on so. I'll just get you some lemonade." Miss Jane was gone before Leighton could tell her he really wasn't thirsty.

The woman's whirlwind of activity accented the silence in the big house now that she was gone. Elliot sat stiffly in the worn chair he had been assigned, staring down at the despised hook in his lap. He pulled on his sleeve, trying to conceal it. The sound of childish laughter outside caught his attention. Looking out the window he saw a gaggle of children tripping toward the house. His gaze narrowed as a dark-skinned woman came into view. She was petite, fine-boned, with abundant dark hair piled high on her head and a heart-shaped face accented by a cleft chin. *Funny*, Leighton thought to himself, *she doesn't look particularly Indian.* She clutched a blonde-headed toddler in her arms and was looking down at one of the children, smiling. *Pretty. Some would say beautiful.* He couldn't begrudge Simon Dane the attraction, that was certain.

Leighton stood up, expecting the entire group to enter the house at any moment, but as he listened, he could tell they were walking around to the back of the house, apparently coming in through the kitchen. Turning to look in the mirror at himself, he straightened his collar and swiped at his long white hair with his hand.

"Uncle Elliot?" A girlish voice sounded from the doorway. Elliot turned around to see one eye framed by a mass of dark red curls peering at him from around the edge of the door.

"Is that Meg?" Elliot said, trying to sound as friendly as possible.

Meg took one step from behind the door. She eyed the stranger suspiciously. "You don't look anything like the picture Grandmother kept on her mantel."

"I expect not," Elliot answered quietly. "The cavalry aged me significantly."

Meg took another step forward. She looked down at the hook protruding from his shirt sleeve. "Did you lose your hand in the war?" she asked abruptly.

Leighton nodded. To his amazement, the child's eyes filled with tears. "I'm sorry, Uncle Elliot," she croaked. "Did it hurt terribly?"

Something in the child's unabashed sympathy touched a place in Elliot Leighton's soul that had been locked away for a long time. Unable to speak without his voice shaking, he simply nodded.

Meg moved to his side and laid her hand on his arm. "Is that what made your hair white too?" she said.

Elliot managed to look at her. Where, he thought, had a child of only eight years learned such honest compassion?

When Elliot didn't speak, Meg said softly, "We saw a lady that got white hair when we were in the Indians' camp last year." She reached up and touched her temples. "Even Gen got some just here. Father said it was being afraid that made her hair do that." She looked her uncle over and smiled. "I like it. You look sort of like a *lion*."

Elliot smiled at Meg with true warmth. He found himself thanking her and meaning it. "I suppose I do look rather fierce. Does it frighten you?"

Meg considered before answering. Then she shook her head.

"Why not?"

"Well," she answered slowly. "I guess you can't always tell what's on the *inside* just by looking at the *outside*, can you?" Her face seemed to age visibly as she said, "What I mean is, when we were with the Indians, some of them looked *terrible fierce*. Daniel Two Stars—he was our friend—he found us one night and he was painted like a very bad Indian." Meg motioned as she spoke, "He had red circles around his eyes, and lightning on his chest. We hardly recognized him! But *underneath* he was just our friend Daniel." Meg shrugged. "You just can't always tell by looking, that's all." She eyed Leighton for a moment and then pointed down at his hook. "Can you pick stuff up with that?"

Elliot nodded.

Meg got a book down from the shelf beside the fireplace. Elliot was demonstrating the mechanics of his metal hand when Genevieve LaCroix entered the parlor, followed by Miss Jane carrying a tray laden with both hot tea and lemonade.

Extending her hand and grasping Elliot's in a firm handshake, Gen said, "I'm sorry to say Simon isn't here. He and Aaron went—"

"West to Crow Creek," Elliot said. "Miss Jane told me."

"Uncle Elliot has a hook," Meg interrupted. "He can pick things up." She nodded at Gen. "Show her, Uncle Elliot."

Elliot said quickly, "Perhaps another time." He turned to face Gen, his face red with embarrassment. "Obviously I was hoping to see Reverend Dane."

"Of course," Gen said. "Won't you sit down?" She offered Elliot a glass of lemonade and then, pouring hot tea for herself and Miss Jane, settled on the couch opposite him. "Including his stint at the prison in Davenport, Simon has been away for some time. One of the mission workers at Crow Creek sent a rather desperate plea for help. Simon is eager to reestablish himself among the Dakota families, so he came back here to regroup and then headed west to the reservation. You only missed him by a week or so."

"When is he expected back?" Elliot asked.

Gen hesitated. "Actually, Meg and Hope and I are just waiting for him to send for us."

Leighton frowned. "I beg your pardon?"

"The reverend and Miss LaCroix are engaged to be married, Mr. Leighton," Miss Jane said.

"I—I thought Simon had written—" Gen interjected, embarrassed.

"He mentioned something about it in a letter," Leighton said.

"But we didn't believe—" He interrupted himself. Looking at Meg, he asked, "Simon spoke of an orphan named Hope. I take it you haven't found her family?"

"As a matter of fact," Gen replied, "Hope's family did eventually answer Simon's notices in a newspaper in Ohio. But when they arrived we made arrangements to keep her with us."

"I see," Leighton said, although it was obvious he did not see at all.

"And how is your brother, little miss?" Leighton addressed Meg.

"He's with Father. They are going to build our new house," Meg said proudly. "Hope and I are going to have our own room," she said. "Father says it will be very much like our house that burned down at Lac Qui Parle. That was a very nice house."

"I'm sure it was," Leighton said. He stood up abruptly. "I don't want to overstay my welcome."

"Please, Mr. Leighton," Gen said, standing up. "Join us for dinner. We'd be honored to have you. Hope will be up from her nap soon. You can meet her. And I know Meg would like to hear more about her Grandmother Leighton." She smiled at Meg. "They formed a close bond while we were in New York."

Elliot declined to stay the afternoon, but promised he would return for supper. He took his leave, bowing to Gen and Miss Jane and promising Meg a special gift when he returned that evening.

As soon as he left, Gen checked on Hope and sent Meg out to pick green beans in the garden behind the house before following Miss Jane to the kitchen.

"Stunning man," Miss Jane said without turning to look at Gen. "Must have been an officer. Regal carriage."

"Yes," Gen said absentmindedly. "He graduated from West Point. Had the rank of major, I believe. He lost his hand at Antietam right before Ellen died. They didn't know where to find him to even tell him. Then he got some horrible infection and spent months in a hospital." She murmured, "His hair was raven black in the picture Mrs. Leighton kept on her mantel."

"Poor man," Miss Jane mumbled. When Gen didn't reply, Miss Jane looked up. She searched Gen's face. "What is it? What's the matter."

Gen walked to the kitchen door and looked toward the garden where Meg had been joined by the Sutton children. Together they were all working away, singing as they made their way down the rows of beans in the garden.

"I don't know," Gen said. A shiver went up her spine. "Something. He doesn't like me. I can feel it." She murmured, "I wish Simon were here."

"Don't be ridiculous," Miss Jane interjected. "Mr. Leighton just doesn't know you. He seemed perfectly nice to me. A bit distant, perhaps, but that's certainly understandable. And imagine his disappointment when he came all this way and Simon and Aaron are gone."

Gen turned back toward the kitchen. She pushed an errant strand of dark hair off her neck. "He didn't write that he was coming. Simon would never have left if he knew his brother-in-law was coming to visit the children."

"Perhaps the letter got lost," Miss Jane said. "Don't jump to conclusions, Gen," she insisted. "You know, he was probably ill at ease after Meg asked all those questions about his missing hand. Poor man. I'm certain things will be fine when he comes to dinner. And you should mention the letter. He mustn't think Reverend Dane knew about his arrival and left anyway. That would be unforgivably rude."

Gen headed up the back steps to get Hope up from her nap. "You're probably right," she said. But instinct told her that Elliot Leighton's surprise arrival had more behind it than a lost letter. And something more than just Meg's questions about his war injury was bothering Elliot Leighton.

# Twelve

"But if from thence thou shalt seek the Lord thy God,
thou shalt find him, if thou seek him with all
thy heart and with all thy soul."

—Deuteronomy 4:29

The night was still, the very air seeming to vibrate with wave after wave of heat. Robert Lawrence and his wife, Nancy, had opened the flap and rolled up the sides of their tent in a vain attempt to catch even the slightest movement of air. They lay a few inches apart, content because of the blazing heat only to touch hands. From where he lay, Robert could see a flicker of light on the opposite side of the parade ground, evidence that someone else had given up trying to sleep in the oppressive heat and come out onto their front porch to smoke.

Robert sat up. Nancy whispered his name. He looked down at her, smiling. "Sleep, best beloved," he said tenderly, bending low to kiss her forehead. The corners of her mouth curled up in a lazy smile. Robert thought of Daniel Two Stars, who slept alone each night longing for the presence of a girl he called Blue Eyes.

Whatever Robert and Big Amos did, they could not seem to drag their friend back from wherever his spirit had fled. He had been almost completely silent since he buried his friend Otter down on Jeb Grant's farm weeks ago. He had become as thin as one of the rails Grant used to fence in his cornfield. He refused to go with them to the daily services conducted by the fort chaplain. When they spoke of God, he found reason to go elsewhere.

Daniel still did good work for the army. Captain Willets had commended him several times. Together, the three men had brought in dozens of frightened Dakota to camp near Fort Ridgely until they could be sent to Crow Creek. From what Robert could tell, the thanks of the people they were helping had no effect on Daniel Two Stars. In the past few days he had taken to communicating more in sign language than anything else. Robert had begun to fear that some morning he would waken to find his friend gone, or worse—dead at his own hand.

A twig snapped just outside the tent. Daniel was just sitting down beside the campfire, opening Etienne LaCroix's journal.

Robert got up and went to him. "If you want to find her," he said, "I will talk to Captain Willets. He recruited us for six moons. That will soon be over. Even if he wants us to stay longer, you could go to Crow Creek. Captain Willets would understand. And someone there might know something."

Daniel stared into the dying campfire and said nothing. He closed the book and tossed it behind him on the bedroll.

Robert reached out and put a hand on his friend's shoulder. "I am losing my friend, and I don't know what to do," he said softly.

Tossing a stick into the fire, Daniel said bitterly, "Do you see that stick? The coals are not hot enough to destroy it, but still the stick feels the heat. You can see the bark cracking and the liquid inside oozing out." He paused. "I am that stick. I wait to be consumed by the flames, but all the life has already been drawn out of me."

"Then go find her," Robert said gently.

Daniel shook his head. "I have nothing to give her anymore. I look at her picture and try to remember how I felt. I feel nothing." He looked up at the sky. "I remember looking up at those stars and seeing God."

"Can you think of nothing to thank Him for?" Robert said quietly.

Daniel was silent for so long, Robert thought he would not answer. But finally, he said, "I am thankful Blue Eyes is not here to see what I have become."

Robert protested gently. "Only a good man would have let Brady Jensen live that day when he killed Otter. Only a good man would bury his friend the way you did, risking the anger of the army. Yesterday you put an old woman on your own horse and walked many miles to bring her to our camp." Robert paused, thinking. "Our world has broken apart. No one can blame you for feeling lost. None of us knows what to expect tomorrow. But *God knows*, Daniel. He says we have a future. We can have hope."

"What future?" Daniel snapped. "What hope?"

"You are not the only one who has lost much, Daniel."

He shot back angrily. "But I am the only one inside *this* skin. I am the only one living *this* empty life. And I seem to be the only one God blesses with His silence."

"Pray," Robert urged him.

"He does not hear," Daniel said bitterly.

"How do you know that?"

"Nothing changes."

"Perhaps He is waiting for you to pray that He will change *you* instead of the things around you."

Daniel pondered what Robert had said for a moment. His voice was calmer when he asked, "Is it wrong to want a home?"

"You already have a home. You have a house not made with hands—eternal in the heavens."

Daniel shook his head. "Simon Dane's wife said those words to Blue Eyes the night their house burned down up at Lac Qui Parle." Thinking of Ellen Dane led him back to Genevieve. "Is it wrong to want a wife?"

"Of course not." Robert swallowed. "But, Daniel, whether God gives you the things you want or not, *He* is always with you. *He* will never leave you. It is enough."

"It is *not* enough," Daniel replied angrily.

"It is. But you will never know that until you decide to accept it instead of demanding God send what *you* want."

"How do I do that," Daniel asked, "when everything inside me cries out against the way things are?"

Robert cleared his throat. "You do it by faith, my brother."

Daniel shook his head. "I don't have that kind of faith."

Robert reached behind him and produced a Bible he had brought with him when he came out of his tent. He tried to hand the Bible to Daniel and was ignored. He quoted, "'So then faith cometh by hearing, and hearing by the word of God.'"

"I suppose you are going to tell me just which passage to read that will answer all my questions," Daniel said sarcastically.

"Do you remember those nights long ago when you came to me—when you were being pulled between Otter's way and God? Do you remember how often we stayed awake half the night reading and arguing? You chose the name Daniel because you said you had found a way to live with the lions without being devoured." Robert put his hand on Daniel's shoulder and shook him gently. "The lions are still roaring, my friend. And I fear that you have decided to let them eat you." Robert's voice broke as he cried out, "Don't let it happen. Listen to *God*, Daniel—not the roaring lions.

Look at *His* face—not the faces around you. Not even the face of Blue Eyes can fill your empty heart." Tears streamed down Robert's cheeks. "I love you, my brother. Don't let this thing happen."

"Go to your wife, Robert," Daniel said. "I know you are my friend."

"I will go," Robert said. "But not to my wife. Tonight, I am going to speak to the Father. If it takes all night and another night and another. I will not stop until He breaks through to your stubborn heart." Robert got up and headed for the parade ground. He paused and turned back. "*Faith*, Daniel. You can only still the roaring lions by faith. Hebrews, chapter eleven."

Daniel sat beside the fire staring up at the blazing stars in the night sky and watched Robert walk away. Somewhere in the distance a wolf howled. And then, echoing from the very gulch where Little Crow's warriors had taken cover when they attacked the fort last year, came the cry of a wildcat.

"It's a terrible assignment," Captain Willets said. "And I'm sorry I have to give it out. But if there's any truth to the rumor that the reservation Indians are trying to cross over the James River and come back into Minnesota, somebody has to talk them into going back. It's for their own good. If they are seen by any of the whites in this area, you know as well as I do they'll be shot as hostiles. They must be convinced to stay on the reservation at all costs." Willets looked at the three Dakota men. "To be honest, I doubt any Sioux headed this way would trust regular army to tell them the truth. Can't say that I blame them, either." He cleared his throat. "And some of my men might be a little too eager to use force." He paused. "Do what you can to find them—and turn them back. Escort them all the way to the reservation if you have to."

The three scouts left the captain's headquarters and headed back across the parade ground to the scouts' camp. Robert and Big Amos went to talk with their wives. But Daniel quickly gathered his things. He saddled his horse, being careful to pack both the journal and Robert's Bible in his saddlebags. He went to Robert and said abruptly, "You can catch up with me. I'll leave a good trail."

Robert frowned. "Captain Willets said we could wait until tomorrow."

"I know," Daniel nodded as he climbed into the saddle.

"What if Captain Willets notices you're already gone?"

"Tell him I'm chasing the mountain lion that was prowling around the fort last night," Daniel said.

"A mountain lion?" Nancy said as he rode away. "This close to camp?" she shivered.

Robert put his arm around her. He called to Big Amos. "Did you hear a mountain lion last night?"

Big Amos shook his head.

"Neither did I," Robert said. He watched his friend ride out of camp. And he prayed.

Jeb Grant had filled nearly half a wagon full of good corn when Daniel Two Stars rode up. "Been hopin' you'd come by," he said, taking off his work gloves and beating them against his pants to shake out the dust. "That stallion's a beautiful animal, but I can't do a thing with him."

"I'm sorry if he caused you trouble," Daniel said.

"No need to apologize," Jeb said quickly. "I was hoping to keep him. But every time I come near him, he throws a fit. I've managed to keep him fed, and some creative herding has gotten him in and out of his stall so I could muck it out, but he's never going to be content living on a farm."

"Captain Willets is sending three of us west to stop the reservation Indians trying to come back to Minnesota," Daniel said. He hesitated before adding, "I'd like to set the horse free out there—if it's all right with you."

"I'd be grateful," Jeb said without hesitation. "Even if I could have tamed him down, I didn't know how I was going to explain a dirt farmer from Kentucky having a horse like that." He grinned. "Maybe he'll make up to you. I been thinkin' he objects to the smell of white folks."

Daniel smiled and headed for the barn. He found the stallion backed into the corner of his stall eyeing him suspiciously. When Daniel put his hands on the edge of the stall, the horse tossed his head and bared his teeth.

"See what I mean?" Jeb said from the doorway.

"*Damakota. Mawaste,*" Daniel said in a low voice. He held out his hand. The stallion neighed sharply and pawed the ground. "*Ihnuhan hecanon kin,*" Daniel continued to speak to the horse in Dakota. As he did so, he unlatched the stall door and stepped in. The horse stretched his neck out and turned his head, eyeing Daniel carefully. As Daniel continued speaking Dakota, the animal lowered its head and stepped forward until its forehead rested against Daniel's chest. It sighed and stood still while Daniel scratched its ears.

"Well, I'll be," Jeb said quietly. "Guess I was right. All he needed was an Indian friend."

"His halter?" Daniel asked.

Jeb handed it over, and in only a few moments the horse was following Daniel around the farm yard calmly.

"Like a big ol' puppy dog," Jeb commented from his observation post near the cabin.

"Can you stay to supper?" Marjorie called out. She was sitting beneath a newly constructed porch, a huge bowl of freshly picked green beans in her lap.

Daniel shook his head.

"You stay safe, my friend," Jeb said.

Daniel lifted his hand in a silent good-bye. Then, for some reason, he urged his gelding back around. "Do you still pray every night?" he asked abruptly.

Jeb looked up at him in surprise. He grinned. "I even been makin' up my own words of late. Guess I decided bein' upset with the Man in Charge was pointless."

Daniel nodded. He almost asked Jeb to include him in his prayers. Instead, he lifted his hand again and rode away.

When the Grants had supper that night, Marjorie said abruptly, "Say a prayer for Daniel Two Stars, Jeb." At her husband's look of surprise she shrugged. "It just seems like somethin' we ought to do."

Jeb prayed.

# Thirteen

"For the Lord seeth not as man seeth;
for man looketh on the outward appearance,
but the Lord looketh on the heart."

—1 Samuel 16:7

"Welcome home," Gen whispered, hugging Simon. Her joy faltered when she realized how thin he was. She looked up at him with a little frown of concern. Fatigue was etched in his face, aging him considerably.

Simon released her quickly and opened his arms to Meg and Hope, staggering backward when they flung themselves at him. "Whoa, there, girls," he said, his voice choked with emotion. "Let your old father sit down." He held their hands and together they went into the parlor where it did not escape Gen's notice that Simon sighed with relief when he sank into a cushioned high-backed chair.

Aaron lingered behind his father, his arm around Gen. He did not miss her look of concern. "It's all right," he whispered. "He's just tired."

Gen patted Aaron on the back and then left his side to join the small group gathered around Simon.

"We want to hear everything," Miss Jane said.

Samuel and Nina Whitney murmured their assent while the children sat quietly on the braided rug, miraculously well-behaved and quiet in the face of Aaron and the reverend's home-coming.

"You talk first, Aaron," Simon said, smiling up at his son. He kissed Hope on the cheek and then let her down with the other children while Meg nestled back against him.

Aaron sat down on the couch next to Gen. He studied the floor for a moment, obviously struggling to organize his thoughts. "Crow Creek is—" He shook his head. "I can't begin to tell you. The worst place possible. The idea of farming there is ludicrous." Aaron looked at his father and shrugged. "There isn't much anyone can do."

"Wrong," Simon interrupted gently.

With a look in his father's direction, Aaron nodded. "We're fairly helpless to relieve the *physical* difficulties." He continued, "Although we helped plow up a few new acres for planting in the spring, it will all be pointless unless the drought breaks." He paused, thinking. "I got to know a few of the old men." He looked around the room. "There aren't many boys my age. Most of them have died. The rest are too sick to do much." The situation Aaron went on to describe was worse than anything the group had imagined. Aaron finally gave up with a helpless shrug. "You can't really imagine it until you've been there."

"But," Simon spoke up, "we have witnessed some amazing things spiritually." He looked at Aaron. When their eyes met, something passed between them.

"Yes," Aaron confirmed. "Father told you how we put up a booth—you know," he said as he held his hands over his head to illustrate for the children, "poles set in the ground with brush for a kind of roof. As soon as we had it finished there was a crowd ready to attend the first meeting." Aaron grinned at Gen. "Amos Huggins would have been amazed if he could have heard the hymn-singing."

"Amos Huggins?" Nina Whitney asked.

Miss Jane explained, "Amos helped translate many of the hymns in the first Dakota hymnal." She lowered her voice almost reverently. "He was among the first killed in the uprising. He had just returned from having the hymnal printed. They found his body on the road."

"Singing is one of the favorite parts of the day," Aaron said. "We sing hymns at every meeting. And they love to hear Father teach." He looked at his father with unabashed pride.

"Tell them about the trip back to St. Anthony," Simon broke in.

"Perhaps over supper," Miss Jane interrupted. "You men must be starving." She was already headed for the kitchen. "We've a roast turkey in the oven and the first harvest of squash." She motioned to the children. "Come along—time to set the table." Aaron got up to help her, but she pushed him back. "You get unpacked and talk to the grown-ups." She flashed a huge smile at him. "I declare, you're very nearly an adult, anyway. I can't believe how you've grown!" She herded the rest of the children into the hall and toward the kitchen.

Simon pushed himself up out of his chair. He sighed. "Miss Jane is right, Aaron. We'd best be getting unpacked and cleaned up." He patted the sides of his vest. "I think there's at least ten pounds of road dust in these rags." He walked by the couch and patted Gen on the shoulder. "It's good to be home."

Gen closed her eyes and put her hand on his. "I'll go help Miss Jane with dinner." She walked to the door with Simon, kissing his cheek when they parted. From the doorway, she watched him trudge up the stairs. "Simon," Gen called from below. When he turned to look back at her, she said softly, "There's plenty of time for you to lie down before dinner. You must be exhausted."

He nodded. "Perhaps I will."

❦

"Where's Father?" Aaron wanted to know. He bounded into the kitchen and swept Hope up in his arms. "I knocked on his door before I went out to the garden nearly an hour ago."

"I'll check on him," Gen said quickly. She flew up the back steps to Simon's door, knocking gently at first, then with more force. When there was no answer, she turned the knob and called softly, "Simon. Supper is ready. Simon?" When the only answer was soft snoring, Gen pushed the door open a little farther. Simon was lying face up on the bed, fully clothed. He did not stir while Gen removed his shoes, then his socks. When she covered him with a lightweight blanket and tucked a pillow beneath his head, he sighed happily. It was not until she gently undid his tie and began to unbutton his top shirt button that he woke. Without opening his eyes, he took her hand and kissed it, whispering, "It seems that I do have a guardian angel, after all." He opened his eyes and stared up at her. "I was dreaming about you, Miss LaCroix."

Gen knelt beside the bed. She stroked the gray hair along his temple. "You're completely worn out, Reverend Dane."

He mumbled, "Guilty as charged." He took a deep breath, obviously fighting the temptation to close his eyes.

"Sleep," Gen whispered gently. She kissed his forehead before getting up. He was sound asleep before Gen got to the door.

❦

"He's resting," Gen said when Elliot Leighton knocked at the kitchen door the next afternoon. She was sitting at the kitchen table, a box of apples on the floor beside her, a pile of peelings in a bowl in her lap. "If you wish," she said without getting up, "I can send Aaron for you when Simon comes down." She cut the apple in her hands in half, cored it, and began slicing it into the first of seven pie shells waiting on the table.

When Leighton did not reply, Gen looked up. "If you are waiting for an invitation to tea, Mr. Leighton, I'm afraid you're to be disappointed. We should be civil to one another for the sake of the children. You needn't pretend when no one else is here. Do you want me to send Aaron for you or not?"

"It's very important that I see Simon right away," Leighton insisted.

"Not as important as it is that he get some uninterrupted rest," Gen shot back. She didn't look away, but stared at him stubbornly. "Aaron just took Hope out for a walk. He should be back soon. As soon as his father is awake, I'll send for you"—she shot him a wilting glance—"not in the servile sense, you understand."

The front door slammed shut and Miss Jane came charging down the hall. She managed to get only halfway to the table when the handle on her market basket broke and everything dropped to the floor with a thud. "Mercy!" she exclaimed, her cheeks burning with embarrassment.

"Let me help," Elliot said, kneeling down and beginning to pick things up and set them on the table.

"Oh, don't!" Miss Jane exclaimed, scrambling to pick up a dozen small packages wrapped in brown paper. "I can do it!"

Leighton shot back vehemently, "So can I—even with only one hand!"

Miss Jane retorted, "It has nothing to do with one hand, Elliot Leighton. It has to do with my embarrassment at being such a graceless ninny." She snatched up the last package, clutching it to her as if it were a priceless treasure. Her cheeks were blazing red, her eyes crackling with a mixture of anger and embarrassment.

Gen looked on with a confused frown. Whatever was going on between those two?

"Will you stay for tea, Mr. Leighton?" Jane asked abruptly.

"Thank you, Miss Williams."

"Well, sit down then and let me get my bearings." Still flustered, Miss Jane stared down at the pile of packages on the table. She pointed to each one, mumbling to herself, "brown sugar, cinnamon, flour—ah—" She grabbed a small package and turned toward the stove. "*Tea.*"

Gen had finished peeling half the box of apples and filled all the pie shells with apple slices by the time Miss Jane had tea ready.

"Care to join us?" Miss Jane asked Gen.

Gen shook her head. "I'll just get the top crusts ready." She turned away, rolled up her sleeves, and began rolling out the dough waiting on the wood counter against the wall. When the seven pies were ready for the oven, Gen washed and dried her hands, rolled her sleeves back down, and excused herself. "I promised Meg we'd finish the story we began at bedtime last night as soon as she came home from school." She glanced up the back stairs and said to Miss Jane, "If Simon comes down—"

"—I'll send him to the parlor," Miss Jane said quickly.

"No, I wasn't thinking that," Gen said reluctantly. "Mr. Leighton came to talk to Simon. Actually, I just wanted you to let me know that he was up."

Miss Jane reached out and squeezed Gen's hand. "He's fine, Gen. I've seen it happen before on the mission field. When men don't have a woman caring for them they don't care for themselves. They don't eat properly, they don't rest—they work themselves into a frenzy and then they fall apart. We'll just have to see that it doesn't happen again." She smiled at Gen, who nodded and left.

Elliot sipped his tea and watched as Miss Jane finished putting away her market packages. She untied a small bundle of cinnamon sticks and put them in a clean jar. Brown sugar and flour were put into crocks in the pantry, tea in a dark brown box on a shelf over the stove. Finally, she slid three pies into the oven and then, pouring herself a cup of tea, sat down opposite Leighton.

"Suppose you tell me what the problem is between you and my friend Miss LaCroix," she said abruptly.

Leighton raised his eyebrows and eyed Miss Jane for a moment. "I don't know what you're talking about," he said carefully.

"Of course you do, Mr. Leighton." Miss Jane sipped her tea. "Every time the two of you are in the same room, it positively frosts over."

Leighton put a teaspoon of sugar into his tea cup and stirred it. "I apologize," he said quickly, "if I've made you uncomfortable. And I don't want to say anything that might reflect poorly on Miss LaCroix, since you obviously care for her."

Miss Jane shifted in her chair. Leaning forward, she said, "Let's be clear on something, Mr. Leighton. I have no use for people who dance around an issue. I've asked you to say what's on your mind, and I'd appreciate an honest answer." She sat back and waited for him to respond.

"Very well," Elliot said abruptly. "I'll be brutally honest." He nodded toward the front of the house where Gen had gone. "That woman's people have committed horrible, horrible, things. You cannot make a silk purse from a sow's ear. And you cannot make a civilized human being out of an Indian."

Miss Jane blinked rapidly a few times and bit her lip, willing herself not to speak for a moment. Presently, she reached across the table and tugged on Leighton's left sleeve. He let her pull his injured arm onto the table where she laid his hook in the palm of her hand. She looked up at him, her eyes glimmering with emotion when she said, "I believe *your* people have done a few horrible things from time to time as well, Mr. Leighton." She arched one eyebrow. "But you don't hear Miss LaCroix saying how much she hates *you* because the United States military killed the man she loved by mistake."

"Please," Elliot said, pulling his arm back and concealing his hook by sliding it onto his lap beneath the table. "Not another story about the great Daniel Two Stars." He brushed his white mane of hair back from his face. "I've heard all about him from Meg."

"He's only one hero from the uprising," Miss Jane said quickly. "If you'd just listen—"

"I don't need to hear stories about Indian heroes to know that I have no intention of letting my sister's children be dragged to the edge of the wilderness just because my brother-in-law has some misdirected notion of piety's demands. And I most certainly will *not* have them raised by a half-breed *Indian*." He sneered the last word.

"I believe," Simon said from the bottom of the stairs, "that that is *my* decision to make, Elliot." He was leaning against the door frame and neither Elliot nor Miss Jane knew how long he had been listening.

Elliot glanced at Miss Jane, whose cheeks were flaming red.

Simon ignored Miss Jane as he walked across the room to perch on the edge of the table, one hand on the table beside him and one hand on his knee. When he spoke his voice was so quiet Leighton had to strain to hear the words. "I thought it was odd that you would trek halfway across the country just to see your niece and nephew, Elliot. Especially when you haven't written them once since their mother's death."

"If you will recall, Simon," Leighton said, putting his hook back on the table. "I had to learn a few things more important than writing."

Simon stood up. "I apologize, Elliot. I truly had forgotten that you were left-handed before you were wounded."

Aaron burst into the kitchen with Hope in tow. "Uncle Elliot!" he nearly shouted. "I came to the hotel to surprise you, but you were gone."

Leighton stood up, obviously flustered by Aaron's exuberant greeting. He extended his hand, but Aaron ignored it, preferring instead to engulf his uncle in a bear hug. When he released him, Aaron stood back. When Leighton grimaced, Aaron apologized quickly, "I'm sorry, Uncle Elliot—I thought you were all healed up. Did I—did I hurt you?" He looked down at Elliot's hook.

"No, no, it's not that—" Leighton mumbled. He recovered and forced a smile. "How tall are you going to get, young man?" Without waiting for Aaron's reply, he looked at Simon. "I think he got the Leighton height, don't you, Simon?"

Simon smiled and followed his brother-in-law's lead. "I think he got *all* of the good things about his mother's family—including height. Isn't he nearly as tall as you were when you were that age, Elliot?"

Leighton surveyed Aaron carefully. "I think he's a bit taller. And he looks much older. You *are* only twelve, aren't you, my boy?" He put his hand on Aaron's shoulder. When Aaron nodded, Leighton frowned. "You're growing up entirely too quickly. Stop it immediately. Your grandmother won't recognize you when you visit."

"Father said we'd have a studio photo taken to send home with you," Aaron said.

"Your grandmother would love that," Elliot said. Then, looking across the room at Simon he added, "But she would much rather have the living, breathing version come for a visit." He looked back at Aaron. "What do you say, my boy? Would you like to go back to New York with me for a visit? We'd take Meg, of course."

"I'd love to." Aaron didn't hesitate. "But I can't." He nodded toward where Simon stood. "Father and I have much too much work to do. I'm to attend school here in St. Anthony this winter. Then in the spring I'll be heading back to Crow Creek."

"You could just as easily attend school in New York as here," Elliot said. Then, sensing the tension rising in the room, he backed off. "But that's a topic for a later discussion." He slapped Aaron on the back. "It's good to see you, my boy." He nodded at Simon. "Perhaps we can have supper this evening? At my hotel?"

"Of course." Simon nodded. "Eight o'clock?"

"Eight o'clock," Elliot said. He thanked Miss Jane for his tea and left. Just when the screen door closed, Gen came down the stairs. "You must be starving," she said to Simon. Going to the oven and opening the door she said, "And I'd say I can offer you fresh apple pie in a matter of moments."

If there was one thing in the world that Elliot Leighton despised, it was a lack of self-discipline. Self-discipline had brought him back from near certain death, had conquered the threat of gangrene, had taught him to use his right hand when he lost his dominant left hand, had wrested a semblance of life from the gloomy existence accepted by other war casualties. Any weakness, any challenge, Leighton reasoned, could be made his enemy. Through self-discipline, he could wage war against it and either bring it under submission or cut it out of his life completely. This exercise in self-discipline was successful in every area of Leighton's life except one. Try as he might, he could not seem to conquer his persistent attraction to women. It caused him unending difficulty and a deep hurt that he barely acknowledged to himself.

He had been slow to accept the reality that any possibility of worthwhile feminine companionship had been blown away with his left hand. For a season he had thought the situation only temporary. Once he was rehabilitated, he thought, women would stop seeing him as an invalid and begin to view him once again as a man. After all, Leighton reasoned, surely they must realize that the loss of a hand did nothing to affect a man's virility.

Strangely, none of the women he had known before the war seemed to grasp this basic truth. One look at his hair, whitened overnight in battle, one glance at his hook, and something happened to them. Their eyes clouded over, their faces took on a pained expression, their voices dripped with unwelcome pity. The day he realized that even Betsy, the maid he had once scolded for her impertinence, seemed to see him as an object of sympathy, Leighton began to think that no woman would ever again see him as anything other than a victim at best, or a freak at worst. *Fools*, he thought.

By the time Leighton headed for Minnesota to rescue his sister's children, he had cut off most of his prewar social contacts and devoted himself almost entirely to managing his father's considerable estate, thereby convincing himself that his self-discipline had eradicated any desire for feminine companionship. Until Miss Jane.

Leighton thought it absurd that after swearing off younger and more beautiful women, he should find a rather plain, willow-thin spinster attractive. Even more absurd was the fact that what he liked most of all about Miss Jane had little to do with either her figure or her features. What he admired was her manner. She was all business, amazingly focused on her duty to God and her adopted family. She had a fiery disposition. She had suffered her own battles, did not consider herself a victim, and apparently did not appropriate the title to him, either. Not once had he seen pity in her eyes when she looked at him.

When Leighton found himself unable to conquer his attraction to Miss Jane, he took solace in the fact that he would soon be returning to New York with Ellen's children. And that, he thought, would be the end of that. It was, therefore, totally disarming when Miss Jane pulled on his shirt sleeve and laid his hook in the palm of her hand, apparently without revulsion. It was equally unnerving when, not two hours after he had left the Whitney kitchen, a hotel maid knocked at his door and presented him with a calling card informing him that a certain Miss Jane Williams was waiting to speak with him in the hotel dining room.

When Leighton descended to meet her, Miss Jane stood up to receive him. She had donned a severe black dress and a magnificently outdated hat and yet, Leighton thought as he walked toward her, her manner lent a measure of grace to the costume. She returned his handshake firmly and sat down, quickly waving a waiter over and ordering tea. It did not go unnoticed by Leighton that she handled the entire exchange as if she did it every day. He suspected that it had been at least ten years since Miss Jane had had any opportunity to order tea in a hotel dining room. He could not keep from smiling inwardly at the woman's ability to adapt to situations.

As soon as the tea was put before them, Miss Jane said abruptly, "I've come to discuss your difficulty with my friend Miss LaCroix." She looked directly at him and he did not miss the spark of emotion in her eyes. "It would appear, based on your previous comments, that you determined to dislike her even *before* you came to St. Anthony." Placing her hands on either side of her cup and saucer, she said earnestly, "I am waiting, Mr. Leighton, for you to say something to convince me that you are not really so simpleminded."

Leighton pursed his lips. He lifted his chin and reached up to adjust his cravat. "Of course I'm not so stupid as that. I'm very well-read on the subject of the Indian problem."

Miss Jane leaned forward. "Tell me something, Mr. Leighton, exactly how many Indians had you known personally before coming to Minnesota?"

He was defensive. "You know the answer to that. It doesn't matter. As I said, I have researched the subject extensively."

"It isn't a *subject*," she snapped. "It's *people*. People who bleed and hurt and love and have families and grieve. People who know what it is to be lonely, to have dreams ripped out of their hands through no fault of their own—"

"Lo, the poor Indian," Leighton said sarcastically.

Miss Jane sat back and eyed him carefully. "Miss LaCroix and I were together when the war party decided to move all the captives farther north. A fellow named Otter had charge of us. Charming fellow. Liked to make things as difficult as possible for his captives. On this particular day, he decided to toughen us up a bit. He decided we shouldn't be allowed on the road with the rest of the group." Miss Jane looked out the window as she relived the event. "Otter drove us like cattle. We walked for miles without water, without rest. He had made it perfectly clear that if we faltered, he would shoot us. He was tired of us by then." She turned and looked at Leighton, satisfied that she had his attention.

"The landscape was dotted with thickets of brambles and berry bushes. Of course Otter rode around these things. But he drove us through them. It wasn't long before the children's legs and arms were running with blood. When it became apparent they weren't going to be able to continue, Gen and I had an idea." Miss Jane stood up. "We put them directly behind us. Had them wrap their arms around our waists. Put our arms over theirs." She clenched her hands in front of her. "Like this." She shrugged and shook her head. "It wasn't perfect, but it *did* get us through those bushes." Miss Jane quickly unbuttoned her cuffs and pulled her sleeves up. Her forearms were covered with jagged red scars. She sat down and continued talking while she rolled her sleeves back down and buttoned her cuffs.

"Miss LaCroix's scars are deeper than mine." She glared at Leighton. "I was able to wear the men's moccasins. But it was a while before anyone could find a pair small enough for her. That afternoon, Gen was barefoot. But she kept going, kept protecting Meg's arms against the worst tears. Finally, she was limping so badly an elderly Indian woman named Mother Friend shamed Otter into putting Gen in a wagon alongside the old woman." Miss Jane went on, "That old woman shared every bit of food, every drink of water, every tepee, every cabin with us for the entire rest of the time we were held. I saw her deprive herself of food so your niece and nephew would not go hungry." Miss Jane leaned forward, her eyes flashing angrily. "So don't you sit there and tell *me* about 'that woman's people,' Elliot Leighton."

Leighton protested gently, "All right, Jane, all right. Perhaps there *are* a few good souls among them. I met a Secesh or two who seemed to be good men too. It doesn't change the fact that hundreds of Indians scalped and raped and murdered hundreds of innocent settlers. Am I really supposed to ignore *those* facts because you have other facts?"

"You are supposed to investigate things and use the brain God gave you, Mr. Leighton," Miss Jane snapped. "Or did the same shot that took your hand off also somehow remove part of your brain?" The moment the words were out of her mouth, Miss Jane winced. Her entire face reddened. "I'm sorry, Mr. Leighton. That was completely uncalled for."

Leighton ignored her apology. Instead, he asked calmly, "And how would you suggest I investigate these matters, since you claim the newspaper accounts are untrustworthy?"

"Go to Crow Creek with Reverend Dane. Meet the people. See what he has in mind for his family."

Leighton snorted. "That's an absurd notion."

"Why?" Miss Jane said quickly. "Haven't you ever wondered what it was about mission work that captured your sister's imagination? Haven't you ever wondered how the Dakota people won her heart? Anyone would agree that your motive to do the best thing for your sister's children is good. But you can't just sweep them away from the life she chose for them without ever having understood it."

"Idealism isn't very practical, Miss Williams," Leighton said abruptly. He held up his hook. "Look what it did for me." He leaned forward and said slowly, "And it killed my sister."

Miss Jane met his gaze and didn't look away. Clearing her throat, she replied, "I don't deny that idealism plays a role in the missionary's call—especially if she is young. But idealism is quickly destroyed in the face of reality. Your sister was a woman of purpose, Mr. Leighton, not an idealistic fool. You do her an injustice not to realize that. She accepted reality and gave her heart and soul to it. It's a pity that her brother cannot follow her example."

Noting Leighton's look of surprise, Miss Jane hurried on. "You have a mental image of Indians that you won't adjust, even when faced with someone like Genevieve LaCroix. You continue to operate on the premise that Reverend Dane is the same self-serving, self-righteous man your sister married, even though you must see that he has changed." She swallowed and persisted. "The tragedy in it all, Mr. Leighton, is that your bitterness and anger and unhappiness hurt *you* the most. Your beliefs won't change the way we all feel about Gen. And they certainly won't change her devotion to us. Nor will they change Reverend Dane's commitment to his calling. But you, Mr. Leighton—" She stood up slowly. "If you let these beliefs and feelings continue to burn inside you, they will destroy you." She laid a gold coin on the table. "It would be a pity for such an attractive, intelligent man to allow that to happen."

She bid him good day and swept out of the room.

# Fourteen

"A fool uttereth all his mind."

—Proverbs 29:11

"I'm going with you."

Simon looked up as Elliot burst into the Whitney's parlor unannounced. Simon nodded, but gave no indication that he had heard or understood what Leighton said. "Good morning, Elliot. We're just reading the story of Daniel in the lions' den."

Leighton looked down at where Rebecca and Timothy Sutton, the Whitney children, and Meg and Hope sat clustered on the rag rug spanning the space between the two stuffed chairs by the fireplace. He smoothed his wild hair self-consciously and opened his mouth to clarify his intention.

"It's my favorite story!" Meg interrupted. She grinned up at him. "Father does *voices*. You should hear it!"

"Indeed," Elliot said halfheartedly.

"I'll be with you in a moment, Elliot," Simon said. "You're welcome to listen—or perhaps you'd like a cup of coffee in the kitchen. I think Nina and Gen are still back there cleaning up from breakfast." He nodded toward the hall.

Elliot exited quickly, but stayed just outside the parlor door and listened while Simon read to the children. Simon did, indeed, *do voices*, as Meg had said. At the first high-pitched roar, Elliot peeked into the parlor. Simon was down on all fours, pretending to devour Meg's arm. The children shrieked with joy and tumbled all over him. He lay on his back for a moment then, panting with the effort to get up, he slumped into the chair. It was a few moments before he caught his breath and by then the children were once again sitting quietly.

Elliot leaned against the wall listening as Simon finished the story without further roughhousing. As the children filed past him and headed outside to play, Elliot was thinking back to something Jane had said to him. *He isn't the same man who married your sister. But you ignore the obvious and maintain your opinion.* Reluctantly, Elliot admitted that in the matter of Simon Dane, Miss Jane might have a point. The Simon Dane he had known back in New York years ago would never have stooped to crawling around on the carpet with a bunch of children.

"Come in, Elliot." Simon appeared at the parlor door and waved him inside. "Thank you for waiting. Did I hear you correctly? Did you say you are going?" He put his hand on Elliot's shoulder and guided him to another chair. He sat down. "I'll take Meg and Aaron down to the photographer's tomorrow so you can take a new print home to Mother Leighton." He paused. "And, Elliot, you can be assured I will send the children for a visit. It's just that right now—"

"You've misunderstood me," Elliot interrupted. "I'm not going back to New York. I'm going with you. To Crow Creek."

Simon blinked a few times, and sat down, trying to absorb the idea.

Elliot shifted in his chair. "I never did understand what it was about missions work that captured my sister's imagination." He cleared his throat and looked down at the carpet. "I certainly never understood her love for the Indians." He looked back at Simon, his gaze steady. "Perhaps I never will. But now it seems even Aaron is caught up in it. I need to see it for myself. Perhaps then I'll understand. But whether I understand or not, at least I will see with my own eyes where it is you want to take Ellen's children." His gaze did not waver. "I don't imagine I'll change my mind about wanting them anywhere but with Mother and me in New York. But at least no one will be able to accuse me of making a decision based on thirdhand information."

Simon looked past Elliot toward the parlor door. "Come in, ladies, come in. Elliot and I were just discussing the possibility of his going with me back to Crow Creek."

The men stood up as Gen and Miss Jane entered the room.

Simon noticed the way Gen's blue eyes were accented by her pale blue calico dress.

Elliot noticed the red curls fringing Miss Jane's lined face. And the triumphant smile as she nodded approvingly and winked at him.

"When he learns his uncle is going, Aaron is going to be furious with you for making him stay here in St. Anthony," Gen said quietly.

"He'll get over it," Simon replied.

Elliot nodded. "The boy needs his education."

"Sometimes," Gen argued softly, "a boy can get a better education outside the classroom." She looked at Simon, her eyes pleading.

"That may be true in another civilization, Miss LaCroix," Elliot said. "But it isn't true for Leightons. Leighton men have always been formally educated. Aaron should be no exception."

"Have you really considered Aaron's wishes?" Miss Jane interrupted. "Or are you men just going to battle it out between you, then hand the boy a life and tell him to live it?" She pushed at the fringe of red fuzz around her face with a gloved hand.

"He's a boy," Leighton said. "He needs guidance."

Miss Jane nodded at Simon. "I realize this is not my business—"

"We know you love our children, Miss Jane. We value your opinion," Simon said.

Encouraged by Simon's response, Miss Jane turned to Elliot. "You forget, Mr. Leighton, that Aaron has lived adventures the Leighton men never encountered. If you put him in a classroom with a bunch of city boys while you men travel west, he'll be miserable. He won't be able to concentrate—"

"He will adjust," Elliot insisted.

"He needs his father," Miss Jane retorted, "and his uncle. You'll be hurrying home to New York soon, and what will he have gained from you? You will have been separated and you will have missed a great opportunity to strengthen family ties."

"It isn't safe out west," Leighton protested.

"The Dakota people at Crow Creek love that boy," Miss Jane said quickly. "They wouldn't let anything harm him."

"If the hostile Sioux attack the agency," Leighton said, "all the love in the world won't protect him."

"Elliot is right," Simon insisted. "It isn't safe. Not yet. I worried about it the entire time we were there this summer. Lord willing the government will send more troops next spring. Then we can reconsider." He looked up at his brother-in-law. "If you are willing, Elliot, I'd welcome your company. I'm trying to arrange for some relief supplies to be shipped with us. An extra wagon driver would be a great help."

Leighton looked down at his hook. "I haven't driven a wagon since—"

"Well then," Miss Jane said quickly. "You'd better get to the livery and get some practice." She touched Gen's elbow and took a step backward. "You've just got time before supper. Try to be back by six." She headed off down the hall toward the kitchen.

"That woman," Elliot said under his breath, "should mind her own business."

Simon smiled and patted Elliot on the back. "Ask for Abe Carver at the livery."

❧

Only the news that an entire family had been massacred on the Dakota border convinced Simon to travel by steamboat instead of heading off across the prairie for Dakota Territory. The Missouri was so low it was barely passable, and Simon often lamented Elliot's exposure to passengers who despised Indians—each one seeming to have an awful story to tell.

A man purporting to have killed Little Crow climbed aboard at St. Louis and regaled the men with a bloody story.

"The problem with him," Simon later told Elliot, "is that his story is a complete fabrication. There was no battle—no shoot-out. Little Crow was shot by a farmer north of Hutchinson. He and his son were picking raspberries when it happened. The farmer didn't even realize it was Little Crow until later."

"Why didn't you say something?"

Simon shook his head wearily. "It does no good to argue with men like that. They have their minds made up about the Sioux. They don't want to be confused with facts."

Elliot blanched, realizing that Simon could be talking about him as well. One evening as he leaned on the steamship railing staring down at the sluggish Missouri, a man swaggered up. When he looked up at Elliot, recognition shone in his eyes. "Major Leighton?"

Elliot looked down at the man, squinting, trying to remember. "I'm afraid you have me at a disadvantage."

"Jensen, sir. Private Brady Jensen." He gave a halfhearted salute and forced a laugh. "I thought you'd be back with the regiment by now, sir."

Leighton raised his left arm and slammed the hook on the railing. He studied the waters of the Missouri carefully and drew on his cigar.

Jensen shifted his weight nervously. "Sorry, sir. I—uh—I didn't know."

"How is it you came west, Jensen?"

"Reassigned. I've been at Fort Ridgely for a few months. Just escorted over a hundred prisoners up to Fort Snelling."

"Prisoners?" Leighton frowned.

"Mostly women and children. Old men. We've been rounding them up all summer. Finally had enough to haul up to the Fort." He spit again. "Then I got leave to see relatives down in St. Louis. I'm on my way back now."

"Why would women and children be made prisoners?"

"Oh, I don't guess they're exactly prisoners," Jensen said. "But we got to get them out of the state before someone kills them." He exhaled sharply. "Leastways that's what our orders are."

"So you are headed back to Fort Ridgely?"

Jensen shook his head. "No. I'm done with that place. Can't stand working with Dakota scouts. Glad to be leaving. I'd rather be a cook at Fort Thompson than a captain if being captain means I got to live and work with them red devils."

"I didn't realize the army had employed Indian scouts," Leighton said, his curiosity piqued.

Jensen spit again. "There's dozens of 'em. You ought to hear Captain Willets up at Fort Ridgely. He's fairly in love with his Dakota scouts. Calls 'em in every evening to talk over what the army should do." Jensen shook his head. "If I didn't know better,

I'd think he was part missionary." He laughed harshly. "Contemptible fools, every one of 'em. How they can justify helping the very people that murdered hundreds of innocent white farmers I'll never know."

"I heard some of them saved white families," Leighton said.

Jensen looked up at him quickly. "Yeah. I heard that too. But I didn't see it happen." He stood back from the rail. "You still in the army, Major? I heard they had a new corps for the wounded men—using them as clerks and such."

Leighton turned to look down at Jensen. His eyes narrowed. He pulled the cigar from his mouth and tossed it overboard. "Fact is, Jensen, I'm traveling with my brother-in-law. He's one of those 'contemptible fools' you were talking about earlier—a missionary. We're headed for Crow Creek with supplies for the Dakota."

"Never thought I'd see the day Major Elliot Leighton turned into an Injun lover," Jensen said.

"And you haven't," Leighton snapped. "But I've heard reports that the United States Army is starving women and children. That's not right."

Jensen mumbled something about "extermination" and backed away. Leighton watched him go. Willing his breathing to even out, unclenching his fist, he pulled a fresh cigar out of his pocket and placed it in his hook while he struck a match. Finally, he took the cigar in his good hand and put it to his lips, taking a long draw and exhaling slowly. He watched cigar smoke drift out over the river and as he did, he remembered the smoke of battle. He hadn't thought about Antietam in a long time. He swore at Jensen for bringing it back so fresh, so raw that he could almost hear himself screaming as his left hand flew off and landed at his feet only to be drenched in his own blood flowing freely out of the stump still attached to his body.

*Fifteen*

"He that oppresseth the poor reproacheth his Maker:
but he that honoureth him hath mercy on the poor."

—Proverbs 14:31

Simon sat back in the dust, holding the starving
Dakota woman in his arms. He and Elliot had been crossing to
the agent's office to arrange for distribution of their supplies
when they noticed the woman weaving back and forth across
the trail where a company of mounted soldiers had just passed.
She would stoop over, picking at the dust, tuck something into
a skin bag at her waist, and then go on a little farther. When she
staggered and fell, Simon ran to her. She whispered something.

"What is it?" Elliot knelt beside Simon.

"Soup," Simon whispered hoarsely. He reached into the bag

at the woman's side and withdrew a few filthy kernels of corn. "She said she was making soup."

The two men looked around them at the steaming piles of manure left in the wake of the cavalry's passing. They looked at the woman, limp in Simon's arms. Her fingers were coated with manure.

"Dear God in heaven," Elliot whispered, disbelieving.

Pulling the semiconscious woman into his arms, Simon struggled to his feet and headed across the barren earth toward the agent's quarters. Elliot walked ahead of him. Together, the men burst through the door unannounced.

"What's this?" Harry Finley looked up from his desk, frowning.

"It's a starving woman," Simon said between clenched teeth. He laid the woman gently on Finley's desktop.

Finley jumped up, wrinkling his nose. "Get this stinking piece of flesh out of here," he barked. "She'll have lice crawling all over the place."

"I want guns," Simon said tersely. "Guns for fifty men—that is if I can *find* fifty able-bodied men. I want you to authorize a hunting party to be led by my brother-in-law and myself."

"Don't be ridiculous," Finley snorted. "I'm not going to arm my prisoners!" He lowered his voice. "Be reasonable, Reverend Dane. I know things are wretched. That's why I'm in the process of contracting locally for supplies."

"You can't get enough fast enough," Simon retorted. "We have nearly a thousand starving people just outside the stockade. The last relief supplies you got were spoiled meat and worm-ridden flour. These people need fresh meat or they are not going to survive the winter." Simon leaned across the unconscious woman's form. "How many more children must die? *You* be reasonable, Finley. These men aren't going to rise up against you. Sending out a hunting party isn't dangerous. It's common sense."

The agent scratched at his grizzled day-old beard. He looked at the unconscious woman on his desk and turned away in revulsion.

Simon spit words between clenched teeth. "If you refuse to do this, Finley, I will personally see to it that you are drummed out of your office if I have to carry this woman to Washington, D.C. and lay her dead body at the president's feet!" He knew he should lower his voice, but he didn't try. He touched the woman's hair. "They aren't animals, Finley." He walked around the desk and faced the man. "She is someone's wife. Someone's mother. In another time, in another place, she could have been *your* wife. *Your* mother. How would you feel if it were *your* mother picking through manure to salvage corn?"

Finley looked down at the sagging flesh on the scarecrow-thin woman's bare arm. She was regaining consciousness, but she made no effort to move. She simply lay on his desktop, her open eyes glazed over.

Simon turned to Elliot. "Take her to Mother Friend," he said quietly. "The tent just outside the east gate." He gestured with an open hand. "A red sunburst painted over the door. Get a bag of grain out of the supply wagon for them."

"Won't that start a stream of people—?"

"I'll be along directly." He nodded at Elliot. "Don't worry about a mob scene around the wagons. These people share everything."

Elliot scooped the woman up and started to leave.

Without turning away from Finley, Simon said, "Tell Mother Friend to spread the word that I need the fifty best hunters in the area to meet me at the gate in an hour."

When Leighton had gone, Simon returned to the opposite side of Finley's desk. Finley grasped the back of his desk chair and leaned over, inspecting his desktop carefully. He balled up a piece of paper and swiped it across the surface. While he worked, he talked. "I'm not an evil man, Reverend Dane. I know the people are suffering. I'm trying to get more help. If the drought had lifted—" He sighed.

"If you know these people," Simon said more calmly, "you also know they are just as terrified of the hostile Sioux as you are. That's why they don't scatter over the reservation and try to build homes. That's why they haven't cultivated more land. You cannot expect them to go away from the protection of the troops and put themselves at the mercy of this godforsaken wilderness without means to protect themselves. Without a way to hunt. It's ludicrous." He pleaded, "You wouldn't do it, Finley. Not with your loved ones. Nor would I." Once again, he asked, "Just give us fifty good rifles and let Elliot and me take a hunting party out. I don't even need your wagons. I can use the ones provided by the Dakota mission."

"All right," Finley said. "But I'm sending a military escort along, and the minute there is any trouble—"

Simon had already turned his back and was headed out the door. He waved his hand in the air. "There won't be any trouble. You have my word."

They had come in under cover of early morning darkness when most of the natives were asleep inside their tepees. Now, as Elliot walked through the open stockade gate an old woman sitting outside a tepee gave a cry and stood up. Immediately, dozens of faces appeared from behind and inside tepees. A small group of elderly men hobbled to the road. They were nothing like the "noble savages" pictured in eastern newspapers. The faces were weathered, the hands so thin they were almost clawlike. Some of them wobbled so Elliot wondered they could walk. He felt as though he were walking through some terrible nightmare, surrounded by surreal, half-human figures. When he finally located the tepee with the red starburst over the tent flap, he felt a huge sense of relief. Just as he arrived, a well-preserved old woman with a waist-length white braid stepped outside.

"Reverend Dane—" Elliot began, feeling awkward about his inability to talk to the woman.

"You are with Reverend Dane?" the woman said in English.

Leighton nodded. He looked down at the still, unconscious woman in his arms. "She fainted inside the stockade—"

The woman gently drew the woman's hair away from her face. "Buffalo Moon," she whispered, stroking the forehead. "Bring her inside."

Elliot ducked and went inside, laying Buffalo Moon on a worn animal skin beside a small fire in the center of the room. He stood up, surprised at the neatness of the meagerly furnished tepee. The old woman dampened a cloth and dipped it in a gourd of water. She knelt beside Buffalo Moon, bathing her face gently while making comforting noises deep in her throat.

"We brought supplies," Elliot finally said. "I'll bring you a sack of flour." He ducked back outside where a group of natives waited quietly. When he returned with the flour, the people gathered around, smiling happily. One patted him on the back, another reached up to touch his white hair, jabbering something that made the others laugh.

Presently Simon drove up with one of the supply wagons. A small crowd gathered to welcome him. When Simon jumped down to greet them, they pounded his back. One old man wept openly. Simon put his arm on the man's shoulder and led him back to Elliot's wagon.

"This is Buffalo Moon's father. He wants to thank you for bringing the flour."

Another woman touched Elliot's hair, eliciting laughter from the group.

Simon grinned. "She says you must be called Silver Fox." He

added, "It's a compliment, Elliot. I didn't get a Dakota name until I'd been among them for quite a while. And even then it wasn't very complimentary." At Elliot's questioning look, Simon shrugged. "They called me Many Words—in honor of my long sermons."

"Do they still call you that?" Elliot wanted to know.

Simon shook his head.

"Well?"

"It's difficult to translate." Simon headed for Mother Friend's tepee. When Elliot followed and insisted on knowing about the name, he said gruffly, "It's something like 'He Who Brings Words That Heal.'" He ducked inside the tepee. "Will she be all right, Mother Friend?"

The old woman had already broken open the bag of flour. She knelt on a ragged rug, mixing a lump of dough in the wooden bowl before her with her hands. She looked at Buffalo Moon and shrugged. Forming a flat cake of dough, she set it directly on the hot coals from the half-spent fire. "Once I get a little of this into her, she should feel better. Whether it is enough to save her, only God knows."

Simon nodded toward Elliot. "This is my brother-in-law, Elliot Leighton. Ellen's brother."

At mention of Ellen, Mother Friend stood up. She approached Elliot solemnly, squinting as she looked up at him, gazing into his eyes. Presently she smiled, revealing two missing front teeth. "She did not carry such sadness in her eyes. Still, I see her in you." She held out her hand. "Welcome."

Simon explained to Elliot, "Mother Friend is the one I told you about who took such good care of Gen and the children during the outbreak."

Elliot bowed stiffly. "Thank you. Miss Jane Williams spoke of you as well."

At mention of Miss Jane, Mother Friend smiled broadly. "You

must tell Miss Jane that I have not forgotten her. I hope she comes back to us soon. We don't have many children now, but those who have survived would love a school. They always loved Miss Jane."

Elliot and Simon left, spending the rest of the day driving their wagons to the various small encampments huddling around the agency, trying to give each one a little flour, a little meat. At one camp, a family insisted that Elliot and Simon come in and join them for a meal.

"This is ridiculous," Elliot protested. "They're starving and they want to share with us?"

Simon smiled. "Not bad for bloodthirsty savages, eh, brother-in-law?"

That evening, the religious meeting was another surprise. Nearly everyone who came in said something to Elliot or patted him on the back. When a congregation of nearly one hundred had gathered, a frail-looking man Elliot had not yet met stood up. Opening what was obviously a Bible, he read a passage and then began to speak in low tones to the assembly. It was a short sermon, for which Leighton was grateful. After the man spoke, several individuals in the congregation stood up. It did not take Elliot long to realize he was witnessing some kind of personal testimonial service. Singing followed for nearly an hour before the assembly broke up and people trudged home.

After sundown, Elliot joined Simon and fellow missionary John Masters, impressed by the latter's obvious level of education coupled with a passion for his ministry among the Dakota. "I wish we had gotten decent housing in time for the Misses Williams and Huggins to join us. The people are fairly clamoring for instruction, both in God's Word and in the basic skills."

"Surely you wouldn't bring women here," Leighton said brusquely. He looked around at the crude buildings inside the stockade.

"Their presence would be a great comfort," Masters said quietly. "Miss Williams was a particular favorite at Hazelwood station. She's a gifted teacher. Once winter arrives in full force, there will be hours and hours of idle time. It would be an excellent opportunity to reach some of the adults."

"What about the children?" Leighton asked.

Masters stared at him for a moment before saying carefully, "There aren't many left."

Leighton swallowed hard. "I'm sorry. I—" He looked at Simon. "I guess you did write that. I just didn't think—"

"You thought I was exaggerating," Simon said. "Most people do." He sat back. "That's why this abominable situation is allowed to continue." He made a fist and pounded the table gently. "We need someone in the East making the citizens aware of things here. Someone trustworthy who has a heart for the Indian." He willed his voice to sound calmer. "I cannot but think that if people knew the extent of the suffering here, something would change." He sighed. "But, in the immediate, there's nothing we can do but hunker down and face the winter." His face brightened. "We must pray that the hunting expedition is successful."

Leighton had thought Simon was speaking in a metaphorical sense. To his surprise, both missionaries immediately bowed their heads and without hesitation prayed aloud, asking God to send game their way.

In the morning, Elliot woke and staggered, half asleep, out of the tent he and Simon inhabited. Simon was nowhere to be seen. Presently, a group of natives gathered on a hillside just beyond the cluster of lodges where Mother Friend lived. Leighton pulled on his dark blue coat and, turning the collar up against his neck, climbed the hill to find Simon down in a hole, shovel in hand. Beside the hole lay what was obviously a dead body wrapped in a threadbare blanket.

Mother Friend came to Leighton's side. "Buffalo Moon," she said tersely.

Leighton thought for a moment. "I'm sorry. I wish Simon and I had arrived sooner."

"It wouldn't have mattered," Mother Friend said. "She had lost the will to live. Her husband is in prison. When her son died last week, she had nothing left to keep her spirit on the earth."

The mourners gathered around the open grave listening as Simon read from the Dakota Bible. A cold wind picked up as they listened, lifting hair off shoulders, sending a collective shiver through the crowd wrapped in moth-eaten buffalo robes and worn blankets.

# Sixteen

"For whatsoever things were written aforetime
were written for our learning, that we through
patience and comfort of the scriptures
might have hope."
—ROMANS 15:4

HE RODE TOWARD THE SETTING SUN THROUGH FAMILIAR territory. Every year until he had lived at least a dozen winters, Daniel had been part of the mile-long trail of women and children following mounted warriors west on the fall buffalo hunt. Glancing behind him at the white stallion, he imagined the joyous shouts of his friends as they chased down a thundering herd. Astride such a magnificent animal, he would have been the envy of every one of his friends. Now, it was so still he could hear the dry grass crackle with the bay gelding's every stride.

He wondered if any of his childhood friends were out there at Crow Creek. The scouts had heard rumors about it from the few wanderers they had brought in to Fort Ridgely over the past few months. It was hard to believe things could be as bad as the wanderers said. But then a unit of soldiers returned from what they called the "Moscow Expedition." What they said about Crow Creek made the men shudder.

*Thank God I didn't have to go there.*

Daniel remembered Robert's challenge, "Can you think of nothing to be thankful for?" He had answered in bitterness, but now he realized he was truly thankful that he was not among the few men at Crow Creek. He had already decided he would remain a scout as long as the army would have him. Anything was better than Crow Creek Reservation.

Daniel rode all day, content to let his horse set the pace, enjoying the feel of the sun on his face, the gentle rhythm of the bay's easy lope. The stallion followed willingly. When Daniel stopped for the night, he apologized aloud to the horse for hobbling him.

"As soon as we are farther west, my friend, I will set you free. For tonight, you must stay near my campfire."

After tending to his horses, Daniel built a fire and set to cleaning the rabbit he had shot earlier in the day. He erected a small spit over his campfire and sat back watching it cook. As the sun went down and the wind picked up, he looked around him at the peaceful scene. It was a nearly perfect night. Cool air brought relief from the day's oppressive heat. Daniel leaned back against his saddle and closed his eyes, listening to the crackling fire, the horses grazing nearby. The colors in the western sky faded as the stars began to shine. Almost, he thought, he could pretend that life was good.

He had nearly dozed off when a soft muzzle brushed against his hair and a horse nuzzled his shoulder. The white stallion whickered softly and nudged him. Daniel stood up and patted the horse's neck. "I wonder who Otter defeated to get you, beautiful one," he murmured, raking his fingers through the long white mane. "In my heart, I want to keep you." He sighed and shook his head at the irony that now, when he was no longer a warrior, he had in his possession the most desired, the most *wakan* of all warhorses—a white stallion. He leaned into the animal, inhaling the horse's scent. "But I am only a poor Dakota scout now. Reminding soldiers of warrior-Indians would be stupid."

Bending down, Daniel took a brush out of his saddlebags and began to brush the sleek white coat. It wasn't easy living among soldiers who knew nothing about Indians besides what they read in newspapers. To them, Daniel was nothing more than a savage using his uniform as a disguise until the day he returned to his wild ways and scalped them as they slept.

Claiming religion did nothing to make life easier for the scouts. Daniel could actually understand that. Even Brady Jensen claimed to be a Christian. Daniel recognized he, personally, had done very little to convince anyone that his faith had any bearing on his behavior. In that regard, Daniel thought with a chill, he was just like Brady Jensen.

He finished brushing the stallion and shoved him away. The aroma of roasted meat reminded him the rabbit was ready to eat. Pulling a chunk of meat off the spit he took a bite, thanking God for his meal while he chewed.

He recalled a night when, after the scouts and Captain Willets had been out hunting, Big Amos had led them all in a prayer of thanks before they dived into a meal of roasted antelope. The incident had led Willets to ask Big Amos about the missionaries' work with the Dakota. When Big Amos's answer developed into a personal testimonial about his coming to faith in Christ, Willets had listened carefully. "I'm not a Christian, Big Amos, but I must admit I'm impressed with you. You seem to live what you believe. And that's more than I can say for half the men in my regiment."

*Captain Willets.* Among all the soldiers stationed at Fort

Ridgely, the tall, blond-haired captain was the exception to nearly everything Daniel thought about career soldiers. The captain preferred to form his opinions about Indians from experience, and he openly admired his Dakota scouts' skills.

On the hunting expedition he exclaimed, "You can hit a running wolf from the back of a galloping horse! Most of my men couldn't hit a galloping Indian while standing still on the ground!" The day after they all got back, he ordered his men to take more target practice.

As it grew dark and Daniel finished gorging himself on the rabbit, he rummaged in his saddlebags for Etienne LaCroix's journal. Once again he watched Blue Eyes grow up in her father's sketches. As the campfire died down, he lay back and stared up at the stars, wondering where she was that very night. He liked to think of her with the blonde child on her lap, rocking, singing a Dakota lullaby. When the thought rose that she was probably married to Simon Dane by now, he turned over on his stomach and tried to sleep. But somewhere in the distance a mountain lion was yowling. The horses were stomping about nervously, so Daniel got up. He added wood to the fire and brought the horses nearer. Tethering them to a bush where they could back up against a rock ledge, he settled back into his bedroll. When the mountain lion screamed again, closer, Daniel thought of Robert Lawrence. *I am afraid,* his friend had said, *that you are letting the lions devour you.* He finally fell into a troubled sleep.

Halfway through the night Daniel knocked his saddlebags nearly into his campfire. The acrid odor of hot leather woke him. He swore softly when he realized Robert's Bible was scorched. Picking it up, he started to pack it away. *Faith comes by hearing . . . and hearing by the Word of God.* Robert Lawrence's challenge came to mind. Since he wasn't really sleeping anyway, he decided to reread the story of that other Daniel and the lions.

The beginning of the book of Daniel had always been hard

to understand. That hadn't changed, but there was one passage that spoke to him. *He revealeth the deep and secret things: he knoweth what is in the darkness, and the light dwelleth in him.* Daniel sat back, wondering that if God revealed deep and secret things, why He hadn't let him understand more of what was going on in his life.

He lay back, thinking about Robert's insistence that what he needed was faith. *Hebrews, chapter eleven, Daniel,* Robert had said. Daniel added more wood to the fire. He leaned back against the sheer rock wall behind him and, stretching his legs out toward the fire, opened Robert's Bible to Hebrews, chapter one.

*Now faith is the substance of things hoped for, the evidence of things not seen . . . By faith Abel . . . By faith Enoch . . . By faith Noah . . .* With each new name, Daniel remembered the stories as told by the missionaries at Hazelwood Station. *By faith Abraham . . . By faith Isaac . . . By faith Joseph . . . By faith Moses . . . Who through faith subdued kingdoms, wrought righteousness, obtained promises, stopped the mouths of lions . . .*

Daniel stopped reading. His faith must be small, he reasoned. He had done nothing great purely because of faith. *They were stoned, they were sawn asunder, were tempted, were slain with the sword: they wandered about in sheepskins and goatskins; being destitute, afflicted, tormented; . . . they wandered in deserts, and in mountains, and in dens and caves of the earth. And these all, having obtained a good report through faith, received not the promise . . .* Daniel stopped reading and stared at the campfire. *They received NOT the promise.*

He reread the chapter. This time, different things leaped out at him. *Faith is the substance of things hoped for, the evidence of things not seen . . . without faith it is impossible to please him: for he that cometh to God must believe that he is, and that he is a rewarder of them that diligently seek him.*

Things were getting confusing. The chapter itself said that

most of those people had *not* been rewarded at all. They had suffered and died and never received any of the promises God had made.

*For he looked for a city which hath foundations, whose builder and maker is God . . . These all died in faith, not having received the promises, but having seen them afar off, and were persuaded of them, and embraced them, and confessed that they were strangers and pilgrims on the earth. For they that say such things declare plainly that they seek a country . . . a better country, that is, an heavenly . . .*

They embraced promises of heaven. That was how they survived. They accepted being strangers on the earth. *A house not made with hands,* Robert had said. *A house not made with hands,* Mrs. Dane had said. Daniel rebelled against the idea. He had wanted to be rewarded for what he had done to save white women and children during the uprising. When it did not happen, he rebelled. He accepted nothing *by faith.* He was not looking to *a better country.* He wanted his farm back. His old life back. The girl he loved back. Here and now. Not someday.

*Look to the future. To the house not made with hands.* This time, when Daniel finished Hebrews 11, he continued reading, and it was as if God spoke directly to him . . . *lay aside every weight . . . run with patience the race that is set before us, looking unto Jesus the author and finisher of our faith; who for the joy that was set before him endured the cross . . .*

*I don't know if I can do it,* Daniel half thought, half prayed. He grabbed up the journal and looked into Blue Eyes' face. What if the race God had set before him was to be alone for the rest of his life? The thought frightened him. Tears welled up in his eyes. He blinked them away and turned back to the open Scriptures.

*Make straight paths for your feet . . . follow peace with all men . . . look diligently . . . lest any root of bitterness springing up trouble you . . .* There it was, Daniel thought. The thing that had almost destroyed him. For months now he had nourished a root of bitterness, had allowed it to flourish and grow until it nearly choked out his weak faith. It was like the vine that grew at the old mission; one small green shoot came out and before long nearly swallowed up the porch. Even now, he thought, that vine had probably swallowed up the rubble left after the fire destroyed the cottage.

No wonder he was so unhappy. The Bible said truly great things were done *by faith*. Men conquered death *by faith*. And they got that kind of faith from God's Word. It had been months since Daniel had opened a Bible. No wonder he felt empty. No wonder there were times when he wanted to die. He almost was dead, spiritually speaking.

Over and over again, the fire waned and Daniel fed it, leaning close, squinting to discern the words on the pages of Robert's Bible. Near dawn he finally settled back against the rock wall and dozed off, completely relaxed for the first time in many, many moons.

⌇⌇

Things happened so quickly he barely had time to react. A scream sounded from above, and in an instant the mountain lion he had heard the night before dropped down the sheer cliff onto the white stallion's back. The horse's rear hooves nearly caught Daniel full in the face as he leaped up, snatching his knife from its hiding place in his right boot. Everything was chaos. The bay gelding hopped and whinnied and bucked, rolling its eyes and working itself into a frenzy while the cat clung to the white stallion's back, scraping the beautiful white shoulders until they ran with blood. The horse went down and the cat sank its teeth into the horse's neck. Then everything grew strangely quiet.

As the scent of dust and fresh blood filled the air, the cat peered at Daniel across the white stallion's mane, flicking its huge tail angrily, watching his every move. The horse lay still. Daniel crouched down, licking his lips, trying not to tremble lest the creature sense his fear and come at him. But, just as he thought it, the great cat released the stallion and flew through the air toward him. Daniel screamed a war cry and met the animal, knife extended. The cat barely had time to slap Daniel's shoulder with one paw before it fell dead at his feet.

Daniel stumbled back onto his rear in the dust, panting, trembling, staring in disbelief at the dead cat. It lay on its side and would have appeared to be asleep except for the handle of a knife jutting out of its neck. His sleeve hung in shreds, but apparently the war cry had startled the animal enough to deflect the worst damage from its claws.

The stallion snorted and began to struggle to get up. Daniel pulled the knife out of the cat's carcass. He went to the horse's head and, grasping the rope lead, cut away the braided hobbles. Able to spread his legs farther apart, the stallion regained his feet. He looked at the dead cat and snorted, dancing away, tossing his head. Relief flooded through Daniel as he checked the animal's wounds. The once unmarred skin would be scarred, but the stallion would live. His legs trembled as he led his horses to a nearby stream. His bay gelding waded in and drank deeply.

Both horses were still jittery. It took a while for Daniel to coax the stallion into the water, to let him wash the claw marks across his shoulders. He wished for a needle. He could have used the cat's innards to sew up the wounds. "I wish I could help you more, friend," he whispered in the stallion's ear. The horse flicked one ear in Daniel's face and shoved him playfully.

By dawn, Daniel had skinned the great cat and hauled the carcass a mile from his campsite. He had located a plant his mother had used for healing and, breaking it open, spread the gooey substance inside across the stallion's shoulders. The animal appeared to be none the worse for its encounter with the mountain lion, and by late in the day, Daniel realized with regret there was no reason to delay letting him go.

At sunset, Daniel led the horse to the top of a distant rise. The hills were flecked with orange and gold as the sun sank behind the horizon. "You belong out there, my friend," Daniel whispered in the horse's ear. "I send you to the place where our fathers hunted the buffalo." He raked his fingers through the abundant mane. Then, laying his hand on the horse's snow-white neck, Daniel looked heavenward. He took a deep breath. "I wish you could have carried Otter to a peaceful life." He blinked back tears before abruptly removing the animal's halter.

The stallion did not at first seem to realize he was free. Daniel slapped him on the rump. "Go!" He waved his arms in the air. The horse tossed its head and danced away playfully before rearing up and combing the air with its front hooves. One step, then two, and the horse leaped ahead, stretched into a run and headed for the setting sun, tail flying, nose into the wind.

Daniel watched the horse go and a sad smile crept across his face. "As he runs to freedom, Father, I send with him all my anger, all my bitterness. Cleanse me of it. Make me white. Let me finish the race with You, my Father."

He stood looking toward the west for a long time before returning to camp and the task of scraping the mountain lion's pelt. He was still working on it when Robert and Big Amos rode into camp shortly after sundown.

"The stallion?" Big Amos asked abruptly.

"Gone," Daniel replied. "I let him go just as the sun was setting."

"And that?" Robert Lawrence asked, nodding at the pelt.

Daniel held it up. "The lions roared, but they did not devour me. Our God and Father protected me—just as He did that other Daniel."

He was surprised to see tears well up in Robert's eyes, surprised when Big Amos strode over and grabbed him and hugged him. After pounding him on the back, Big Amos looked heavenward and shouted "*Wakantanka waste!*" "God is good!"

*Seventeen*

"Be not wise in your own conceits."
—ROMANS 12:16

ELLIOT LEIGHTON LAY ON HIS BACK LISTENING TO SIMON cough. He sat up. "We have to get you to a doctor, Simon."

"I'm sorry, Elliot," Simon said. "I don't mean to disturb you—" He collapsed in another fit of coughing.

"Don't apologize," Elliot said harshly. "I'm not concerned about me. It's you I'm worried about. You came back from the hunting expedition half dead from fatigue. If that weren't bad enough, the thermometer has dropped through the floor—"

"I'll be all right," Simon wheezed.

Elliot got up and crossed the narrow room to where Simon lay. Feeling his forehead, he said abruptly, "You're burning up."

"It's not that serious," Simon insisted. He clutched his blankets beneath his chin, trying to will himself to stop shivering.

"Maybe not," Elliot snapped. "But I'm going to get Mother Friend in here anyway. She's the closest thing to a doctor available. Maybe she'll know what to do." He pulled on his overcoat and stumbled outside.

Simon listened as Elliot's footsteps retreated in the distance, breathing a prayer of thanks. For a man who despised Indians, Leighton had come a long way since their arrival at Crow Creek late in the summer. Outrage at the conditions at the reservation had been followed by grudging respect for the men on the hunting expedition. Elliot's going for Mother Friend signaled yet another change in attitude.

In an attempt to fend off another coughing fit, Simon stood up, breathing deeply, trying to ignore the pain across his chest. For a moment, he felt better. But then a wave of dizziness sent him crawling back beneath his blankets, where he lay shivering until Elliot came back.

"She wants you in her tepee," Leighton said gruffly. "Said she has everything she needs there. Says the white man's buildings are full of bugs. Doesn't want to have anything to do with them." He looked down at Simon. "Do you think you can walk?"

"Of course I can walk!" Simon said indignantly. He pushed his covers aside and stood up. Grabbing his coat, he had thrust one arm through a sleeve when he nearly toppled over. Elliot ducked just in time to get Simon to fall on his right shoulder, where he could hold him with his good hand. He braced himself and stood upright. "Just relax, Simon," he ordered. "I'll carry you up there." Throwing a blanket over Simon's back, he headed outside and up the hill, frowning to himself at how little his brother-in-law weighed. He didn't think it possible, but Simon had lost more weight since they arrived at the reservation.

Mother Friend fussed over Simon like a mother doting on a

grown child. She prepared a foul-smelling poultice and painted Simon's chest. She burned noxious-smelling weeds and made him breathe deeply, inhaling the smoke. It sent him into another fit of coughing that brought the congestion up out of his lungs. Mother Friend inspected it and nodded with satisfaction. Elliot watched for nearly an hour. When he saw Mother Friend take the weed she had just burned and add it to boiling water and force Simon to drink it, he decided he was watching worthless incantations and witchcraft.

Mother Friend looked at him and smiled. "Go to bed, Silver Fox. I will send for you if there is a change." She waved Elliot out the door. "Say a prayer before you sleep," she said, patting him on the back. She lowered her voice and added, "Helping Words is very sick. You should have brought him to me before this."

Elliot walked back up the hill toward the narrow shack he and Simon moved into when winter arrived. The night was clear. As far as Elliot could see, there was no glow of civilization. At home on a night like this, there would be glimmers of light in the distance from other villages. Here, there was nothing. Only the vast canopy of stars arching over black velvet that stretched away into the distance. Around him, the cooking fires in the center of each tepee made the skin and canvas shelters glow like Chinese lanterns. A wolf howled. Elliot shivered and rubbed his arms, imagining mounted warriors racing toward the peaceful scene, intent on killing. *But Simon said they don't attack at night,* Elliot reminded himself.

Once back at the narrow cabin he shared with Simon, Elliot could not sleep. He stirred up the fire and sat beside it, watching the flames devour stick after stick of wood, remembering a conversation he and Simon had had only a week before. They were sitting before their meager little stove, alternately picking meat off a small roasted bird and drinking coffee when Simon began to talk about the days before the uprising.

"In the old days," he explained, "each band had its own government. In camp, each band had its place in the circle." He scratched a circle on the floor with the tip of his knife. "The circle was open toward the east for the rising sun. Another opening at the north or south provided a corridor through which the young boys took the horses to pasture and water. Each separate camp was grouped around a council tepee. Everything well organized, everything in order. I have seen a camp of hundreds be totally packed and moving in less than two hours." He sat up and reached for his coffee cup. "They are a remarkable people. Perfectly suited to the land. They know how to use everything around them." He gestured toward the door. "When you go out in the morning, look at the arrangement of the tepees and bark houses. You can still see the same circular design if you know what to look for. Even here the people tend to cluster by their old camp associations." He shook his head sadly. "If we whites had left them alone, they wouldn't be starving."

Elliot listened, more interested in Simon's feelings about the Dakota people than the customs he was describing. As the weeks went by and he saw the people reacting to Simon, he began to see some of what Simon had said about their willingness to share, their caring for one another. He began to see them as people, and when he began to do that, he began to change.

"They have always been a very spiritual people," Simon explained another time. He and Elliot had ridden out together after a herd of antelope someone had seen beyond reservation lines. When they came upon an odd arrangement of buffalo skulls, Simon said, "Almost everything in their lives has a spiritual significance. Of course most of us discount it all as godless super-stition. But there is a haunting beauty in the symbolism of their ancient ways. Even the war paint means something. If a man wears black, it means he killed an enemy. Blue means victory." He smiled. "There is language in the way the men wear their feathers. A scout's feathers are painted yellow or white—and worn hanging down. Feathers standing up means he killed an enemy." He paused. "Of course some of it we'll never know, because they will never tell us what it means. I once asked Buffalo Moon to tell me the meaning of a symbol on her moccasins. It was something I'd never seen before. She only smiled and said it was just a design she liked. I know better. But she took that secret to her grave."

Elliot mused, "Someone should be writing these things down before they're lost." He was surprised to hear himself say it but even more surprised to realize he meant it. The culture was obviously going to change, and much of it would be lost if no one documented it.

"Yes," Simon said quietly. "Someone should." He smiled at Elliot. "Perhaps that will be your ministry, brother."

"Not me," Elliot said quickly.

Simon studied his face carefully. "No," he said finally. "Perhaps not." He grinned and nudged his horse forward. "But I can't tell you how pleased I am—how pleased Ellen would be—to hear you even voice the idea. It's quite a departure from your previous position. And I don't know anyone else who thinks Dakota culture worth saving. Most either want to exterminate it completely or at best let it die a natural death through assimilation."

"What do you think, Simon?"

Pulling his horse up, Simon thought for a moment, then shook his head. "I don't honestly know. Part of me wants them to change as quickly as possible because it will save their lives—and their souls. Part of me wonders if there isn't a way to save their traditions and still win them to Christ."

"Jane said she struggles with the same things," Elliot said.

"Jane?"

"Jane Williams." Elliot gestured toward a distant ridge where a huge buck antelope stood silhouetted against the gray sky. "Outspoken woman. Exasperating."

"Pure gold, Elliot. There isn't a finer woman in all of Minnesota."

"Or Dakota Territory," Elliot added under his breath. He put his reins in his hook and withdrew his rifle from its scabbard. "Unfortunately, she is completely dedicated to her beloved Indians. Whereas I am completely dedicated to returning east and seeing that my niece and nephew receive a proper education."

"We can talk about that," Simon said, lowering his voice and watching the antelope as it crossed toward them.

Elliot did not hide his surprise. "We can?"

Simon nodded. "Yes. *After* we get that big buck back to the agency." He kneed his horse ahead of Elliot's.

Later that evening, after they had returned to the agency with two carcasses on their pack mules, Simon resumed the subject.

"The fact is, Elliot, I don't see any evidence of things quieting down any time soon. Sibley has yet another campaign planned for next year that will keep the western bands stirred up. And believe it or not, he plans to remove most of the small detachment of troops we have in the spring. Even the cannon."

"He can't be serious!" Elliot interjected. "That will leave the entire agency vulnerable to attack!"

"Yes." Simon nodded. "And it will keep everything in an uproar. I can't believe the government is really going to keep the reservation located at Crow Creek. Superintendent Thompson's glowing letters notwithstanding, someone somewhere is going to have to listen to the truth. Until the situation is more settled, I'd be a fool to bring my family out here. It really isn't safe, and it wouldn't accomplish anything." He looked at Elliot. "Time in New York with their grandmother would be good for the children. I didn't want to admit it, but I had thought about it even before your arrival. The difficulty was I thought it was too much to expect of Mother Leighton alone. But now that you won't be returning to your regiment—" He stopped abruptly.

"It's all right, Simon," Elliot replied. "Perhaps it's all for the best." He smiled slowly. "I do rather like the idea of having children, and since marriage is out of the question—" He gestured toward the door. "Coming here has changed the way I look at the situation. I don't share your passion for the ministry, Simon. God hasn't called me that way. But as much as a layman can, I understand why you feel you have to be here. These people need what you have to offer. And if the children come to New York, I'll do my best by them. And"—he put his hand on Simon's shoulder— "I won't be your adversary in the matter of Dakota ministry."

Simon cleared his throat. "You know that I still intend to marry Genevieve. If she'll have me."

Elliot shifted uncomfortably in his chair. "Yes. I expected you would." He looked at Simon. "It will cause you difficulties."

"Not with anyone I care about."

"What about your children?"

"They adore Gen."

"That's not what I meant. Will they be—hampered in some way—looked down upon? I'm sorry, Simon. I'm trying to be realistic. White children with an Indian mother. People will wonder."

"The children will rise above it," Simon said firmly. "They know skin color doesn't matter."

"Of course it doesn't matter in a person's *worth*," Elliot said. "But it certainly *will* matter in the way they are treated by people in New York. Is it fair to ask the children to endure that? To knowingly put an obstacle in their future?"

Simon didn't speak for a moment. When he did, his voice was calm. "I have considered all of this already, Elliot. I'll agree that perhaps it changes the situation a little that the children will be in the East where people might not be exposed to such marriages as much, but—I love her, Elliot. With no disrespect and with every sacred memory of your sister intact, I can tell you that I love this woman and I think she and I can have a good life together. And I truly believe the children will be better off with her as their mother."

Elliot pursed his lips together. He sat with his head bowed for a long while. When he looked up he said quietly, "Then I will stand by you, Simon. You and Genevieve."

"Thanks be to God," Simon said immediately. Then he asked, "Tell me what you meant earlier—about wanting children but knowing you won't marry."

He gestured with the hook. "Women positively recoil from this."

"Has Miss Jane ever done that?"

He shook his head. "But then I've never approached her as a man interested in her as a woman."

"Why not?"

"Because I know better."

"Risk, Elliot. You have to take the risk."

"Taking risks got my hand blown off at Antietam."

"Which is worse, Elliot? Taking the risk and suffering loss, or shrinking back and living with the knowledge that you're a coward?"

Thinking of Brady Jensen, Elliot was quiet for a moment. "I was in the hospital for weeks, Simon. I nearly died. I can't begin to tell you what it was like." He shuddered.

"But you came through. You survived. You should hear the Dakota men talk about you. They watched you struggle to learn how to handle that rifle on the hunting expedition. They were proud when you finally bagged that antelope. You are what we call a 'man's man,' Elliot Leighton." Simon nodded. "And again I say, you misjudge Miss Jane Williams if you think she sees nothing but a metal hook when she looks at you."

"I would give anything to know that's true," Leighton said.

"You will have to give everything, Elliot—because you are going to have to overcome your pride and bare your soul to find out what Miss Jane Williams is really made of."

Elliot smiled wistfully. "Isn't it amazing that a man who has lined up and gone into battle quakes in his boots at the thought of rejection from a mere woman?"

Simon laughed. "There's nothing 'mere' about Miss Jane, my brother. And I expect some day you'll look back and know that the risk was worth the result."

That had been a few days ago, Elliot thought as he sat alone in their tiny shack, worrying about Simon, worrying about Meg and Aaron's future, and thoroughly terrified at the prospect of trying to court Miss Jane Williams. She would be polite, Elliot thought. She would hide her revulsion. But under no circumstances would she be interested in a freak. Elliot sighed and got up. He stepped outside and looked up at the moon. In the west, a bank of clouds was moving in. It had been a dry year. Elliot worried that just when he might have to convince Simon to return east for his health, it looked like it might snow. And he had heard about the storms that blew across this awful place.

*Don't let it happen, God,* Elliot prayed. *Not if we are going to need a doctor.*

# Eighteen

"[Love] . . . seeketh not her own."
—I Corinthians 13:5

December 18, 1864
St. Louis, Missouri

Dear Miss Williams,

I have just returned from an extended trip abroad. How it is that of all my acquaintances in St. Louis, no one would have informed me of your notices in the newspaper, I cannot say. However, it appears that you may have my niece and nephew, Rebecca and Timothy Sutton, in your care.

Perhaps some family history is appropriate. My sister Felicia and I were twins. I regret to say that we caused our *departed parents a great deal of stress for many reasons, not the least of which was their complete inability to understand the rather intense religious conversion Felicia and I experienced in our early twenties. Further difficulties arose when neither of us fulfilled our parents' plans for our lives. They never forgave Feleicia for marrying Philip Sutton against their wishes. When Felicia and Philip moved to the frontier, the estrangement worsened.*

*When I met and married my Richard, it was the final blow to our parents. They never accepted our marriages to men who would not be bullied into submission—men who shared Felicia's and my commitment to personal Christianity. When both Richard and Philip staunchly maintained their own ideas of leadership and independence, when it became clear that we would not be living the life of ease our parents had provided, we were virtually disowned.*

*Once my husband, Richard, and I went abroad, Felicia and I were able to exchange a few letters. I even have a photograph or two of Rebecca and Timothy.*

*Felicia's letters stopped abruptly at the end of 1862. My mother and father did inform me of Felicia's and Philip's deaths, which were a great shock to my parents, who were in ill health. I think they were terribly grieved by their obstinate behavior. In a letter to me after Felicia's death, my mother sounded truly brokenhearted. While we were able to mend our relationship, both my parents succumbed to old age and illness within a few weeks of one another at the beginning of last year. I was indisposed at the time of their death and unable to make the long journey home to see to their affairs.*

*My husband and I have at last returned to St. Louis. Upon going through my parents' papers (their house was closed up and has awaited my return for the finalization of business and estate matters), Richard and I became aware that the fate of Felicia's children was not exactly known. We are unhappily childless, Miss Williams, and the prospect of finding Felicia's children has ignited a flame of hope in our hearts that words are insufficient to relay. To think that our prayers for children may soon be answered is almost more than we can believe.*

*I enclose a photograph of myself and Richard. While my very human desire is to rush to St. Anthony and throw myself at Rebecca and Timothy, Richard has convinced me that we should pray and wait upon your wisdom as to how best to introduce them to the idea of a new family. Timothy is too young to remember me, but Rebecca might have a glimmer of recognition if you mention the lady who used to send the oranges. (I managed to have a crate or two delivered to the frontier.)*

*I am certain the children have become attached to you, and I am most concerned that after all they have endured, they be spared any more pain if at all possible. Not being familiar with your situation, I hesitate to request this, but I wonder if you would be able to consider traveling with them to St. Louis? We would be happy to provide your passage and a salary as their nurse until the children have made the adjustment to their new home.*

*No amount of money could possibly repay you for what you have done, Miss Williams, but we hope that the enclosed will in some measure assure you of our heartfelt gratitude and our goodwill. We also offer a letter from our dear Pastor Irvine as a sort of "recommendation" regarding our character and suitability as parents. We eagerly await your response.*

*Most Sincerely,*
*Fanny & Richard Laclede*

Miss Jane Williams waited, her hands clenched, while Gen and Nina Whitney sat at the kitchen table leaning over the letter.

Gen held up a check. "It's for a thousand dollars," she said in disbelief.

"I know," Miss Jane said. "Go ahead and read what Pastor Irvine says about them."

After reading the letter, Nina said softly, "They sound too good to be true."

"Yes," Miss Jane said. She sat down abruptly. "It's wonderful, don't you think?" She looked from Gen to Nina before hiding her face in her hands and bursting into tears.

Gen put her arm around Miss Jane.

Miss Jane accepted Nina's offered handkerchief and cried for a few moments before wiping her eyes and saying, "I—I've been praying for guidance. I've felt so at loose ends. I've felt almost trapped, and then guilty for feeling that way when Rebecca and Timothy need me. I've spent more nights than I care to admit pacing around my room, wishing I could return to the mission work, trying to be content if I don't. And now, the Lord seems to be making the very thing I want possible and I dissolve in a puddle. Honestly!"

Nina spread the letter on the table and reread a few passages. "They sound like sincere Christians. And they are obviously well off." She looked up. "What are you going to do?"

"Tell Rebecca and Timothy, of course." Miss Jane took a deep breath. "It will help immensely if Rebecca has some memory of the oranges. It would at least be a connecting point."

She pushed herself away from the table. Standing up, she balled Nina's handkerchief into the palm of one hand. "I don't see any reason to put this off." And she headed up the back stairs to Rebecca's room.

❧

Rebecca Sutton had more than a vague memory of a woman sending oranges to her parent's farm. "Mama talked about Aunt Fanny all the time," Rebecca said. "She has dark, dark hair and eyes, just like Mama did. She married Richard and they went away to France. And they were very happy. We had their picture in an album that Mama kept in the bedroom." She frowned. "But the Indians tore it all up when they killed Mama and Papa." Her expression changed and she murmured, "I guess it burned up in the fire." She looked at Miss Jane. "They burned lots of our things after they took Timothy and me. They made us watch." Something glimmered in her eyes, and almost as if a switch had been turned, she changed the subject. "Mama said Aunt Fanny was the first one to learn to read, and the first one to say she loved Jesus. And she taught Mama to sing the doxology. They used to put on plays in the attic together . . ."

"Well," Miss Jane said quietly, "I'm glad to see you remember so much, because your Aunt Fanny wants you and Timothy to come live with her in St. Louis."

The two children looked at one another. After a moment of silence, Timothy frowned and said, "Don't *you* want us Auntie Jane?"

Miss Jane suppressed a sob. She hugged Timothy. "Oh, you dear boy. Of *course* I want you. But I'm just a poor spinster. Your aunt and uncle have been very sad for a long time because God hasn't given them any babies."

"God hasn't given *you* any babies, either," Timothy said abruptly. "If we go away you'll be all alone."

Rebecca gave her brother a little shove. "You have to be *married* to get babies, Timothy. And anyway, when Miss Jane goes back to the mission she'll have lots of Dakota children to love." Rebecca looked up at Jane. "Isn't that right, Aunt Jane?"

Jane nodded. "I've been asking God to show me what I should do. Not just about you dear children, but about many,

many things. And I think if He gives you a wonderful new home in St. Louis, perhaps that means I am supposed to return to the reservation and teach again."

"What if we don't like St. Louis?" Rebecca asked abruptly.

"I think you will like it very much," Miss Jane said quickly. "I'll be coming with you to make certain."

"You're coming too?" Timothy asked.

Miss Jane nodded. "Just to help you get settled."

Rebecca and Timothy sat side by side on the edge of Timothy's bed, thinking. Finally, Rebecca looked up. "I'd like to meet Aunt Fanny," she said with confidence. "Mama always said I'd like her a lot. She didn't say too much about Uncle Richard. But we'll try him, too." She hesitated before adding, "I've been worried you would go back to the Indians and take us there." Her voice lowered a moment as she said, "Please don't be mad at me, Aunt Jane, but—I don't want to go back to the Indians." She shivered. "I'd be scared all the time."

Miss Jane knelt down and put her arms around both children. "Thank you for telling me that, Rebecca. I'm sorry you've been worried." She cupped Rebecca's chin in her palm and touched her nose. "I'll go right to the telegraph office and let your aunt and uncle know that we want them to come as soon as possible."

The children bounded off the bed and out into the hall. Rebecca hurried downstairs to tell Meg and Aaron the news. Timothy followed, obviously deep in thought. At the top of the stairs, he turned around. His dark eyes flashed as he said, "If I don't like St. Louis, I'll come find you. They won't stop me. I won't be afraid of the Indians, and I won't let them stop me!"

"If you don't like your new home, Timothy," Miss Jane said solemnly, "I will personally come and get you."

"Promise?"

Miss Jane nodded. "Absolutely."

With that, Timothy followed his sister downstairs. Miss Jane donned her wrap and hat. By the time she reached the telegraph office, she had almost stopped crying. She told herself on the way back to the Whitneys' that the tears were tears of joy. Over the next few days, she said it often enough that she began to believe it.

# Nineteen

"Delight thyself also in the Lord;
and he shall give thee the desires of thine heart."
—Psalm 37:4

Winter, which had lulled the residents of St.
Anthony into thinking it might be mild, arrived with a
vengeance. Thermometers dropped to forty below zero and then
froze solid. Business on Main Street slowed to a trickle. Even
Christmas failed to bring the locals out in force. At the
Whitneys', the holiday was celebrated quietly with little emphasis on the few homemade gifts exchanged, but great emphasis on
cookie baking and games, the love of God's family for one
another, and the love of God for them all.

Aaron complained of having to thrust his legs into what he called
"hollow icicles" each morning, but after hearing Samuel Whitney's

Christmas sermon on the manger in a stable, he began to get up early and start a fire in the kitchen stove while the household slept.

The rest of the children got in the habit of leaping out of bed each morning and racing down to the kitchen half-dressed, where they huddled around the stove pulling on stockings and thawing out shoes while Aaron heated water for hot cocoa and tea. He learned to make coffee and began leaving a steaming cup outside Gen's door early every morning.

When the cold did not abate, Samuel Whitney hitched up a rickety sleigh and began to haul neighborhood children to school a half mile away. The corporate transportation had the effect of familiarizing the town's permanent residents with "those mission-ary kids."

As she had at the Dakota Mission, Miss Jane took to keeping her pockets stuffed with nuts and other small treats for the chil-dren. She met the sleigh each day and quizzed the children as they descended. Every correct answer to her scholarly challenges won a treat. By the beginning of February, "those Injun-lovers that bought Avery Criswell's run-down place" had become simply, "the neighbors"—and good ones at that.

Once the river had iced over and steamship travel halted, St. Anthony no longer received its weekly mail delivery. The Lacledes sent a telegram: *Rejoicing at news. Love to children. Arriving on first steamship in spring. Fanny & Richard Laclede*

Miss Jane replied: *Train available St. Paul to St. Anthony. Eight departures daily. Less than an hour from station. Children excited. Rebecca remembers Aunt Fanny. Miss Jane Williams.*

A flurry of telegrams ensued.

*Will you come to St. Louis? Will make room adjoining children's suite ready.*

*The Lacledes*

*Yes to St. Louis. No special treatment necessary. Happy to be of help. Funds used to give children special Christmas. Most retained in their name at bank.*

*Miss Jane Williams*

❧

*Funds meant for you as well. Please telegraph for more when needed.*

*Fanny & Richard*

❧

*Will discuss monetary issues after you arrive. Children well.*

*Jane.*

❧

On Valentine's Day, Rebecca and Timothy sent their own telegram. *Your favorite color, please. And does Uncle Richard smoke?*

The reply came: *Favorite color red. No smoking.*

Rebecca and Timothy made gifts for their aunt and uncle. Miss Jane began to make plans for her return to mission work. Aaron and Meg earned certificates for outstanding scholarship. Hope chased up and down the stairs and halls and learned to turn somersaults. Samuel and Nina Whitney selected a board of directors for their boarding school and made plans to open for their first session the following fall.

And Gen worried. That Elliot Leighton, who sneered when he said the word Indian, would be a hindrance rather than a help.

That Simon would overdo. That supplies would run out and snows would hem them in and leave them vulnerable to illness and starvation.

When the thermometer stayed below zero and snows deepened, the boarders at the Whitneys' were housebound for days at a time. Gen grew restless. Whenever she thought about spring something tightened in her midsection. Samuel and Nina had plans for their boarding school. Miss Jane had plans to go to St. Louis. Only she did not have a clear vision of what the future held.

Every day when she rose, Gen prayed that God would make her His servant. She prayed to be a good mother. And she prayed to love Simon Dane. She bowed her conscious mind and her will to doing love. But at night, when she dreamed, it was not Simon who came toward her in the moonlight.

Less than a week after he carried an ailing Simon to Mother Friend's tepee, Elliot was awakened by the sound someone pounding on his cabin door. "I'm doing all I can Reverend. I don't want 'em to freeze to death either."

Realizing it must be Simon, Elliot jumped out of bed, cursing his missing hand as he clumsily tried to pull on his drawers and simultaneously get to the door. He flung the door open just in time to admit a blanket-clad Simon Dane.

Once inside, Simon pushed the blanket away from his head and let it fall around his shoulders. He was thinner than ever, and he coughed a little, but there was purpose in his gleaming eyes as he said, "I need to talk to you."

A knock sounded at the door and Simon admitted an old brave Elliot recognized as Ironheart, one of the few Dakota near the reservation who spoke fluent English.

Elliot snatched his prosthesis up off the floor, fumbling with the buckles on the leather straps. Simon added wood to the small stove in the corner of the room and sat on the edge of his cot.

Ignoring Elliot's obvious self-consciousness about his disability, Ironheart touched the hook and pressed on the stuffed false forearm. "Not bad." Looking at Elliot with honest curiosity, he asked, "White man make legs too?"

Elliot nodded, "Yes."

"I hear many white men lose legs in that war they are having towards the rising sun."

"The War of the Rebellion," Elliot provided the name for what would one day be called the Civil War. He buckled the last buckle attaching the prosthesis to his upper arm and then shrugged into his shirt. "Yes, many terrible wounds have been inflicted."

Ironheart asked, "Is it true that those white men make war by standing with shoulders touching and walking towards the enemy?"

"That's the way it's done." Elliot began the laborious process of buttoning the row of buttons down the front of his shirt. He looked at Simon. "Something tells me you didn't bring Ironheart over here to discuss battle strategies." He threw some coffee grounds into a pot and set it on the stove. "I'm sorry I wasn't prepared for company." He looked at Simon. "It's good to see you feeling better."

Simon's voice was hoarse, but other than that and a slight cough, he was much improved. "It would appear, brother-in-law, that you owe Mother Friend an apology."

"I didn't say anything to offend her."

Simon chuckled. "You didn't have to say anything. She knows exactly what you thought about her treatment—which, by the way, is a time-proven remedy—unlike some of the things the last white doctor I saw tried." He grimaced. "Downing a fingerful of goose grease followed by a teaspoonful of turpentine." He made a gagging sound and shuddered dramatically.

"All right, Simon, all right. Once again I stand corrected on my opinion of all things Dakota." Leighton sat down and motioned for Ironheart to join them. "What is it?"

"Ironheart's band is leaving the reservation," Simon said calmly.

Elliot stared, dumbfounded, at Simon. "Leaving? When? For where? Why?" He shook his head and waved one hand in the air. "Never mind. I understand why." He nodded at Ironheart. "But where can you possibly go that's any better?"

"We are going home," Ironheart said. His eyes glittered with determination. "The white man is not going to let us live. We see now that anywhere he takes us, it will be only to watch us die." He sat up straight, placing a hand on each knee. His voice was tinged with sadness. "We have no quarrel with the white man. We have always been his friend. If he had brought us to a place where we could live, we would plow the earth and do as he says. We would learn to live as he wishes. But in this place, there is nothing. Mother Earth is barren. Some of our people stayed in Minnesota near Fairibault. Some near the Redwood. We wish to be near them. Then as we die, our brothers will bury us with our fathers."

Ironheart spoke for a long time. He talked about his childhood in the Big Woods, about the changes that came upon the people. He spoke of the coming of the missionaries, of the reservation, of broken treaties and injustice. He was not complaining, Elliot realized, only telling the history of his people because, of some impossible generosity, he really wanted Elliot to understand what was in his heart.

The man's tale carried Elliot back to the days in the army hospital when he had ridden the roller coaster of betrayal and anger and rage against the men in his regiment who turned and fled in the face of death. Unlike the Brady Jensens Elliot had known, Ironheart was looking death in the face, walking toward it, accepting it—and yet wresting a semblance of his own terms from it. It was a humbling kind of courage.

Cold air blew in between the unchinked logs in the little shack, and Elliot shivered. *The wind had shifted,* he thought.

As if he could read Elliot's mind, Ironheart said quietly, "This dryness is about to change. We must leave before the snow. At sundown tonight we will be going."

Simon broke in. "The plan is to leave the tepees and tents here. It will be a while tomorrow before anyone knows they are gone. If the snow moves in as expected, I doubt Agent Finley will risk any soldiers to come after us. He doesn't care that much about his Indian charges."

*"Us?"* Elliot looked from Simon to Ironheart and back at Simon.

"The thought is that if we travel with them, they'll be less likely to get killed by some overzealous settler." Simon hurried to add, "I had to talk nearly half the night to convince Ironheart to let us go along. He doesn't like the idea. He's afraid that if any harm comes to us, the army will use the excuse to kill them all. But then I suggested that we might be useful in other ways." He paused and waited for Elliot to absorb the information.

"How many people are we talking about?" Elliot asked.

"Less than a dozen," Simon said quickly. "They have a few ponies. You'd be amazed at what they can fit on a travois."

"How far is it to the Redwood?"

Ironheart said something in Dakota that made Simon laugh. He translated, "He says ten days or less for Indians. Two weeks for whites."

Standing up, Elliot reached for an old carpetbag sitting on the floor. He took out a cigar and, opening the stove door, lit it. He had just sat back and prepared to draw on the cigar when he caught something in Ironheart's expression. He handed the cigar to the old man, who drew on the cigar and exhaled slowly, obviously savoring the flavor of the fine tobacco. He ceremoniously passed it back to Elliot. "Keep it," Elliot said.

"No," Simon said quickly. "Share it. Ironheart honors you."

Frowning slightly, Elliot obeyed, then passed the cigar back to Ironheart, who took another draw and passed it to Simon. To Elliot's amazement, Simon puffed on the cigar without collapsing into a fit of coughing. The men sat quietly until the cigar was a glowing stub. When Elliot finally got up and tossed the butt into the stove, Ironheart stood up to go. "I will knock," he rapped a distinctive beat on the door. He looked at Simon. "You will see no one but you will know what to do."

Simon nodded. When Ironheart had gone, the two men sat talking for a long while.

"If these people were the warriors who had started this whole mess, I wouldn't give them any quarter." Elliot said. "I'd be the loudest advocate of the most overwhelming force. But standing by and watching defenseless and innocent people die sickens me." He stopped abruptly. "One question," he raised his eyebrows and looked at Simon. "What happens after we get to the Redwood?"

"You and I keep going. All the way home."

"You mean back to St. Anthony?"

Simon nodded. "If the weather allows it. We'll get another supply train together and do our best to get back to the reservation as quickly in the spring as possible. We'll organize a letter-writing campaign to Washington." He stood up and began to pace back and forth across the tiny room. "I want to see Finley gone. He's nearly heartless. The idea of Sibley being allowed to take troops away from here is ridiculous." He pounded his open palm with his fist. "Someone has to get them to listen. Someone."

Elliot went to Simon and put his hand on his shoulder. "Someone will," he said resolutely.

Simon looked up at him. "Are you telling me that you are willing to be that someone?"

"Perhaps I am," Elliot mumbled. He lifted his left arm and slapped his prosthesis. "It is one thing this wouldn't interfere with. In fact, if I were to don my old uniform, I suspect I could get through a few closed doors in Washington."

Simon slapped him on the back. "Thanks be to God, Elliot. Thanks be to God."

"Don't be too premature on the thankfulness," Elliot warned. "I haven't done anything yet. And we still have to keep from getting frozen or killed in the next two weeks." He shook his head. "I can't believe I am doing this. It's insane."

# Twenty

"For the Lord your God is God of gods,
and Lord of lords . . . He doth execute
the judgment of the fatherless and widow,
and loveth the stranger, in giving him food
and raiment. Love ye therefore the stranger."
—Deuteronomy 10:17–19

WITH THE RELEASE OF THE WHITE STALLION, SOMETHING inside Daniel Two Stars had broken free. The same longings were still there deep inside him, and yet when he indulged in a cursory look at the old journal he realized that bitterness had mellowed into regret. Gradually he was able to channel his restless energy into a need to help as many wanderers as he could.

More than a hundred scouts were left in Minnesota to help the army stand against the hostile Sioux on the frontier. While Daniel, Robert, and Big Amos stayed at Fort Ridgely, the rest were sent out to make nearly a dozen separate camps all along the frontier at places like Cheyenne River, Twin Lakes, and Bone

Hill, so named because of a three-foot ring of buffalo bones found atop a hill. All through the winter of 1863 and into 1864, these scouts chased hostile Sioux and rounded up peaceful wanderers. By early in 1864, they had killed a few hostiles and collected more than a hundred innocents who were taken to Fort Snelling until arrangements could be made in the spring to transfer them to Crow Creek Reservation.

And so it was that Daniel, Robert, and Big Amos were about to break up their camp on the banks of Lake Hanaska one frozen morning early in 1864 when movement along the snow-dusted horizon caught Daniel's attention. He did not stand up, but motioned silently to his two friends, who turned around and faced the horizon, squinting to make out what it might be. Before long, Big Amos, whose eyesight was sharper than his friends', grunted and said under his breath, "Six ponies. Travois." All three men relaxed. Warriors did not travel with such encumbrances.

Daniel and Big Amos stayed behind to guard the campsite while Robert crept noiselessly across the landscape to learn what he could about the travelers.

While Robert was gone, Daniel and Big Amos rounded up their horses and led them behind a row of evergreen trees.

Robert's voice was charged with emotion when he came back. "They ran away from Crow Creek," he said. "I don't know how they made it this far. They have been surviving on the roots they could dig out of the frozen ground." He paused, choking back tears. "These are the worst we've found so far."

"How many?" Daniel wanted to know.

"Half a dozen," Robert said. "Two men. Ironheart and Singer. They lost at least four on the way here."

Daniel swung into the saddle. "Let's bring them to camp," he said. He reached into his saddlebag and tossed a small sack onto the ground beside the fire. "If we boil that salt pork in water and add what you two have, we can probably come up with enough soup for at least half a meal. More than they are accustomed to, anyway." He looked at Robert. "What do you think of keeping them here overnight?"

"It's a good idea," Robert said quickly. "They could use some rest before we take them in." He motioned to the thick line of evergreens. "If it snows, we're in a good spot." He grinned. "Maybe we'll have an excuse to try fishing." He put his hand on his friend's knee. "It's not going to be easy convincing them. The one called Ironheart is a leading man. They've heard about the band camping at Faribault. Ironheart says they will keep going until they get there." He shook his head. "That's at least five more days away. I doubt they'll make it."

"We'll think of something."

Robert said quietly, "Ironheart is adamant that he's not going to put himself under the control of any more military men or agents."

Daniel bowed his head for a brief second, then picked up his horse's reins. "I'll bring them in," he said, and headed out to meet the group of wanderers.

When Daniel dismounted and approached Ironheart, an old woman nearly hidden within the folds of a faded blanket ran up to him. Lifting her hands to the sky, she began to call Daniel's name and cry. She reached up to pat his face with her gnarled hands, then took his hands in hers and kissed them.

Hardship and starvation had changed her so that he would never have recognized Mother Friend if she hadn't spoken up. Daniel grasped her bony shoulders and smiled at her like a son looking at his own mother. Rage flickered inside him when he saw the ravages of Crow Creek in the woman's face, but he channeled the energy into affection and hugged her fiercely before lifting her into his saddle. Turning to the rest of the group, he waved them after him. "We are making soup for you." He pointed to the low bank of dark clouds racing toward them. "We are in a good spot to weather that storm. Come. Make camp beside us." He squeezed Mother Friend's hand. "Soon you will be sitting beside a warm fire, Mother Friend. And then I want to know everything."

Six of them crowded into the tent, sitting shoulder to shoulder, no longer shivering, watching as Big Amos sliced every fragment of meat the scouts had into a pot of boiling water. While Big Amos cooked, Ironheart told the scouts why they had left Crow Creek and what they hoped to do.

"We cannot return to that place," he said quietly but firmly. He motioned around him. "These people helped the whites. For this they are hated by the Sioux who fight in the West. For this they will be killed if Little Crow can accomplish it."

"Little Crow is dead," Robert said.

Ironheart raised his eyebrows in surprise. "I thought it was only a rumor."

"It's true," Robert said with conviction.

Ironheart shrugged. "So there is one less warrior who wants to kill us. We still are not safe at Crow Creek." The others nodded their assent.

"We will take you to Fort Ridgely," Robert promised. "No more hunger. No more shivering in the cold. You will be treated well. In the spring, the soldiers will probably transfer you to Fort Snelling with the rest of the"—he hesitated—"with the rest of the prisoners."

Ironheart shook his head. "They said we would be free on the reservation. We were not free." He held up his arm and pulled up his sleeve to reveal sagging flesh. "We were prisoners of our own hunger. We were prisoners of sickness. There was no doctor. We were prisoners of death, watching our children die, able to do nothing." He looked at Robert as he said firmly, "We will be prisoners no longer. We will die as free men, on the land God gave to us."

As Daniel listened to Ironheart insisting that they would live on their old lands, he thought of Jeb Grant saying, *I never learned to be afraid of Indians. I hope it don't get me killed.*

Big Amos lifted the pot of thin gruel off the fire and set it aside. The three scouts contributed their tin cups for dishes, and while the starving Dakota shared the pathetic meal, an impossible possibility began to form in Daniel's mind. It had barely taken shape when Mother Friend smacked her lips with appreciation and, looking at Daniel with a big smile said, "Our white friends have gone on to Fort Ridgely. They will be glad to see you, Daniel Two Stars." She patted his arm affectionately. "We all thought you were dead."

At Daniel's questioning look, Mother Friend parted her lips in a toothless grin. "Many Words has a new name. He is Helping Words now. He was with us at Crow Creek. And one we called Silver Fox. Mrs. Dane's brother." She swept her hand over her head. "He has long white hair." Mother Friend made a chopping motion with her right hand, pretending to cut off her left. "And only one hand." She drew a question mark in the air with her finger. "A metal hook for this hand." She sighed and shook her head. "Helping Words is sick."

Ironheart interrupted. "We sent them to Fort Ridgely." He looked at Daniel carefully. "They promised not to tell the soldiers about us."

Daniel scooted toward the tent door. Mumbling something about checking to see if a storm was brewing, he lunged outside. Inhaling deeply, he stood up and began to pace back and forth across the entryway.

Robert joined him. He nodded toward the horizon.

When Daniel followed his gaze, his heart sank. "Do you think we can make it back before it hits?"

"Not a chance," Robert said. "I'm going to bring the horses around and tether them closer to the tent." He headed off. Daniel followed him, grateful they had pitched the tepee-sized tent up against a low ridge. Whatever was coming, they would be ready. Except for food. But they could live off horseflesh if they had to.

He cast a glance in the direction of Fort Ridgely before ducking back into the tent. Mother Friend was asleep, her head resting on one of his saddlebags. He pulled a blanket across her and sat down, listening to the stamping of the horses' feet as they huddled just outside the tent wall. He didn't need to look outside to know that by morning the landscape would be covered with a fresh layer of snow. He only wondered how long the storm would last and if Mother Friend knew any more about Simon Dane than she was telling him. Looking behind him at the old woman's sleeping form, he realized he would have to wait. It was probably for the best, he thought. Waiting would give him time to think. Time to plan. Time to convince Big Amos and Robert that perhaps *this* group of wanderers should be helped in a different way.

Daniel prayed. For Simon Dane. For Blue Eyes. For himself. For every individual inside the tent. And for Jeb Grant, who had no idea what he was about to be asked to do.

"You want me to *what?*" Jeb Grant didn't shout, but Daniel saw disbelief in his eyes as the little man scratched his scraggly day-old beard and stared up at him. He looked around Daniel and toward his barn where the sorriest group of Indians he had ever seen sat with Big Amos and Robert Lawrence.

"They are only six," Daniel coaxed. "Ironheart—the one on the spotted pony—is a leading man. You will like him. All together, they will take up only a tiny corner of your land." His voice was cool, convincing, as he added, "They can help you with the farm. No one around here will mind if you hire a few old Sioux to do some of your chores."

Jeb snorted. "Indians don't know a thing about farming. They hate it. I heard the braves think it's worse than death to do that kind of work."

Daniel nodded. "But some are changing. Ironheart set the example for his men last year. He works hard."

Jeb peered doubtfully at the gray-haired man sitting on the spotted pony. "Don't seem possible."

"We could build them a cabin," Daniel argued. "A cabin and a tepee. And if they work for you, if they live quietly—and they will—they might be allowed to stay. There is a similar arrangement with a man in Faribault—"

"I heard about that," Jeb said quickly. "But them Indians is family to the farmer's wife. She's a half-breed. That's different." He frowned up at Daniel. "What do you mean if *we* build them a cabin? Who's *we*?"

"Robert. Big Amos. Me."

Jeb laughed. "What do you know about building a cabin?"

Daniel looked past Jeb. "We built the one you live in."

"You what?"

"We built it. Robert and me." Daniel lowered his voice and leaned closer. "Before the outbreak this was Robert and Nancy Lawrence's home." He nodded up to the ridge where a pile of charred logs was silhouetted against the sky. "That was mine."

Jeb inhaled sharply. "I took over your place?"

Daniel nodded.

Jeb flushed with embarrassment. "Look here, Two Stars—nobody ever told me—I didn't mean—"

"It doesn't matter," Daniel interrupted him. He cleared his throat and gestured around him. "This will never belong to us again. We know that. I never would have said anything, except—"

"Except my knowin' now might make me feel like I owe you," Jeb said half angrily.

"*Jeb,*" a strident female voice called from the house.

"Marjorie's not well," Jeb said quickly. "I can't be putting this on her." He turned to go. Hesitating, he said, "Look, Two Stars, you're a good man. I know that. Your friends can stay the night. But I can't—" When Marjorie called Jeb's name again, Daniel heard fear in her voice. He frowned. Telling himself he shouldn't, he followed Jeb to the door.

"I'm here, darlin'," Jeb said gently. He was leaning over the bed in the corner.

Daniel couldn't see anything, but he heard enough to know that Marjorie was expecting a baby and things were not going well. He hurried away from the cabin toward the waiting Indians.

"We can stay the night," he said to them. "We'll use his barn." He went to Mother Friend. "His wife—" He looked down, embarrassed.

Mother Friend headed for the cabin. She disappeared inside, only to reappear, waving Daniel toward her. "Get me fresh water."

She ordered Jeb to light a lamp and fire up the stove, then turned back to Daniel, motioning toward the well with both hands. "Hurry!"

If Daniel expected to see Jeb chase the old woman away, he was surprised. Relief spread over the man's face as he headed for the door to fulfill Mother Friend's demand for a roaring fire in both the fireplace and the stove.

As Jeb Grant had feared, his wife, Marjorie, did not give birth to a healthy child. She gave birth to two. And she did not die. Instead, she slept for nearly two days and then woke to sit up in bed and feed her two tiny but remarkably healthy infants who had been taught to nurse on a twisted piece of cloth repeatedly dipped into warm goat's milk by Mother Friend and another old woman named Standing Tall. Between the two of them, the women kept the twin boys contented and warm until Marjorie was ready to feed them herself.

Big Amos brought the news down from the house to the Indians who had taken up residence in a box stall at the far end of the barn. Resting his forearms on the top of the stall, he grinned. "It seems Mrs. Grant trusts Mother Friend and Standing Tall more than she trusts her own husband with those babies. Mr. Grant says he hopes you can be convinced to stay."

# Twenty-One

"Be kindly affectioned one to another with brotherly love;
in honour preferring one another."

—Romans 12:10

"I TOLD YOU IT WAS INSANE TO LEAVE THE RESERVATION in the middle of winter," Elliot almost yelled. "This is even more ridiculous." He grabbed Simon's bony shoulders. "Look at yourself, man. You're half dead. You said St. Anthony is two days' hard ride from Fort Ridgely. We should spend some time here at the fort. You're in no condition—"

Simon jerked free of Elliot's grip. "Don't tell me what condition I am in," he said between clenched teeth. "I made it this far and I'm not letting another two or three days' ride keep me from home." He leaned over, resting his hands on his knees, waiting to catch his breath. When Elliot moved to help him, he waved him away. After a moment of silence, he said quietly, pleading, "Please, Elliot. I want to get home. To see my children. To see Gen. Try to understand."

Leighton knelt down in front of him. "The doctor said you shouldn't try it. He said you're on the verge of pneumonia now."

"We'll stick to the trail. It isn't hard traveling. Not like coming from the reservation across the wild territory. Nothing like it."

"You still have to sit on a horse and handle the cold. And what if it snows again?"

Simon forced a weak smile. "There's a doctor in St. Peter. If I can't make it, you can dump me on him." He coughed again. "But I promise you it won't come to that."

Elliot still argued. "You aren't God, Simon. Unless you have some secret powers I don't know about, that's a promise you may not be able to keep."

Simon pushed himself to a standing position. "You'd be surprised what kind of power I can muster when it comes to my children and Gen." He walked toward the door. "I am going home, Elliot. With or without you." He leaned against the door weakly. "Come, Elliot. You know you don't really want to spend the next few weeks wondering what Miss Jane Williams has been up to."

"Very amusing, Simon." Elliot studied his brother-in-law. His cheekbones stood out prominently, casting shadows across his face in the waning light. And yet, deep within the feverish eyes there was determination and a will that would not bend. Elliot almost believed the man *could* will himself to do the impossible. He went to the door. "All right, Simon. We'll go." He leaned close. "But I had better not have to explain to your children why I didn't keep you at Fort Ridgely until you felt better. Why I let you die on the trail."

Simon straightened. "You won't have to do that. I promise."

"Promises," Elliot grunted. He shook his head and grabbed

the door latch. "God help you keep your promises, Reverend Dane." He pulled the door open. "I'll get some provisions over at the sutler's. When I come back, I'll have the horses saddled up."

"If we leave right away," Simon said, nodding, "we can be at St. Peter by nightfall."

Elliot nodded and headed out the door. As soon as he was out of earshot, Simon collapsed in a fit of coughing.

"Yeah. I seen 'em." The soldier leaned against the guardhouse door and blinked up at Daniel Two Stars. He scratched his dirty blond head. Inspecting his filthy nails, he flipped something into the air. Swearing against lice, fleas, and a few other choice vermin, he finally said, "One of 'em's sick. The missionary. They got him over to the hospital. The white-haired one just rode by." He nodded across the road at the log store. "That's his horse."

After staring toward the fort hospital for a moment, Daniel opted for meeting Ellen Dane's brother first. He nudged his horse into a trot and headed across the road to the sutler's store. His hands were trembling as he dismounted and wrapped the reins around the hitching post. He lingered, his hand on the saddle pommel, wondering what to say. His emotions were crazy, alternating between anticipation and fear. Anticipation of knowing. Fear of hearing that Blue Eyes had married him.

He had been arguing with himself since he left Jeb's farm before dawn. No one in his right mind would have expected her to grieve for this long. After all, he told himself, *she* wasn't riding across the wilderness staring at his picture every night. She was living in that other world—the normal one. In that world, a person would get used to having a house and children. Certainly she wouldn't want to remember the fear and the awful days they spent running away from the hostiles. She would be glad to forget all that. And gradually, he told himself, she would have forgotten him too.

Standing before the sutler's, he ran the entire thing through his mind a few times. When he finally backed away from his horse, he had to grab the porch post to steady himself as he approached the door. Just when he had mustered the courage to go inside, the door was flung open and a tall slim stranger with long snow-white hair nodded politely and shoved past to tie the bundle in his arms to the saddle horn. Behind the stranger came Edward Pope with a second bundle.

"Hey," Pope said, nodding. "Didn't know you were back." He paused. "You get me some fresh meat, I'll cook you up a welcome-home pot of stew." He looked toward the scouts' camp near the granary, frowning slightly. "Are Robert and Big Amos all right?"

Daniel nodded. "They stayed up by the old agency for a couple of extra days." He paused. "We thought we saw signs of a small group headed that way. I'm—" He hesitated again. "I came ahead to tell Captain Willets." He felt guilty lying to Edward Pope like that. But he couldn't tell anyone attached to Fort Ridgely about Ironheart and Mother Friend and the others. Not yet.

The tall stranger had turned around and was looking at him with curiosity. He held out his hand. "Elliot Leighton. You must be one of the famous Dakota scouts. I haven't had the pleasure— although I've heard a lot about your work."

Daniel returned the handshake and stood, speechless, not knowing what to say.

Edward Pope filled the silence, pounding Daniel on the shoulder. "This here's one of the best scouts in all Indian territory." He flashed a smile. "I could tell you stories about Two Stars . . ."

"Two Stars?" Leighton said. His eyes flashed with surprise. "You aren't by any chance related to Daniel Two Stars?"

"Related?" Pope said loudly. He laughed. "He ain't just related. This is him."

Leighton stared in disbelief. "That can't be. I was told—I mean, we all believed—" Leighton stuttered. "They said you were dead." While Daniel tried to steady his own breathing, Leighton sputtered awkwardly, "Everyone said you were dead."

"Well, everyone's wrong," Pope said. "I followed him and his two friends all over this territory for half of last year. Believe me, Major Leighton, Daniel Two Stars ain't dead."

"Forgive me," Elliot finally said. He removed his hat and perched it on his saddle horn. Wiping his forehead with a trembling hand, he observed Daniel carefully. So this was the hero Meg regaled so often. The man Aaron said was the bravest man he'd ever known. He didn't look particularly heroic, with his trail-worn uniform and his unkempt black hair. Searching the weather-beaten face, Leighton thought he looked older than his—how old would he be, Elliot wondered—no more than his early twenties. He looked a decade older, that was certain.

"I'm sorry, Mr. Two Stars," Elliot said again. "It's just that I've heard so many stories about you—" He stopped abruptly. Putting his hat back on, he turned to Edward Pope. "Would you excuse us, please?"

Shrugging nonchalantly, Pope headed back inside. He paused at the door. "Don't forget about supper," he called back to Daniel. Looking at Leighton he said, "And bring your friend if you want to."

Leighton stared at Pope, waiting for the door to close.

Daniel said quietly, "He's the best cook in the army. At least that's what the soldiers say." He looked up at Leighton with a faint smile. "An invitation to Edward's mess hall is worth accepting." He felt calmer now. He didn't have to face Simon Dane yet.

He looked up at Elliot and decided there was little resemblance between the tall one-handed man and his sister. He suspected the silver hair and the metal hook were somehow connected. He had seen one of the white women captives' hair turn white almost overnight during the uprising.

For something to do, Two Stars unwrapped his horse's reins. He stood looking down at them and said, "Mother Friend told us you left them to go to the fort. She said Reverend Dane was ill." At Elliot's look of surprise, he explained, "There are many scouts' camps across this territory. Just last fall we took More than a hundred stragglers up to Fort Snelling."

"Is that what will happen to Mother Friend?"

Daniel hesitated, but then something in Leighton's expression made him trust. He shook his head. "No. Mother Friend and the others will be working on a farm up by the old agency. The white farmer said they are welcome to stay."

"How did you convince him to allow it?"

Daniel shrugged. "It wasn't too hard." He looked up at Leighton again. "Since the farm he lives on used to be ours. Since I helped build his house before the uprising. And," he added with a slight smile, "Mother Friend helped his wife give him twin sons."

"I'd say that man owes you a debt."

Daniel shrugged again. "He's a good man."

"What about your Captain Willets here? Will he allow it?"

"I think between the three of us, we will be able to convince him." Daniel had an idea. "If you would tell him what it is like at Crow Creek, it would help. He is a reasonable man.'"

"I've already done that," Elliot said quickly. "And I'm going to see to it that a lot of other people know about it as well. People who can make a change."

As Leighton talked, Daniel thought of Mrs. Dane. It wasn't pronounced, but something in the controlled intensity in Leighton's voice reminded him of her. "Your sister was the first white woman I learned not to hate." He looked off toward the horizon and then back up at Elliot. "The first one who showed me Christ. Instead of preaching Him at me. She saved my life."

"Yes," Elliot said softly. "Meg and Aaron told me the story." He shook his head. "They also told me what they thought was the story of your death. Meg still cries about it."

"Are Meg and Aaron well?" Daniel asked. He suppressed the question about the blonde-haired child, afraid he would learn too much about Gen. And he wasn't ready. Not yet.

"They are wonderful," Elliot said with enthusiasm. "I can't imagine what they are going to think when they learn I've seen you." He hesitated. "Reverend Dane is over at the hospital. They cleared out a little storeroom for us. He refuses to be considered a patient." Leighton nodded toward the bundles of supplies hanging off his saddle horn. "We're supposed to be leaving today." He gathered up the reins to his horse. "Can you come with me now?"

Daniel nodded and together the men walked across the road, past the guardhouse and the commissary, beyond the stone barracks, and toward the hospital. With every step, Daniel's heart beat faster, until, when they stepped up onto the porch that ran the length of the log building, he thought surely Simon Dane could hear the pounding as he approached.

He could hear Simon before he saw him. Heard the coughing and wheezing, frowned and looked up at Leighton, concern shining in his eyes. Leighton shook his head. "He's been fighting it for months. Mother Friend helped for a while. Then it came back. But he insists on going home."

"Home?" Daniel wanted to know.

"St. Anthony."

As Leighton opened the door, Daniel realized with a jolt that his Blue Eyes might be only two days' ride away.

Leighton led Two Stars inside the hospital and toward a small storeroom at the back of the building. "The doctor wanted to keep him isolated from the others. To protect his health." He tapped on the door with his hook. When Simon didn't answer, he slowly opened the door. "I've someone here to see you, Simon."

The man Daniel saw sitting on the floor looked nothing like the Reverend Dane he remembered. He was leaning back against a pillow half asleep, his mouth sagging open, his cheeks sunken. When Elliot stepped into the room Simon started, rubbed his eyes, and pushed himself to a sitting position. "Ready to go?" he said to Elliot and forced himself to stand up, albeit unsteadily.

With a frown, Leighton grabbed Simon's arm. "Sit down, Simon. I've brought a visitor."

Simon blinked a few times and looked stupidly toward where Daniel stood beside the open door. Finally, his eyesight adjusted. His expression changed from intense concentration to utter amazement. And then, behind the amazement, a glimmer of something else, something almost animal in intensity.

"You?!" Simon gasped. He sat down abruptly. "It can't be!"

Daniel knelt before Simon, surprised to feel himself fighting back tears.

Simon put a trembling hand on Daniel's shoulder. "They told us you were dead! Your name . . ." Simon's voice lowered and he said with wonder, "Your name was in the paper. The list of men hanged. It was right there!" He lifted both hands to cover his mouth and began to cough and sputter. Daniel hurried out to get the doctor while Leighton made Simon lay back on the cot. It was a few moments before Simon could speak again. When Daniel finally went back into the little storeroom-turned-bedroom, Simon lay on his back covered with several blankets, his head once again propped up on a pillow.

He extended his hand toward Daniel, who went and sat down on the chair Leighton pulled up. Daniel leaned forward, nervously twirling his hat in his hands while Simon just stared at him, still disbelieving. When he finally spoke it was to ask, "How could it be? Where have you been? I looked for you. We all did. We kept thinking the paper was a mistake, but they cut the bodies down and used them for—" He broke off. "I guess it doesn't matter now."

"I was in prison at Mankato," Daniel said. "With Robert Lawrence."

"But I went to Mankato. I was there for weeks. I didn't see you."

"Sacred Lodge came for us in February. He was hiring scouts for General Sibley."

Simon shook his head. "I went down in March."

Daniel nodded and pressed his lips together, forcing himself not to ask the obvious question.

Simon took a deep breath. He started to say something, then stopped. Finally, he only asked, "And the scouting—you like it?"

Daniel studied the floor. He swiped across his forehead nervously. "I was a walking dead man for a long time. It all seemed too much." He paused. His voice was a hoarse whisper when he finally said, "Too much to lose. I couldn't understand why God would do that to me."

Simon nodded.

Daniel looked at him, surprised when Simon didn't offer a quick response, a Bible verse, some easy answer to heartbreak. Instead he lay quietly, honest sympathy shining in his feverish eyes.

"I can't even imagine what you've been through, Two Stars," Simon said. "It surely is a miracle that you haven't abandoned your faith."

Daniel shifted nervously. "Meg and Aaron?" he asked.

"They are—wonderful," Simon said. "And Hope. The child you saved. She is still with us. She's walking now."

"You never found her family?"

Simon pursed his lips. "They found us. But we convinced them to let her stay with us."

The silence in the room hung heavy. At last, Simon said, "Genevieve is well, Two Stars. She is with us. As is Miss Jane

Williams. We are all living with another missionary couple in a big, drafty house in St. Anthony." He hurried on, "Miss Huggins and Miss Stanford were with us for a while. They spent some time at Fort Snelling, but they've both gone back east now until the Dakota Mission's future is known. They hope to come back. Reverend Masters is at Crow Creek. He's started a small school." Simon stopped as abruptly as he had begun. He had said much, but it was as if the name Genevieve still hung on the air in the room. He shifted uncomfortably.

Daniel got up. "I heard the doctor say you need rest."

"Nonsense," Simon said abruptly. He started to get up. "We're heading out today. Going home." But a spasm of coughs put him back on the cot.

Elliot started to get the doctor, but Simon called him back. "There's nothing—" He gasped, put his hand up to his chest, took a deep breath. "There's nothing more he can do, Elliot. Leave him alone." He sat back down.

"There is more snow coming," Daniel said abruptly. "You should stay. Let the storm pass. Blue skies make for better travel." He paused at the door and nodded at Elliot Leighton. "I will bring you both some of Edward's 'welcome back' stew."

He was already in the hall when he heard Simon weakly call his name. He turned around.

"She's—wonderful, Two Stars. Healthy. Happy. The children adore her." He took a deep breath and said quickly, "We're to be married in the spring."

Daniel leaned against the door frame, feeling as if he had been struck. But he hid it. He nodded slowly and finally willed himself to look into Simon's eyes. Something flashed between the two men. Something even Elliot Leighton noticed.

"Tell her I wish her great happiness," Daniel said. And then he was gone.

# Twenty-Two

"Look not every man on his own things,
but every man also on the things of others."

—PHILIPPIANS 2:4

DANIEL PLUNGED INTO GOD'S WORD. HE WAS NOT, HE told himself, going to sink back into the colorless existence, the solitary hell he had lived in for nearly a year. Somehow, he was going to deal with the reality of Genevieve LaCroix becoming Genevieve Dane. Deal with it and get on with his own life.

*But things are different now,* his heart argued. *She isn't married yet. If she knew—*

*But she will never know,* he reasoned. *I'll make Simon and Elliot promise not to tell her. She deserves a better life. Meg and Aaron and Hope deserve a mother.*

According to Leighton, the children remembered him as a

hero. There was a certain comfort in that. It was even appealing. He would do the right thing. By God's grace, he would choose against himself and do the right thing for Gen and the children.

*Love seeketh not her own . . . love looketh not out for itself, but also for the good of others . . .* It was right to do what was best for the person you loved. Wasn't that what Christ had done? *He laid down His life for us: and we ought to lay down our lives for the brethren.*

He could think of no reason beyond his own selfish desire to force himself back into Genevieve's life. If she had said she would marry Simon, then she had grown beyond whatever they had shared.

As for his feelings about Simon Dane, Daniel could not blame the man for loving Gen, could not blame him for wanting to protect that love and the future. He had seen the glimmer of emotion in Simon's eyes when they first saw one another. He knew what it meant. Simon had staked a claim, and he didn't want Daniel to challenge it.

*If a man say, I love God, and hateth his brother, he is a liar.* Christians were to be like Christ. He would not fail. Everything in him cried out against letting Gen go. Everything in him yearned for life with her. And yet, he told himself, he would let her go to a better life than he could ever give her, where people lived in houses and had plenty to eat and were surrounded by friends. He would give her to Simon Dane, who loved her. She would be cherished. Knowing that would have to be enough for him.

For two weeks Daniel read Scripture, prayed, and tended Simon for all he was worth. He did it for Gen. And because it was right. He provided fresh meat for Edward Pope's soup and poured it down Simon's throat by the quart. When Simon's cough persisted, he rode up to Jeb Grant's farm to get Mother Friend, introducing her as the nurse to a white farmer's children. Up north.

"Mother Friend and a few others work for Jeb Grant," he told Captain Willets. To his credit, Captain Willets never asked where they had come from. He seemed content to assume they were like the group at Faribault, peaceful Indians with connections in the white community who had never been involved in the uprising and were quiet citizens, accepted by their neighbors and therefore allowed to stay put.

Mother Friend's ablutions once again brought Simon back to a measure of health. He stopped coughing and began to put on weight. Within a week of her arrival, he was haranguing Elliot about heading home. By the end of the second week, he was well enough to conduct a worship service for the scouts' camp.

"You should start a church," he urged Robert Lawrence. "The group up at Jeb Grant's would gladly come to services. You'd have a dozen members." He looked at Daniel. "And you already have a deacon."

The weather finally broke late in March. The snow melted and the promise of spring burst from the moist soil, sending a pungent aroma into the air. The horses began shedding their winter coats and the post's veterinarian sounded the news of two foals making their appearance in the stables just across the road.

Simon and Elliot prepared to leave. The morning they were to go, Daniel and the other scouts gathered to say good-bye. Simon led them all in prayer and then climbed up into the saddle.

Before mounting his own horse, Elliot grasped Daniel's hand. His blue-gray eyes flickered with emotion as he said, "When Simon and I started this trip I hated Indians. Hated everything about them. Didn't want my sister's children anywhere near them. I said the word *Sioux* like it was a swearword." He squeezed Daniel's hand tighter. "I just want to tell you that after what I've seen of Indians, both here and back at Crow Creek, I'm ashamed of myself. Indians being human, I suspect there's a few cowards and liars among 'em. But all I've met are honorable men. And among those honorable men, you are one of the best." He nearly crushed Daniel's hand before he released him. Shaking Big Amos's and Robert's hands, he mounted and prepared to head out.

Simon leaned down to put his hand on Daniel's shoulder. The unspoken name passed between the two men. Reaching into the wide blue sash at his waist, Daniel withdrew Etienne LaCroix's journal. "I don't know if you'll ever be able to explain how you got this without mentioning me," he said, choking back the emotion that clutched at his throat. "But"—he handed the journal up to Simon—"I think you should have it." Simon opened the book. When he saw the sketches of Gen, his eyes filled with tears.

Daniel pointed to one of the sketches and said, "She will have a good man for a husband. And I think she will have a happy life with him." Impulsively, he put his hand on Simon's saddle horn and said, "When you get home, put your arms around your children for me." He glanced at Elliot to be certain he, too, could hear, and then he stared into Simon's eyes and said, "And forget you ever saw me."

And then he walked away.

Gen hated gas lighting. She didn't trust it, cringed every time she heard the hiss of the gas coming through to light a lamp. And so it was that she sat alone late one night in the Whitneys' kitchen, bathed in the soft, golden light of a kerosene lamp sitting beside her half-finished letter to Miss Jane. *We haven't heard from the men in weeks, and I am beginning to worry.* She paused and sat back, inspecting the nib of her pen. Rubbing her arms briskly, she got up and headed for the stove to heat water for tea.

"She's beautiful, isn't she?" Simon said, preventing Elliot from knocking at the back door.

"Yes, Simon. She is. Now let's get you inside where it's warm."

Stifling a cough, Simon shook his head. "Wait just a minute." He drew in a wheezing breath. "We haven't talked about what Two Stars said—"

Through the window, Elliot saw Gen whirl around and head for the door. "Thank God!" she exclaimed, pulling it open.

Simon would have fallen into the room if Elliot had not braced him up.

Gen put her hand to Simon's forehead. "You're burning up." She glanced at Elliot. "You had him out in this weather like this?"

"Don't be angry with Elliot," Simon wheezed, stumbling to the table and falling into a chair. He summoned a smile. "I told him I was coming home to my girls with him or without him."

Elliot looked over the top of Simon's head, shaking his head apologetically. "He was adamant."

"You're a big boy, Mr. Leighton," Gen snapped angrily. "I think you could have made him stay put."

Simon grabbed her hand and pressed it to his cheek. "Not unless he tied me down, dear." He kissed her hand. "This is all the medicine I need."

Gen snatched her hand away. Her eyes blazing, she settled her gaze on Elliot. "Dr. Abernathy. Two doors up from the hotel." She leaned over and put her hand on Simon's shoulder. "The Whitneys went to St. Louis with Miss Jane, Simon. Do you think you can make it across the hall to their room?"

"St. Louis?" Elliot asked abruptly. "Jane's gone to St. Louis?"

"Rebecca and Timothy Sutton's aunt and uncle—" She shook her head. "I'll explain later. Please, Mr. Leighton. Dr. Abernathy." She whisked out the door and across the hall. Elliot could hear her moving around in the Whitneys' quarters.

He put his hand on Simon's shoulder. "Do you need help getting across the hall?"

Simon shook his head.

After turning back the Whitneys' bed and building a fire in

the tiny fireplace in a corner of the room, Gen found Simon, his head resting on his crossed arms, half laying across the kitchen table, shivering. "Dear Lord," she whispered, wondering how she was going to get him across the hall and into bed alone.

"Can you—can you walk, Simon?"

He raised his head, bleary-eyed. He didn't seem to recognize her.

She took his hand and pressed it to her cheek. "Simon," she said gently. "It's me. It's Gen. You're home. Please, dear. Come to bed."

Somehow he managed to stand up and wobble across the hall. He collapsed into bed, oblivious to Gen's gentle hands as she removed his coat and shoes. He was shivering uncontrollably by the time Elliot arrived with Dr. Abernathy.

"I'll make some tea," Gen said, backing out of the room as Dr. Abernathy and Elliot began to undress Simon, who was only semiconscious.

"Forget the tea," the doctor said over his shoulder. "This man needs a good shot of whiskey."

Gen hesitated. "He won't want—"

"I said whiskey, woman!" the doctor half shouted. "This is no time for a temperance lecture."

"I'll get the whiskey, Miss LaCroix," Elliot said quickly. "As soon as we get Simon undressed. Don't worry about it." He smiled kindly. "But *you* could probably use some tea. And I know I could. Strong tea."

Gen nodded and fled to the kitchen, her eyes misting over with tears as she listened to Simon coughing.

In a moment, Elliot came out of the Whitneys' quarters and headed outside to tend the horses. When he came back, he took a bottle of whiskey in to Dr. Abernathy before returning to the kitchen where he found Gen staring at a half-finished letter on the table.

Elliot made the tea and handed her a cup. "The whiskey helped. He's resting more quietly."

"It probably knocked him out cold," Gen said wearily. "I don't think he's ever even tasted whiskey."

"The doctor is going to stay the night. He said he'll call if he needs anything."

Gen cupped her hands around her teacup. She nodded at the half-finished letter. "I was writing Miss Jane." She looked up at Leighton, a bit surprised at the intensity of his interest. "Rebecca and Timothy Sutton do have family, after all. It turns out they didn't respond to our efforts to find them because they were in Europe." She sighed wearily. "They asked Miss Jane to spend some time in St. Louis. To help the children adjust to their new home."

"So she'll be away for a while?"

Gen nodded. She watched Leighton's reaction. He made no effort to hide his disappointment. "Perhaps you could enclose a note in my letter—"

"Yes," he said and nodded eagerly. "Thank you. I will."

Dr. Abernathy came in. "I need hot water. I want to make a poultice. See if I can't break up some of the congestion."

Elliot went to sit with Simon while Gen helped the doctor. He lay beneath a mountain of quilts, muttering to himself.

When the doctor finally settled back into his chair beside Simon's bed, he ordered them both out. "Get some rest," he said. "We're all going to be worn out before this is over."

Gen and Elliot lingered in the kitchen. "Please, Mr. Leighton," Gen said quietly. "Simon's room is the second door on the left upstairs. Go ahead." She headed back to the kitchen. "I don't think I can sleep right now."

Elliot followed her into the kitchen. "He was insistent, Miss LaCroix. I would never have thought—"

"I—I apologize for accusing you earlier. I shouldn't have

struck out at you that way." She looked past him and out the window. "I know how he can be."

"He wouldn't be dissuaded," Elliot said. "He said he wasn't going to let three days on horseback keep him from his girls."

"Three days?" Gen asked abruptly.

Elliot nodded. "We were at Fort Ridgely."

"But—why? How?"

They both sat down at the table. Elliot took a deep breath. "First, there's something I should say." His blue-gray eyes sought hers and held.

She headed for the stove and poured herself another cup of tea. "It changed your opinion of a few things. About Indians."

He raised his eyebrows and nodded. "How did you know?"

She set the teakettle down on the table and pointed at his teacup. "The way you're drinking your tea," she said.

"What?"

"The first time I poured tea for you, right after you came, I thought it was just an odd habit from being in the army. But then I noticed you only did it when I was the one who served you."

"What are you talking about?" he mumbled. But he hung his head. He knew.

"You always picked up your napkin and wiped the rim of the cup before you drank anything I handed you. As if my touching it contaminated it somehow."

Elliot held out his hand to her, palm up. "I wouldn't blame you if you never forgave me for that."

Gen slipped her hand into his and squeezed. "Tell me what happened at Crow Creek." She released his hand and sat down.

For all the long hours while they waited on Dr. Abernathy and took turns sitting with Simon, Elliot told Gen about the weeks at Crow Creek. When he described the flight back to Minnesota with the Dakota he paused abruptly. "I forgot. You know one of them. Mother Friend?" he asked.

Gen gasped with surprise. "Yes, oh yes. Is she all right?"

Elliot nodded. "She tended Simon twice. Once at Crow Creek. Once at the fort. Brought him back from bouts worse than this." He leaned forward and whispered, "Burned some plant and wafted the smoke around the room . . . then made him drink some of the most disgusting concoctions ever. But it worked."

Gen nodded. "I remember the 'stinking weed.' Every time I sniffled my mother hauled some into the cabin." Gen wrinkled her nose.

"Well," Elliot agreed, "all I can say is I hope whiskey and Dr. Abernathy's powders and quinine do half the good." He stretched and rubbed the back of his neck. "I want to know about Jane," Elliot said quietly. "But not tonight." He stood up. "Can't I convince you to go upstairs and get some sleep? It will be dawn soon."

Gen shook her head. "I'll go into the Whitneys' little parlor and lie down on the couch. I want to stay close." She smiled up at him. "Thank you, Mr. Leighton, for bringing him home."

"Elliot. Call me Elliot." He climbed the stairs, surprised at the weariness that overtook him with each step. When he sank onto Simon's bed, he sighed with relief.

∞

To his credit, Dr. Abernathy remained at Simon's bedside for the better part of the next three days, leaving only once for a few hours to attend a female patient's confinement. He applied hot and cold compresses, administered Dover's powder and quinine, and once threatened to sit on his patient if Simon did not cooperate and drink the prescribed whiskey.

Elliot Leighton proved to be not only an able nurse, but also a good baby-sitter.

"No, you may not skip school today," he insisted, saving Gen from an argument with Aaron. "The Leighton men have always been well educated. Your father would not approve."

"Ouch!" he exclaimed in mock anger when Hope pulled his long silver hair. Then he tickled her until she screamed for mercy.

"Don't, Unka Lee," she demanded. Then she tugged on his hair again with a mischievous grin.

"All right," he said one morning, and showed a curious Meg how his hook attached to his upper arm.

"Sleep," he insisted late one night, when Gen was completely exhausted. He nodded toward Simon's room. "His fever has broken. I'll sit with him." And he sent her to bed.

Not long after Simon and Elliot left Fort Ridgely, Captain Willets organized a battalion to head west to join General Sully's 1864 campaign against the Sioux in South Dakota. Daniel Two Stars traveled with them.

Robert had protested when Daniel said he was going. "Reverend Dane said there was talk of asking the government to give us each eighty acres near the old reservation. We might get farms again, Daniel."

"I hope it happens," Daniel said. He looked down at the metal cross hanging around his neck. "But I can't stay here. Too many times I have headed my horse that way." He nodded northeast, toward St. Anthony. He touched his forehead, "My head knows it would be wrong. My heart still wants her back."

# Twenty-Three

"But what things were gain to me,
those I counted loss for Christ."

—PLILIPPIANS 3:7

"WE THOUGHT—DEAD—HOW—" SIMON TOSSED IN HIS sleep, muttering and frowning.

Gen roused from her chair and went to him. Dipping a clean cloth in cool water, she wrung it out and laid it on his forehead, then sat on the edge of the bed stroking Simon's cheek.

"The doctor says you're going to be fine, dear," she whispered, trying to comfort him. "Just relax and sleep. Your fever broke a few hours ago." She reached down to squeeze his hand. He squeezed back, but he didn't return from wherever his dreams had taken him. He continued talking, jagged, illogical mutterings about Crow Creek and Mother Friend, about starvation and dying . . . and then, about something impossible. Something that made Gen's hands tremble as she prepared another compress and laid it gently across his forehead.

The mutterings of illness, she reminded herself. He had been delirious only a few hours ago. It was just a dream.

As soon as Simon fell into a deeper sleep, Gen made her way across the hall into the kitchen and sat down, leaning forward to rest her head on her crossed arms.

Elliot came hurrying down the back stairs. "What is it?" he asked, rushing to Gen's side. "Is he—should I go for the doctor?"

Gen didn't look up. She shook her head. "He's all right. Just a few bad dreams. He's quiet now." She sat up and brushed her tangled hair back out of her face. Supporting her head with one hand, she said, "He was back in the past somewhere." She took a deep breath and forced a smile. "It just brought back some memories. That's all." She sighed. "Do you mind if I go up and lie down for a while? The children will probably sleep a little later this morning, since it's Saturday."

Elliot went to sit with Simon and Gen dragged herself upstairs and crept into the room she shared with Hope and Meg. They were both still sound asleep. When Gen sank onto the mattress, Meg snuggled close. Closing her eyes, Gen tried in vain to fall asleep. When she could not, she got up to head back down to the kitchen and start breakfast.

Then she remembered Simon's bedroll and saddlebags, still sitting in his room since his return. *Saturday . . . wash day.* Creeping into Simon and Aaron's room, she picked up the bedroll, slung the saddlebags over her shoulder, tiptoed out of the room and headed downstairs. When she pulled one of Simon's shirts out of the saddlebag, something hit the floor. Thinking it was Simon's Bible, she bent to pick it up and set it aside on the kitchen table while she emptied the bags, unrolled the bedroll, and hauled in the washtub from the back porch. She put water on to heat and then went to set Simon's Bible on the stairs to take it up with her when she went to get Hope out of bed. It was then she realized the smooth leather book was not a Bible. Something about it was familiar.

Her heart pounding, Gen backed up to the table and half fell into a chair. She opened the book and with a little "oh" saw Etienne's beautiful script. She turned a page and saw herself, a baby in her Dakota mother's arms. Another few pages and she was a toddler. Another, and another, and another, and with tears flowing freely Gen watched herself grow up, saw her father's love and the end of a way of life unfold in his words.

She was almost sobbing when the sound of footsteps made her look up. Elliot was standing in the doorway, a strange expression on his face. "Where did you find that?"

Gen motioned toward the pile of laundry in the corner. "I couldn't sleep. I thought I'd just start with Simon's laundry . . . Saturday is always the day we do . . ." Her voice faded away.

Leighton sat down at the table and leaned toward her. "I think you should hear it from Simon," he said. "I'm not trying to put you off, Gen. Really, I'm not. It's just not something I want to—"

"I want to hear it from you," Gen said. Her dark eyes flashed with emotion. "I want to know how Simon came to have this." She nodded toward the bedroom. "And I don't want him upset."

Elliot looked away for a moment. "He made Simon promise never to tell you," Elliot said slowly. "I heard it. He said, 'You should have this.' And then he said, 'And forget you ever saw me.'"

"Who? Who said that? Who had my father's journal?" Gen demanded half angrily. When Elliot didn't say anything, Gen raised a trembling hand to her throat, then up to cover her mouth. She closed her eyes, but tears flowed freely from beneath her closed lids, down both cheeks. "Is he—is he—well?" she croaked out.

"He is," Elliot said.

"Was he a prisoner?"

"No," Elliot shook his head quickly. "He's one of the scouts at Fort Ridgely."

"Fort Ridgely," Gen said mechanically. *So close. So impossibly far away.*

"Gen," Elliot said, reaching across to put his hand over hers. "He was the one who brought Mother Friend to take care of Simon. He's quite a man."

Gen nodded. "Yes," she whispered. "Yes he is." She swiped at the tears.

"I heard him beg Simon not to tell you," Elliot repeated softly. "I think he wanted you to—" Elliot broke off. "He asked Simon to hug the children for him. And he pointed to your picture in that journal and said something about you having a good husband and a good life. It was right before we left to come home."

Gen swallowed and nodded. She looked up at the ceiling while fresh tears spilled out of her eyes.

"What—what do you want me to do, Gen?" Elliot said. "What can I do to help you?"

Gen looked down at her father's journal. She closed it and held it for a moment. Presently, she held it out to Elliot. "Take it," she whispered. She stood up, then wavered a little and grasped the back of her chair. Taking a deep breath, she said, "When the children come down, would you remind them to bring their laundry down? Have Aaron fill the washtub. And, would you mind—breakfast—"

"I'll scramble some eggs. Whatever you want," Elliot said quickly.

Gen nodded. "Thank you. I think I'll just take a walk." Without looking at him she headed for the hallway. "Elliot," she said from the doorway.

"Yes?"

"I need to be able to trust you with this," she said. Her voice broke. She nodded toward the Whitneys' apartment where Simon lay recovering. "He must never know." She took a deep breath and finally managed to look at him. "Promise me."

"What are you going to do?" he asked softly.

Gen looked around her. Footsteps sounded in the upstairs hall. She forced a smile. Looking back at Elliot she said quietly, "I'm going to take a walk. And then I'm coming home to do my family's laundry," she said.

"I will." Genevieve LaCroix looked up into Simon's eyes and smiled. Just over his shoulder, she caught a glimpse of Aaron grinning at her. And beyond Aaron, Elliot Leighton stood nodding his approval.

"Will you, Simon Dane, take this woman to be your lawfully wedded wife?" Samuel Whitney intoned.

"I do," Simon said, then corrected himself, "I will." The small crowd gathered in the Whitneys' parlor laughed.

Samuel pronounced Genevieve LaCroix and Simon Dane to be man and wife. "Let us all join in a prayer of blessing for our friends," Samuel said. He raised his right hand. "The Lord bless thee and keep thee, the Lord make his face shine upon thee, and be gracious unto thee, the Lord lift up his countenance upon thee, and give thee peace." He opened his eyes. "And now, Simon, you may kiss your bride."

Meg giggled, Aaron blushed, and Hope broke away from Nina and ran to Gen, pulling on her skirt and shouting "Up, Ma! Up!"

Laughing, Simon leaned over and planted a chaste kiss on his bride's cheek before sweeping Hope into his arms. Settling Hope on one side, he put his left arm around Gen and hugged her close, inhaling the fragrance of the wildflowers woven into her hair.

For a moment, all movement and sound in the parlor was suspended, then Aaron said, "We'd better get going, Father, we have a train to catch!" The rest of the day was bedlam. While Gen hurried upstairs to change, Elliot and Simon loaded one buggy with valises and boxes and hauled them to the train station. They returned just in time to meet Gen, who had walked up to the church for an informal wedding luncheon hosted by the Whitneys' at the church.

By late afternoon, everyone crowded back into the buggy and rode to the train station. Amid hugs and wishes for happiness, Gen and Simon, Aaron and Meg, Hope, and Elliot Leighton climbed aboard the Chicago and Northwestern Railway's Iowa-Minnesota Division headed south.

"What's dat, Unka Lee?" Hope demanded, bouncing on Elliot's lap and pointing out the window.

As soon as one question was answered, another arose, until Gen reached over and tugged on Hope's dress. "Come here, little miss. You're going to wear your Uncle Elliot out."

Elliot shifted Hope to his other shoulder. "She's fine," he protested. "She just fits right here." He sat Hope on his knee so that her eyes could just barely peer out the window and watch the landscape pass. As if on cue, Hope snuggled against Elliot's arm.

She cast a triumphant smile toward Gen, who laughed and shook her head. "Not even two yet, and already bossing the men around."

"Takes after her mother that way," Simon interjected.

Gen slapped his knee. "I beg your pardon! When have I ever bossed you around, Reverend Dane?"

"Oh, let's see . . . convincing me to accept Dr. Riggs's invitation to help him proofread the new Dakota Bible at the printers in New York instead of returning to the reservation—"

"The doctor said you need a good long rest before you even *think* of going back to the reservation!" Gen protested mildly.

"Conspiring with Elliot to take the entire family for a visit to their grandmother's . . ."

"That was Mr. Leighton's idea!" Gen pleaded with Elliot, "Give a little help here, 'Unka Lee'!"

Elliot raised both hands palm up and shook his head. "Sorry, Genevieve. You're on your own."

Simon looked down at her, "And proposing marriage when I was on my deathbed!"

"I did no such thing!" Gen said indignantly.

"You did," Simon insisted. "Praise God."

Aaron slid onto the bench occupied by Meg, Elliot, and Hope, facing Simon and Gen. "It may be faster than the steamboat," he said grumpily, "but it's noisy and dirty. Give me steamships any day." He hunkered down and, pulling a book out of his pocket, put his feet on the bench next to his father and began to read.

Meg yawned and leaned against her brother.

Simon leaned over and whispered, "It looks like getting up at dawn is catching up with everyone."

"Mm-hmm," Gen murmured, resting her head on his shoulder. It wasn't long before the rhythm of the rails lulled them all to sleep.

The train car jerked and everyone stirred. Elliot shifted Hope to his other arm; Meg slumped down onto Aaron's lap. Almost without opening his eyes, Aaron removed his coat, rolled it up, and tucked it under his sister's head. Looking up at Simon, Gen smiled.

"I look old enough to be your father," he had grumbled that morning when he met her at the base of the stairs just before the ceremony.

"You look like a man with character. A man who has lived," she had told him, touching his gray sideburns and kissing him lightly.

"I promised you I would never demand anything you don't freely give," he had said, blushing furiously. "That promise is still in effect."

She had been standing on the second step when he said it, her eyes level with his. She put her hands on his shoulders and leaned forward whispering, "And I promised you I wanted passion in my life. *That* promise is also still in effect, Reverend Dane." She had looked into his eyes then and said, "I'm only twenty years old, Simon. Don't expect me to act like an old married woman for another thirty years or so."

Something had flickered in his eyes, and then he had kissed her gently.

The train slowed, rousing Gen enough that she opened her eyes. She looked outside just in time to see a small herd of horses tearing across a vast pasture. The gray stallion in the lead reminded her of the first time she ever saw Daniel Two Stars. It seemed a lifetime ago that he had ridden into her father's trading post alongside his friend Red Thunder and a dislikable brave named Otter. Some argument had ended in a fight between Red Thunder and Two Stars. When it was over, Daniel owned the gray stallion.

As the train clattered south toward Iowa, Gen took Simon's hand and guided his arm up and over her head and then around her shoulders. With an expression that was both surprised and pleased, he pulled her closer. Gen closed her eyes. She was going to be the best wife, the best mother, the best sister-in-law, she could possibly be. And she would be happy. Because it was right.

# Twenty-Four

"Be ye therefore merciful, as your Father also is merciful . . .
Forgive, and ye shall be forgiven."
—Luke 6:36–37

DANIEL TWO STARS URGED HIS BAY GELDING OUT AHEAD
of the squad of Dakota cavalry, tearing across the landscape, closing the distance between himself and the two Indians ahead. He
finally came alongside one. While his gelding matched the
Indian's pony stride for stride, Daniel slipped his square-toed
boots out of the stirrups. One leap and he and the rider both
tumbled to the earth, rolling over and over. The brave got the best
of Daniel and leaped up, knife in hand. Daniel spun to one side
just as a rifle went off and the brave toppled over.

"Good work, Two Stars," Captain Willets said, dismounting.
He rolled the dead brave over on his back.

"Yanktonais," Daniel said. "Probably half-breed."

"How can you tell?" Willets asked.

"Pale skin," Daniel said. "The beadwork on the moccasins." He bent over to catch his breath, then rounded up his bay gelding. He was standing beside the dead warrior when Brady Jensen rode up, dragging the body of a second brave behind his horse.

Captain Willets glowered at Jensen. "I said capture them, Private," Willets snapped, "not treat them like animals."

Jensen shrugged. "He wanted a fight. I obliged him." He reached behind him and pulled out a sheaf of papers loosely tied together with a piece of twine. "I'd say these are the ones that killed Fielner." He handed the bundle to Captain Willets, who leafed through the pages, glancing at the fine drawings of plants and flowers, a half-finished sketch of a prairie chicken. Willets could almost hear the bird's unique "boom-boom-boom" as it courted the ladies. He shook his head and tucked the notebook in his saddlebags. Darned fool. Talked his way onto the expedition so he could draw plants and flowers. They had found his body early that morning. He must have wandered out of camp alone at dawn, probably to draw the prairie chicken.

"Let's get them back to camp," Willets said.

Jensen climbed down and prepared to tie a second rope to his saddle horn.

"Not you," Willets said abruptly. He waved toward Daniel. "Let Two Stars take them in."

Jensen shrugged and walked away.

It took a while to round up the Indian ponies. When he finally had them, Daniel tied the two braves' hands and feet together, then laid them across one of the horse's backs, secured the bodies to the saddle, and rode off toward camp followed by the rest of the men. If he had known what General Sully would order be done, he would have refused. It took a few moments for him to realize Edward Pope wasn't just repeating an ugly rumor. "I tell you, Daniel, he's going to do it. Jensen volunteered."

Daniel and some of the other scouts strode across the encampment to see for themselves. Unbelievably, it had been done. The two warriors had been beheaded and their heads mounted on high poles. Daniel turned around before he got very close and hurried away, his stomach churning.

The next morning as the troops packed up, Jensen and some of his cronies made it a point to saunter by the scouts' campfire. "Guess that'll send a message what they can expect if they keep killin' whites."

Daniel pretended not to hear. He and a few of the other scouts exchanged glances and went about their business. They were headed out of camp when Captain Willets rode up. "General says to offer you that renegade's rifle and horse if you want them."

"Is it a Spencer?" Daniel asked.

"Nope," Willets said, looking down at the rifle. He grinned. "If it was, I'd have to be asking the general to reward the scouts' commanding officer instead of the scout." He held the weapon out for Daniel's inspection. "Looks pretty worn out."

Daniel cocked the rifle and looked down the barrel. "It's better than no rifle." He handed it back to the captain. "Give it to Edward Pope," he said. "I owe him for some help he gave me at Fort Ridgely."

Willets nodded. "What about the horse?"

"The gray stallion?" Daniel asked.

"He won't let anybody get near him this morning. Kicked Jensen in the rear twice."

Daniel climbed into the saddle. "He just needs someone that speaks his language," he said and headed toward the herd.

❧

The news that General Sully had beheaded two warriors at the Little Cheyenne spread like a prairie fire through every Dakota camp from the Platte up into Canada. But instead of discouraging further bloodshed, the mutilation only convinced the Santees and Yanktonais to withdraw farther west where they ended up in a vast encampment with several other tribes in the Badlands. From camp they sent out their own scouting parties to monitor Sully's plodding march westward through Dakota.

The scouts found old camps, buffalo carcasses, and bones, but no Indians. And yet they knew Indians were all around them. During the day mirrors flashed in the distance as the army's progress was signaled between bands.

At night, while the soldiers sat around their campfires smoking pipes, rolling chews of tobaccos, reliving the battles they had fought back east, burning arrows in the sky communicated their location.

Finding water was a constant challenge. More than once they marched thirty miles before finding water. Sweat soaked through their uniforms, their tongues swelled, and horses died. Some days they rose at two in the morning and marched until noon, trying to avoid the heat of the day. Once they marched along a river where the grass had been burned for ten miles all around.

One particularly awful day the men rode over a ridge and down into a creekbed only to find a narrow puddle of muddy water full of tadpoles and lizards. In desperation, Edward Pope jumped off his mule and started digging. He became a hero when, about four feet down, he struck a vein of clear, cold water. The men threw their hats into the air, shouting and singing and making such a racket Brady Jensen, now a lieutenant, came tearing down the hill, shouting angrily, "Do you want to bring the entire Sioux nation down upon us?!"

Daniel looked up at him, laughing, "With all respect, Lieutenant, I assure you the entire Sioux nation knows exactly where we are." He scooped a hatful of water and poured it over his head. "They don't want to fight, Lieutenant. They are hoping the Great Father's soldiers will get tired and go home and leave them in peace."

"They will discover," Jensen said harshly, "that the Great Father's arm is very long when his children have been murdered."

For all the army's talk of glory, little happened throughout the weeks of July other than the loss of a few stragglers, picked off by small roving bands of warriors. They moved at a pace so slow the scouts wondered if they would find any Indians at all before winter set in. Several bridges had to be built to get mule trains across creeks. Broken wagon tongues, locked wheels, and the ever present search for water plagued the days, while the nights were one long battle with mosquitoes, oppressive heat, and poisonous snakes.

One night Daniel joined Edward Pope at his campfire. Edward looked up at the starlit sky and said, "You know what I think, Two Stars? I think when God Almighty created the world, He just didn't have time to come out here, so He just left the original chaos." He slapped the back of his neck and flicked a dead mosquito away. "I should have stayed at Fort Ridgely."

Dust enveloped the entire column as they marched. One day they found several scaffolds erected, a warrior buried atop each one. Daniel and the scouts stood quietly, looking down at a circle cut in the ground with five buffalo heads set around it, the noses pointed toward the center.

That night Daniel saw Brady Jensen showing off a medicine bag beautifully worked with an intricate bead design.

"Where'd you get that?" Captain Willets asked sharply. "Don't tell me you desecrated those burial scaffolds."

"Now Cap'n," Jensen said. "That warrior didn't say a thing when I climbed up and ripped open his buffalo robe." He snickered and took another swig from a flask being passed around.

"That was holy ground," Willets snapped. "And I'd better not hear of you doing a fool thing like that again. You can bet the men signaling our progress with those mirrors saw what happened. And you can bet they won't forget."

Jensen sobered up a little. Shrugging, he mumbled, "Didn't mean anything by it. Didn't think it'd matter."

"Would it matter if it was your papa's grave somebody tore open?" Willets asked.

Jensen shrugged. "All right, Cap'n. I get your point." He tucked the medicine bag inside his shirt.

On the twenty-seventh of July, the troops marched forty-seven miles through the broiling countryside. They stumbled into camp that night, their tongues swollen with thirst, only to be told several thousand Sioux were camped only a few miles away up against Tahakouty Mountain.

"Uncpapas, Sans Arcs, Blackfeet, Minneconjous, Santee, and Yanktonais," the scouts reported.

"Thicker than fiddlers in hell," one of the soldiers said.

General Sully would later estimate that his two thousand men engaged more than five thousand Indians in the Battle of Kildeer Mountain. As an old man, Daniel Two Stars would read Sully's report and laugh. "That proves one thing," he would say, "two thousand warriors riding out ready to fight look like many more—even to a very brave white man."

Daniel did his best to stay out of the fight. He had no stomach for chasing women and children into the ravines and the hills, for destroying everything in their camp, for burning tepees and ruining stored food.

The night after the battle, a few Indians crept close enough to camp to let a few arrows find their mark. One of them was Brady Jensen, who was standing up leaning against a wagon when an arrow sliced into his abdomen. The doctor cut it out, but by morning Jensen realized he was going to die. He sent for Daniel.

"I don't want to meet my Maker with this on my conscience," he gasped, and held the medicine bag out to Daniel. "I give the arrow that killed me to Edward Pope. I got a sister down in Nebraska Territory. Brownsville. Name Polly. Polly Jensen. Edward said he'd see she gets it." He shuddered and gasped. Then, his eyes, two black slits in his face, he muttered, "That feller I killed at the fort. Your friend. That wasn't right. I should- n'ta done it. It wasn't a fair fight." He grasped Daniel's arm, clutching so hard his filthy nails broke the skin. He swallowed. "Cap'n says you're a Christian. Reckon you got to forgive me fer what I done." He died clutching Daniel's arm.

With the Indians scattered and their camp destroyed, Sully turned his troops and headed back down the Missouri. Daniel and the other few dozen scouts spread out across the frontier. Some went to Crow Creek, hoping to find remnants of their fam- ilies. Daniel turned east. Crossing the James River, he spent a few weeks at the newly constructed Fort Wadsworth. Ever restless, he moved south toward the other camps scattered north to south along the frontier between Minnesota and Dakota.

Mother Friend and Standing Tall bent low in Marjorie Grant's huge garden, filling an empty grain sack with green beans as they moved down row after row of plants. The garden was nearly weedless and had been a great success, thanks to Jeb's having had time to rig an irrigation system. Up at the house Marjorie sat beneath the shade of her new porch, sewing for all she was worth on a new treadle sewing machine. It was the first one in the area, and had caused quite a stir when Jeb hauled it out from New Ulm. Marjorie was beginning to think she might earn extra money if she offered to sew for the officers' wives at Fort Ridgely, just up the road.

To the east of the house and up on the ridge near the ruins of Daniel Two Star's old house, Ironheart and Jeb had filled Jeb's wagon half full of corn and just stopped to get a drink of water when a man mounted on a gray stallion trotted up the road from Fort Ridgely.

Daniel Two Stars had come home.

# Twenty~Five

"Whoso findeth a wife findeth a good thing . . ."

—PROVERBS 18:22

"AUNTIE JANE!" TIMOTHY POKED HIS HEAD IN THE library door and hissed. "*SHHHH!* It's a surprise!"

Jane looked up from her reading just in time to see Timothy's round face wreathed in a smile. Then he giggled and disappeared. Frowning slightly, Jane returned to her reading.

Fanny Laclede came next, inviting Jane downstairs to tea. "I know it's a bit early," she said, smoothing her dark hair with a gloved hand. "But Richard and I have an engagement this evening, and we were hoping to speak with you about something."

When Jane closed her book and stood up, Fanny said,

"Perhaps you'll want to freshen up. Richard and I—" She hesitated, then said quickly, "We might have guests."

"I certainly don't want to interrupt your entertaining, Mrs. Laclede," Jane said, trying to hide the hurt she felt at Fanny's intimation that her appearance was too dowdy for the Lacledes' social circles.

"Oh, no. It's not that. It's just—" Fanny hesitated again, pursing her lips. "Oh, bosh. I'm no good at this." She sighed. "There *is* a surprise, and you'll want to look your best. Now don't say another word. Just freshen up and hurry downstairs. We're waiting." She hurried away.

The idea of someone waiting on her sent Miss Jane into a flurry of activity. She rushed into her room and pulled down her best dove-gray walking skirt. The white waist she always wore with it was missing the top button, but she pinned a cameo over the space and hoped it looked all right. Looking in the mirror, she pressed her lips together with displeasure at the state of her hair. "Ah well," she muttered, "it will have to do." Her frizzy hair had been the bane of her existence since she was a girl, and there was no willing it into place on a humid day like this. She pushed a few pins into it and with a last adjustment of her skirt, a quick glance at the full-length dressing mirror in the corner, she headed out into the hall.

Rebecca and Timothy were waiting at the top of the stairs, their faces bright with excitement. They both looked behind them as Miss Jane approached, then back at her. When she reached the top of the stairs, cries of "Surprise! Surprise!" echoed up toward her. Before she could react, Meg and Aaron Dane were charging up the carved mahogany staircase. "Surprise, Miss Jane! Surprise!"

"Goodness!" was all Miss Jane could manage in the way of a greeting. She let herself be led down the red-carpeted stairs, across the foyer, and into the Lacledes' opulent receiving room where

Richard and Fanny stood to one side, smiling happily as they watched Gen and Simon Dane greet their friend. Elliot Leighton held himself apart until Miss Jane caught his eye.

"I never!" she said. "What—how?" She finally just laughed and shook her head as Elliot bowed low and kissed her hand.

"They're married!" Meg said, pointing to Gen and Simon. "And we're on our way to Grandmother Leighton's. And we stopped to say hello!"

Simon smiled at Meg and then looked back to Miss Jane. "I guess that about summarizes it," he said. He motioned her onto the sofa next to Elliot. Miss Jane blushed and opened her arms to Hope. "Don't tell me you've forgotten me!" she said as Hope leaned shyly against Gen's skirt, eyeing Jane carefully.

Reaching into her pocket, Jane smiled triumphantly and produced a peppermint. Hope grinned and threw herself pell-mell into Miss Jane's lap. "Bribery," she laughed. "It works every time."

"Unka Lee!" Hope shouted, reaching up to pound Elliot on the shoulder.

"Uncle, is it?" Miss Jane handed Hope into Elliot's outstretched arms, smiling when Hope grabbed a handful of silver hair and hung on.

And so began a reunion that was to last for nearly two weeks. The Lacledes insisted the Danes and Elliot stay with them. "It's an half-empty albatross," Fanny said of her parents' mansion. "Having you here will relieve some of the stodginess."

Early every morning Aaron walked the mile down to the riverfront, fascinated by the never-ending activity as steamships arrived and left, were loaded and unloaded. Richard was delighted at his interest and the astute questions he asked about the import business.

Meg and Hope, and Timothy and Rebecca, played together as if they had never been apart.

And Miss Jane and Fanny conspired to see to it that Simon

and Gen had a real honeymoon. One evening a coach arrived and swept the unsuspecting couple away to the finest hotel in St. Louis. They were taken into a private dining room and served by a French waiter who began by being stuffy and ended by being completely charmed when the lady at the table addressed him as *Monsieur,* and pronounced the menu flawlessly. After dinner, the waiter slipped Simon the key to Room 215 and offered his *felicitations.*

When he bowed low and disappeared, Simon said, "Well." And sat looking at Gen. He took a drink of water and fiddled with his napkin. "We've been on a train for an eternity, my dear. You must be exhausted."

"I am a little tired," Gen said. She slipped her hand beneath Simon's.

They went upstairs and gasped when Simon unlocked the door to their room.

"I didn't know things like this existed," Gen said, stepping across the threshold and crossing the room to touch the velvet and satin drapes.

"We can't stay here," Simon said. "It's—"

"It's obvious Fanny and Richard can afford it, Simon. It would be rude to refuse their generosity." She sank onto the sofa before an Italian marble fireplace and sighed.

Simon stood by the window looking out. "You can see the river." Behind him, the lights grew dim.

"I'll look at the river tomorrow," Gen murmured. She came up behind him and touched his shoulder.

He swallowed. "Genevieve. I should tell you—I'm—not very good at this sort of—"

"Sometimes, Reverend Dane," she said softly, and reached up to stroke his beard. "Sometimes you talk too much."

Elliot Leighton paced back and forth in front of the Laclede mansion for the better part of the morning before he managed the courage to go inside and ask for Jane. When she came downstairs, rumpled and not in the best of moods, he almost backed down. The meeting began very badly.

"We'll be leaving tomorrow," he said abruptly when she came in the door.

"Yes. I know." She stood ramrod straight, holding her hands clasped before her.

"I've a meeting arranged with Senator Lance next month. He's an old friend from West Point. I'm hoping to get something done on behalf of the Indians."

Miss Jane raised her eyebrows. "Yes. I heard Reverend Dane mention it."

"I'm hoping to get him to listen, since I've been west now." He smoothed his mustache. "Eyewitness and all that. Of course I'm not an expert by any stretch of the imagination. I wanted Simon to go with me, but the doctors have said he shouldn't travel. He's not fully recovered yet—the last two nights notwithstanding." Elliot cleared his throat nervously.

"Yes." Miss Jane nodded. "He seems—fragile, somehow. I can't quite put it into words. But he isn't his old self."

"He'll be fine, they say. Just needs to be careful for a few months. Take care not to get chilled, that sort of thing."

Miss Jane nodded. "Gen will see that he behaves himself."

"I think they'll be happy together. Don't you? I mean—the age difference and all doesn't seem to matter."

"When two people are determined to make a marriage work, it usually works," Miss Jane said vaguely. "At least that's been my observation, limited as it is. And they have the children."

Elliot muttered agreement and scratched his eyebrows.

"Would you like some tea, Mr. Leighton?" Miss Jane said,

obviously wondering when he was going to get to whatever point it was he had come to make.

"No," he said abruptly. "No, I—I don't need tea." He motioned to a chair. "Would you sit down, please, Jane—may I call you Jane?"

Jane sat down.

Elliot began pacing back and forth again. "I have some things I need to say."

"Obviously," Jane said.

"First, I was wrong. About Indians. About a lot of things. And Simon tells me I've been wrong about women too. Women in general. And then one woman in particular—that is, you." He stopped pacing and looked at her and grimaced. "I must sound completely mad."

Jane nodded. "You do." She smiled kindly. "Perhaps you are the one who needs to sit down."

He felt like a puppy, guilty of breaking some household rule, and yet receiving its mistress's kindness in spite of having been naughty. He sat down opposite her. After another awkward silence, he smiled weakly. "It's—hard to know where to start."

"Well," Jane said. "You had started to say something about women."

"Yes," Elliot said. He ran his index finger along the metal hook, frowning. "It took me a long while to realize that the women I knew at home would never be able to look at me without thinking about this—this *thing*."

"I'd say you have some very foolish women in New York, Mr. Leighton," Miss Jane said quickly.

"You're different."

"Thank you. I think."

Elliot took a deep breath. He looked at Jane with such desperation that she reached out and put her hand on his arm—on his left arm—just above the hook. And she did not withdraw it, but simply sat, looking at him with interest. No pity shone in her eyes, no sympathy. And in that one moment Elliot Leighton realized that he loved her.

"The thing is, Jane. The way you look at me—"

"I'm sorry if I offended," Jane said and snatched her hand away. "I didn't mean to be in the least forward—"

"Oh, stop it," Elliot said quickly. Grabbing up Jane's hand, he kissed it. "What I've been bumbling around like an idiot about is this, Jane. You don't seem to care about the hook."

"I don't. It doesn't matter." Her heart skipped a beat or two when Elliot didn't release her hand.

"You find me—attractive?"

Jane laughed softly. "Is the Mississippi muddy?"

Elliot searched her face as he said, "Miss Jane, will you go with me to Washington when I try to get someone to listen? Will you help me get aid sent to the Dakota? Will you be my partner in the effort to help our friends somehow? And, above all, Miss Jane, will you marry me?"

"Will I—what?" Miss Jane leaned back in her chair, eyeing him with a slight frown.

"You heard me, Jane," Elliot said quietly. "Will you marry me?" He rushed ahead, "Because you find me attractive," he said quickly. "Because we share an interest in helping the Dakota people. Because we are compatible. Because no one on this earth exasperates me as much as you. Because you don't need a husband to make you happy. And," he said, taking in a deep breath, "because I think I am in love with you."

"Repeat that, Mr. Leighton," Miss Jane said softly.

"What?"

"The last part."

He leaned over and kissed her hand gently. "Because, Miss Jane, I believe I am in love with you." He looked up at her, his blue-gray eyes warm with emotion. "We'll test the theory on the train trip to New York. With Simon and Gen as chaperones."

Miss Jane studied his face for a moment. "You know, Mr. Leighton," she said carefully, "I've prided myself on being content. On making my spinster's life count for Christ."

"And it has." He leaned forward earnestly. "But I'm thinking we could make our lives count even more if we worked together." He groped for her hand again. "Like Simon and Genevieve."

Miss Jane looked at him, at the beautiful silver hair, the strong jaw, the cleft chin, the purposeful blue-gray eyes. She allowed her heart to do at least two flip-flops before she said, "It wouldn't do for my friends to think I'd just desperately thrown myself at a man after all these years."

"You didn't throw yourself at me, Jane," Elliot said with an edge of frustration in his voice. "Anyone who thinks that doesn't know you. Just come with us to New York. That's all I'm asking. If you decide you hate me, you can run away."

"All right, Mr. Leighton," Jane said carefully. "I accept. We'll try the trip, with the Danes as our chaperones, and see what we think. And if you decide you hate me, you can send me away." Then she smiled. "But if you decide to keep me, Elliot Leighton, you must agree to marry me immediately. I hate long engagements and I'm not getting any younger."

# Twenty-Six

"To everything there is a season, and a time to
every purpose under the heaven: . . . A time to weep,
and a time to laugh; a time to mourn,
and a time to dance."

—ECCLESIASTES 3:1,4

"DON'T TELL ME THERE'S A WAR ON, AVERY!" ELLIOT
Leighton slammed his hook down on the senator's desk.

Glancing down at the new scratch on his polished walnut
desk, Avery Lance adjusted his tie and motioned to Elliot.
"Please, Elliot. Just sit down and we'll discuss it like gentlemen."

"I'm worn out from discussing things like a gentleman,"
Elliot said wearily. "I've spent most of the fall 'discussing things
like a gentleman.' And accomplished nothing." But he sat down.

"I have the document right here," Lance said, tapping a sheaf
of papers with a quill pen. "Superintendent Thompson reports
that the Sioux are pleased with their location at Crow Creek."

Raising one eyebrow he said, "He also indicates that if it were not for whites telling the Dakota the reservation is no good, everything would be fine."

"He's a liar," Elliot said bluntly. He reached inside his coat pocket and withdrew his own piece of paper. "Agent Bolcombe says that if they aren't moved, the entire group at Crow Creek will become extinct."

"Agent Bolcombe's hysterical reports do not inspire confidence," the senator said quickly.

Elliot leaned forward, pleading, "Avery, this isn't right. You know it isn't right. We were friends at the academy. You know I'm not a hysteric."

"My hands are tied, Elliot." Lance held both hands up in a gesture of despair. "I am sorry, but there's simply nothing I can do. The Indians are still causing untold trouble in the west. It's hard to be sympathetic when I have reports of hostiles still breaking through into Minnesota and killing innocent white families."

"A few isolated incidents, Avery. It has nothing to do with the people at Crow Creek." Elliot leaned forward and rested his forearm on the desk. "I've seen it, Avery. They are harmless old men, women, and children—at least there were still a few children left when I was there early this year. They may all be dead by now."

"There's no need to be overly dramatic, Elliot," Avery said primly. "I'm certain something can be done. But change takes time. You are not the only person saying these things, you know. Governor Edmunds of Dakota Territory has been preaching the same message—judicious superintendence, not soldiers."

"And for all his trouble he's been forbidden to enter Indian country or to attempt any negotiations with the hostiles apart from the army," Leighton said. "I'm not a fool, Avery. I keep myself informed. And I won't be put off." Seeing the obstinacy in his friend's eyes, Elliot sighed. Trying to calm himself, he said quietly, "At least get them to send a physician. Surely that isn't asking too much."

"I'll see what I can do," Avery said, standing up.

"Am I being dismissed?" Elliot said.

"I'm sorry, Elliot. But I have meetings." He sighed dramatically. "You saw the line of people waiting in the hallway." He put a hand on Elliot's shoulder. "But please come back again. And bring your lovely wife with you. Louella gives a tea for all the congressional wives every Wednesday afternoon. I'm certain she'd love to have the new Mrs. Leighton join her."

Before he could think what to say, Major Elliot Leighton found himself in the hallway outside the senator's office. There was, indeed, a long line of people waiting to get in. He supposed he should feel grateful that Avery had made time for him on short notice. But he did not.

"What do I have to do, Simon?" Elliot said later that week over dessert in the elegant Leighton dining room. He tossed his fork aside and stood up. "Maybe you had the right idea back at Crow Creek when you threatened to carry Buffalo Moon back here and lay her at the president's feet. Perhaps that's what it will take." He sat back down. "How is the Bible project progressing?"

Simon nodded. "Very well. It will probably take most of the winter, but in the spring we should be able to go back to Crow Creek with the Dakota New Testament, Proverbs, and a revised Genesis." He cleared his throat and pushed his half-eaten breakfast away. "It will be a long winter. I really do want to get back to the West. We both do. Gen is patient with me, but she hates living in the city."

"Well, perhaps by then we'll have made someone listen. Perhaps there will be a new reservation. Where the Dakota can actually prosper."

Simon looked at Elliot for a moment before saying, "You

know, Elliot, every time I look at you I think what a miracle God has wrought in that heart of yours." Gen came downstairs, poured herself a cup of coffee, and slid into the seat beside her husband. Simon smiled at Elliot. "Miracles all around, brother-in-law. Miracles all around."

Through the winter of 1864–65, Genevieve Dane bent her own will to her heavenly Father's and was rewarded with family love and an inner peace she had never thought possible. She helped Simon proofread the new edition of the Dakota New Testament, she did her best to be an obedient daughter-in-law to Margaret Leighton, and she tried to be content living in New York. She and Elliot Leighton never again mentioned the existence of Etienne's journal. She didn't know what had happened to it, and she didn't care to know. It was part of the past she must put away. And she succeeded, except for once or twice, when she woke with a start and for the briefest moment thought she was back at Hazelwood Mission. On those nights, she allowed her mind to wander into the past, beginning by reminiscing and ending by crying. After the second time it happened, she no longer lay awake looking at the ceiling, thinking. She always crept out of bed and went to the Scriptures, reading away the memories, clinging to the present.

The children were Gen's and Simon's constant delight and dilemma. Mother Leighton spoiled them. Meg and Hope began to test the waters of rebellion against parental authority. Aaron began to talk of West Point. Gen and Simon spent more than one night half arguing the finer points of child discipline until they could present a "united front" to the children. Trying to obey "Do not let the sun go down on your anger" resulted in their seeing the sun rise together more than once—and they forged a stronger union.

Gen refused to act like "an old married woman" when they were alone, and Simon easily learned to rejoice in the wife of his middle age. At times she woke to find him watching her with such love in his eyes she thought her heart would break.

~

Meg skipped into her grandmother's sitting room one day after school, her eyes glowing with enthusiasm as she announced, "Miss Burnside is giving a party!"

From where she sat beside the fireplace, Mrs. Leighton said, "The Burnsides have given the village a party every January for generations. But this year Miss Burnside is in mourning." She looked toward where Jane and Gen sat on the sofa. "Her brother was killed in some minor battle a few weeks ago. An only son, I'm afraid. The family was devastated." She turned to Meg. "Are you certain she said she was giving a party? It hardly seems appropriate, given the circumstances."

Meg nodded briskly. "Uh-huh. She said her brother was in heaven and he loved parties. She said some people thought she should be sad for a year and not have any fun, but she said her brother James loved parties and he wouldn't want everyone sitting around just looking sad all the time."

"Indeed?" Mrs. Leighton replied. She shook her head. "I don't know about these modern ideas. No one seems to observe a proper period of mourning anymore."

"Tell us about the party," Gen urged Meg.

"They have an old barn in the woods and they light a million candles and it's beautiful. They have a dance and we can ice-skate on the pond at night because they put lanterns everywhere. And there's a big bonfire and people can eat until they get sick if they want to and they stay up all night." Meg giggled. "Miss Burnside said last year everybody put their babies to sleep all snuggled into the hay in one of the old stalls. She said somebody changed all their blankets, and the next day when people got home they had the wrong babies! And it snowed and people couldn't change the babies back for nearly a week!" Meg held her hands over her mouth and laughed again.

"That sounds like quite a party," Jane said. "But I bet they won't serve cocoa nearly as good as Betsy's. Come on, little miss"—she held out her hand—"let's go get some."

After Meg and Jane left, Gen stood up and walked to the window, looking out on the streets, already nearly knee-deep in snow. "I remember hearing about the Burnsides' festival when we were here before. Do you think Simon will allow the children to go this time?"

"Of course," Mrs. Leighton said. "They don't have an ill mother to worry over. And Simon—" She hesitated. "Simon himself enjoys life more now. The winter festival has been superb entertainment for the children for years. It's something to look forward to after Christmas." She sighed deeply. "I suppose Millicent is right. James *would* want it to go on. He loved a good party, dear boy." She lowered her voice, talking more to herself than to Gen. "Come to think of it, if we all observed the mourning traditions completely, this village would be permanently shut down. Hardly a family has been unaffected by the unpleasantness down south." She returned to her knitting while Gen went to the library to speak with Simon about the Burnsides' winter festival.

"Of course we'll go," he said. "I remember Ellen telling me the Burnsides were among the founders of this town. Every year people wonder if they will have the festival because every year they expect the barn to fall in, the bridge across the creek to rot out, or some other tragedy to occur that will end the tradition. But the Burnsides always manage. They have the bridge repaired, the barn reroofed, the pond cleared away. Wait until you see it. They light a pastor's annual salary's worth of candles and lamps. It transforms their old place into a wonderland." He pulled Gen toward him and kissed her cheek. "I'll be the envy of every man there with you on my arm."

Gen pushed him away playfully. "Reverend Dane," she said in mock horror. "Remember your piety, sir!"

"I cannot remember anything, dear girl, when the sunlight pours in the window and makes you shimmer like a beautiful butterfly."

"Butterfly!" Hope's voice sounded from the door. "Where's it?" She ran to the window and looked out.

"There's no butterfly, Hope. But there's a snowflake on the windowpane." Gen pointed to where a cluster of ice crystals formed a circular pattern on one of the small panes of glass. "Look there. See how they glisten in the sun?" She bent down and helped Hope count the snowflakes. "When I was a little girl," she began, "my papa used to tell me a story about snowflakes. It's naptime, and if—"

"No nap!" Hope shouted, frowning.

"Yes—nap," Gen insisted. "But I'll tell you my papa's snowflake story before you fall asleep." She took Hope's hand and led the reluctant toddler toward the door. "Piety, Reverend Dane," she chided when she caught Simon staring at her. She pointed to the open theology books spread out on his desk.

He glanced down at them and then leaned back in his chair. "Beauty, Mrs. Dane. Beauty." And he watched her until she left the room.

All day Meg and Aaron had lingered by the windows along the street, watching the procession of farm wagons and chaises, buggies and phaetons, headed north out of town toward the old Burnside homestead. As the hours passed, Meg fretted, "We're going to miss the best part!"

"Don't be silly," Mrs. Leighton said. "The *best* part is when it gets dark and they light the candles. The ice-skaters glide onto the pond, the violins play . . ." She sighed. "The late Mr. Leighton proposed to me at a Burnside winter festival." She looked up as if surprised at the sharing of so personal a detail. Then she grinned at Meg. "So now you know the Burnsides really have been doing this for generations. Almost back to Noah!"

"Oh, Grandma!" Meg said, shaking her head. She looked out the window again. "Where *is* Father?"

"He'll be along," Gen said, going to Meg and standing behind her to look out the window. "He promised he would come back as soon as he could."

When another hour passed and Simon still had not come, she said, "Mrs. Leighton, what if I keep Hope with me and the rest of you go on ahead? Simon and I can come later in the wagon."

"Could we?" Aaron spoke up from where he had been pretending to read.

"And what makes you so eager to get to the party, young man?" Elliot teased.

"Amanda Whitrock," Meg said.

"You be quiet!" Aaron ordered.

"Amanda Whitrock," Elliot murmured. "Is she that ravishing blonde I saw you talking to after school yesterday?"

Aaron's cheeks blazed. "I'm not old enough to care about girls," he murmured. "Amanda's hair isn't blonde. It's light brown. And she isn't ravishing. She's just kind of pretty, that's all."

The adults in the room exchanged glances.

"What time is Amanda going to the party?" Elliot asked innocently.

"Her family drove by about two hours ago," Aaron said miserably.

"And," Meg interjected, "he's worried because Thomas Bannister likes Amanda, too, and if he gets there first—"

"I told you to keep quiet!" Aaron said and stormed out of the room.

It was decided that Elliot and Jane, Mrs. Leighton and Aaron, would use the buggy to head to the winter festival. Gen would stay behind, along with Meg and Hope, and drive the wagon to the festival as soon as Simon returned. Clearly disappointed but submissive to her grandmother's demands that she help entertain Hope, Meg sat down before the fireplace and enticed Hope to build a tower with an assortment of wooden building blocks.

Margaret Leighton paused at the door. "Now remind Simon he must take the *north* branch of the pike. We don't want you two floundering through the woods looking for us!"

With a crack of the buggy whip above the horses' heads they were gone.

Nearly two hours later Simon still had not come. Watching Meg fight back tears of disappointment as she looked anxiously at the darkening sky outside, Gen finally said, "Get Hope bundled up, Meg. I'll get the wagon and we'll go check on your father."

At that moment, the doorbell rang. A message bearer handed Gen a note that read, "Delayed with family. Needed here. Please go on. Will catch up if at all possible."

"But we don't know how to get there," Meg protested slightly.

"We don't need to know how to get there," Gen reminded her. "We've been watching a stream of wagons head out of town all day long. There will be a trail almost as wide as a village of Dakota leaves when they are following the buffalo!" She headed for the door. "I'll hitch up the wagon and be back in a moment."

# Twenty~Seven

"Hide not thy face from me in the day of trouble;
incline thine ear unto me: in the day when
I call answer me speedily."
—PSALM 102:2

LOST. IT WAS ABSURD, GEN THOUGHT. SHE WAS HALF
Dakota Indian. How could she have missed following a clear path
through the woods? Just because the wind had begun to fill in the
furrows made by the other partygoers was no excuse. Just because
it was nearly dark was no excuse either. They had crossed the
bridge and taken the fork to the north, just as Mother Leighton
said. But now, as she sat contemplating the woods all around
them, Gen began to doubt. Could Mother Leighton really have
said to take the fork to the left? She had said *north*. Gen thought
the right fork led north. Certainly her sense of direction couldn't
be so faulty. But it was. They would have to go back.

As they retraced their path through the woods, they came to an old bridge. It certainly looked like the same bridge. And yet, Gen thought, Simon had said the Burnsides kept their bridge in constant repair. She remembered feeling uncertain the first time they had crossed it. Looking down at the icy water rushing beneath it, she felt even more uncertain. As if her nerves were transmitted through the reins, the team stopped the moment their hooves touched the first two boards. They stood shivering, their ears alert. Then, without warning, they backed up. The bridge groaned as if it, too, were a living animal. Gen thought it tilted imperceptibly.

"What's happening?"

"I don't know," Gen said, shaking her head. "But I don't think we dare try to cross the bridge."

"But we have to," Meg said. "To get back."

"I think we'd better wait until help comes," Gen said. She backed the team up a little farther. Reaching into the wagon box behind her, she pulled an extra blanket out and wrapped it around the three of them. "Your father will be along soon. He'll know what to do." She peered into the gathering darkness trying not to shiver. "Let's sing," she said. "Do you remember the Dakota Hymn?" she asked Meg. When Meg shook her head uncertainly, Gen said, "Well, you'll want to know it when we get back with our friends in the West. Let's learn it now. Your father will be very pleased."

"I don't want to go back west," Meg blurted out. "I like it here. Why can't we stay where it's safe and we have a good school?"

Gen put her arm around Meg. "Because this isn't your home, Meg."

"It *feels* like home," Meg said defiantly. "I don't hardly remember Minnesota anymore. Except St. Anthony. And Father says we aren't going to live there. We're going back to the Indians. To a log house."

"Don't you remember your log house?"

Meg shrugged. "It was all right. But I like Grandmother's house better."

"I cold, Mama," Hope whined, snuggling against Gen.

Shuddering inwardly, Gen closed a gloved hand over the leather whip handle. She searched the gray horizon, watched the pink blush from sunset fade. She glanced down at the girls, barely visible except for a fringe of blonde and red hair peeping above the edge of the blanket.

"I'm c-c-cold, too, Gen," Meg said.

Gen nodded. "I know. So am I." She shivered and stamped her feet against the wooden floor of the wagon. They were so numb with cold she couldn't feel them anymore. With all her senses, she peered into the gathering darkness, hoping to hear voices, to see a light, to pick up some hint of where the Burnsides' homestead might be. Surely they couldn't have wandered too far off the trail. But not a sound could be heard, not a sliver of light pierced the gathering darkness to hint at which way she should go.

Picking up the whip, she said, more to herself than to Meg, "We can't wait out here in the dark. We'll freeze. Something must have happened to keep your father in town. We'll have to cross ourselves."

Getting down from the driver's seat, she searched the creek-bank for a possible crossing place. The wind was picking up, and with every blast she could hear the rotten boards of the ancient bridge creaking. There was no doubt they could not chance the bridge. *The creek isn't so wide,* she encouraged herself, squinting across to the other bank, trying to decide the best place to cross. Finally, when she thought she had located the least dangerous route, she returned to the wagon and hauled herself up, encouraged when she guided the team towards the creekbank and they did not refuse. She approached the creek at an angle, relieved when the wagon didn't tip dangerously.

Gen forced herself to concentrate on the team's ears instead of the icy, swirling water. Her heart sank when a tree branch rushed by. The water was deeper than she had judged. Daisy stopped, snorting and stamping her foot.

"I know, Daisy, I know," Gen said. "It's cold and it's running fast. But you can get us across. And when you do, I promise you molasses on your feed tonight!" She forced herself to look down at Meg and smile with more confidence than she felt. "Wrap your arms around Hope, Meg. And then hold on to the seat behind her with both hands. Whatever you do, don't let go!" She urged the team forward down the steep incline, relieved when Daisy obeyed. But the minute the horse's front hooves felt the cold water, she paused. Gen stood up and rattled the reins. "You! Daisy! Darby! Go *on*!" she shouted at the top of her voice. She barely had time to sit down when Darby lurched forward, nearly throwing Meg off the wagon seat.

"Hold on!" Gen yelled, just as the wagon wheels were lifted off the creek bottom and the rushing waters threatened to sweep them downstream. Gen screamed at the team, lashing their broad rumps over and over. The horses strained against the current, and just when Gen feared they would be swept away, the wheels struck bottom again. A flash of relief faded instantly when it was apparent they were stuck in midstream. In spite of Gen's screams, the team could not free the wagon. Hope and Meg began to cry. The rushing water roared past the wagon. It was growing dark as the horses began to thrash wildly against the weight of the wagon holding them in the middle of the stream.

Gen stood up and pulled the blanket off her shoulders. Tying the reins fast to the wagon seat, she ordered Meg to stay put. Taking a deep breath she slid down from the wagon seat, into the icy water until one foot found the singletree. With one hand clutching the wagon front, Gen leaned forward until she had a firm grasp on Daisy's harness. Following the traces under the water, she labored to unhitch Darby. The horse seemed to sense when he was free, and the second Gen had untied the reins, he pulled away from the wagon and swam for the creekbank. Pulling himself out of the water he shook himself off before turning toward the wagon and whinnying sharply to Daisy.

"Whoa, girl!" Gen pleaded as Daisy lunged ahead in a desperate attempt to follow Darby to shore. "Whoa, now," Gen repeated, patting Daisy's rump, forcing herself to remain calm. She could no longer feel her feet and legs. Her hands were almost too numb to work the harness. *Please, God . . . help.*

"Set Hope down here," Gen ordered Meg, patting the bottom of the wagon between the seat and the board that formed the wagon's front. Meg obeyed, wide-eyed with terror.

Gen patted Hope's head, wrapping her in a blanket. "You stay right there, Hope. Meg's going for a ride on the big horse. I'll be back for you." Hope regarded Gen with wide blue eyes as Gen looked up at Meg. She patted her shoulder. "I'm going to turn around and I want you to climb on piggyback."

Meg shook her head uncertainly. "I'm too big. You can't hold me."

Gen ignored her. "From me to Daisy's back. Grab onto the harness strap right across her fat rump. *You hang on.* If I slip and fall in the water, you still hang on." She put one icy hand on each of Meg's cheeks, staring coldly into her eyes. "Understand? Pull yourself up. Don't worry about me. I can swim." She nodded firmly at Meg, then turned around and patted her shoulder.

Trembling with fear, Meg perched on the edge of the wagon. Gen backed up, and Meg slipped down, wrapping her legs around Gen's tiny waist.

Gen took a deep breath and grabbed Meg's legs. Pinning them to her she locked her hands together. Bracing for a moment against the wagon, she lunged forward toward Daisy. She slipped, falling into the horse. But Daisy didn't move. She looked back over her shoulder and snorted and shook her head, but she didn't move. Meg grabbed the harness and hung on while Gen helped her unwrap her legs and scramble up onto Daisy's broad back.

"Ma!"

Hope had pulled herself to a standing position at the front of the wagon and was bouncing up and down on her sturdy legs. "Ma! Ma! Ma!" She reached her arms toward Gen, who looked up at Meg and patted her leg.

"I'm going to get Hope and hand her to you. Turn her to face you, and wrap her legs around your waist like this," Gen said as she motioned. "Then wrap your arms around her and grab the harness in front of both of you. When I get Daisy unhitched, she's going to move fast for the bank. It won't take her long to get there, but you have to hang on."

"What about you?" Meg began to cry.

"I'll hold on to the harness and when Daisy swims, she'll pull me along with you. Don't worry. I'm not going anywhere." Gen bit her lips to keep her teeth from chattering. *One more pass, Lord. Only one more. Just let me get Hope.*

Gen lunged for the wagon. She dragged Hope into her increasingly numb arms, burying her face in the blonde hair for a second before turning back toward where Meg waited atop Daisy. "Ready?" she called. When Meg nodded, Gen counted, "One—two—*three!*" and lunged forward, forcing Hope up over her head and toward Meg. At the moment Meg's arms closed around Hope's body, Gen slid off the singletree. She threw out her hand and managed to grab onto submerged wood. She was thoroughly soaked now. Every movement was agony. She inched her way along, her teeth chattering, willing herself to unhitch the harness. Her fingers fumbled with every step. She prayed herself through, not knowing how she managed to work with buckles she could not feel. Only when she was back at the wagon untying Daisy's reins did she realize her numb fingers were bleeding.

"Go on, Daisy, go on!" Gen called to the trembling horse. The instant the reins were free, Daisy moved forward. "Hang on, Meg!" Gen said, just as she slipped into the icy waters. She realized she no longer felt cold. She was no longer shivering. It felt pleasant, somehow, floating along in the water, surrendering to the control of something else. She looked toward the creekbank and saw that Meg and Hope were safely across. At that moment, the wagon was washed free. It came after her, swirling and tumbling. As she slipped beneath the surface of the water, Gen was vaguely conscious of someone screaming her name.

# Twenty-Eight

"Precious in the sight of the Lord is the death of His saints."

—PSALM 116:15

SIMON STAGGERED ASHORE WITH AN UNCONSCIOUS GEN in his arms. Shaking so violently he could barely walk, he managed to get back to where the team waited. Meg clutched Hope tightly, but both girls were shivering in the cold. It was pitch-black, the only light coming from a sliver of moon just now rising above the trees. Kneeling in the snow, Simon braced Gen across his lap as best he could, trying to protect her from the snow while he considered what to do. *Wisdom, Father. I need wisdom.*

He struggled to his feet, and in one colossal shove positioned her in his saddle. Taking his belt off, he did his best to tie her arms around his horse's neck.

"Can you hold on to Daisy's harness without falling off?" he asked Meg.

"I th-th-think so," Meg chattered, beginning to cry.

"Try not to use up your energy crying, Meg. I know you're cold. But you have to help me or Gen is going to be very, very sick. You must wrap your arms around Hope and keep her from falling off. We are going to go as quickly as we can. We must get help." He climbed up behind Gen's unconscious form and urged his horse forward, but the moment they began to trot Meg screeched, "Father—I can't—hold—on."

Immediately Simon pulled up, continuing at a maddeningly slow pace through the woods. The wind died down as he plodded along, and moonlight shone through the woods, at last illuminating the way. He could feel his pants and shirt freezing solid, but he went on. After a few moments, he realized he wasn't cold anymore, but a pleasant flush of warmth was working its way up from his midsection and into his head. He didn't hear anything, didn't see anything, but simply plodded on, intent on reaching the party, on dancing with Gen, on watching Meg try ice-skating.

After what seemed an age of time, he saw the light flickering through the trees. He could hear music and laughter. It took every ounce of self-control for him not to kick his horse to a lope. Finally, they staggered into a clearing. Voices were shouting, hands reaching up to take him down, to untie Gen's body, carrying them into the barn, rubbing their limbs. Someone raised blankets around a stall to give privacy and amazingly, Dr. Merrill was there, removing their clothing, wrapping them in warm blankets, giving orders so quickly Simon's conscious mind could not decipher them.

"My girls," he said weakly. "My girls are—"

"In good hands, Reverend Dane," the doctor said. "We're taking you back to town. Now drink this." A flask was pressed to his frozen lips. He swallowed and sputtered. *Brandy*, he thought. He looked over at Gen and saw that other hands were thrusting a flask at her, parting her nearly blue lips, forcing liquor down her throat. The last thing he remembered was the odd sight of her dark hair, frosted over with ice. It was melting, and little rivulets of water were running down the sides of her face, dripping off her chin, spotting the blanket just beneath her chin.

The four of them were lifted into the back of a wagon piled full with fresh straw. Jane knelt beside Gen, rubbing her limbs continually. Aaron worked on Meg, and Elliot on Hope while the doctor concentrated on Simon. Mother Leighton rode beside the driver, a man known for owning the best team of Percherons in the state. He lashed their broad black rumps, forcing them to head for the village at a furious pace. At the Leighton house, Betsy was roused to help create an infirmary in Mrs. Leighton's parlor. Four beds were lined up and a long few days of vigilance began.

Gen woke suddenly. "Girls!" she gasped and sat up, her head pounding.

"Shh, shh," someone said in the dark. "The girls are fine."

Gen rubbed her eyes, which for some reason would not focus. To her left she could see the dull golden light of a fire.

"Thank God you're awake," the voice said. She realized it was Jane. For a moment, she thought she and Miss Jane were captives again, sleeping inside a tepee with a fire in the center.

"Where—are—we?" she mumbled, rubbing her eyes.

"You've had an accident." Miss Jane sat down beside the cot and touched her hand. "Do you remember? You tried to cross the creek and the wagon got stuck."

Gen frowned and closed her eyes. She reached up to touch her forehead.

"Twelve stitches. That's why it hurts so." Jane stood up and put an arm around her shoulder. "Lie back. There's plenty of time for questions. You need to rest."

Exhausted, Gen obeyed and fell immediately asleep. The next time she woke, she was in bed upstairs in what had been Ellen's room when she was a girl. No one sat beside her, but a glance at her nightstand revealed quite an array of medicines. She reached up to touch her forehead again. The headache was gone. The door opened and Simon came in. His skin was ashen, but when he saw that her eyes were open, he smiled happily. "Good morning."

"The girls?"

"They're fine. They have colds, that's all. Nothing serious. A few more days and Dr. Merrill says Meg can return to school."

She blinked, trying to clear her vision. "I remember falling into the water and something hitting my head. Just when everything went dark, I thought I heard someone calling my name . . ." She paused. "Was it you?"

Simon sat down beside the bed. He nodded. "I couldn't believe it when I saw your wagon tracks diverge from the trail. I was so worried. The old bridge on that road was half rotten when I was courting Ellen." He traced her hairline. "You were very brave, Gen. You saved the girls."

"I was stupid," she said quickly. "I should have waited to be rescued."

"I would have done exactly what you did," he said quietly. "Daisy and Darby are strong and unusually trustworthy. I would have driven them in and trusted them to get me across. It's not your fault."

"Tell me what happened after—after I went under," she demanded.

Simon recounted the story, pausing only long enough to get a drink of water when he began to cough. When Gen expressed concern, he waved his hand in the air, shaking his head. "It's only a little cough hanging on. I'm fine. The doctor is amazed. And frankly, so am I. Everyone says that after a winter like the last one, I should have a permanent weakness in my lungs. Everyone says I should be barely clinging to life." He stood up and smiled down at her. "Obviously everyone is wrong." He leaned down and kissed her cheek. "The only thing that remains is for you to get those stitches out in a few days. I'm afraid you're going to have to leave your hair down until that gash heals. You cannot believe the amount of blood—" He stopped abruptly. "Never mind."

It wasn't long before Gen's stitches came out, her hair went back up atop her head, Meg returned to school, Hope felt well enough to throw her share of temper tantrums. Life returned to normal, and except for Simon's slight, persistent cough, no one seemed any worse for the ordeal that would forever mark the Burnsides' Festival of 1865 as the most memorable ever.

It began as such a little thing. But Simon's persistent cough would not go away. Everything Dr. Merrill prescribed failed. They visited other doctors, who could offer no help. And while Simon insisted he would be fine, as the weeks went on, Gen saw hints that all was not well. He began to sleep later and seemed to have unusual difficulty rousing himself out of bed. He eschewed his walk to church in favor of riding with Jane and Elliot. Gen noticed he was short of breath after any little exertion. Even climbing the stairs to go to bed at night left him wheezing and out of breath. Finally, he began to have frequent fevers. He would spend a few days in bed and then proclaim himself well and drag himself off to mission meetings or other activities.

By the time he finally admitted that something might be seriously amiss, he had been in bed for nearly a full week, fighting raging fevers. When he began to cough up blood, Gen went against his wishes and called for Dr. Merrill's return. When the doctor came out of Simon's room, he looked at the circle of adults waiting for his verdict and said, simply, "Pneumonia."

Gen looked at Elliot and Jane, and at Mrs. Leighton. "I think we already knew." She paused. "How long?"

"Impossible to say," the doctor replied.

"Months or weeks?" Gen demanded to know.

"Weeks," the doctor said. "But I may be wrong. I often am. He's a determined man. He's fought it more than once and won." He shook his head and put his hat back on his head.

The moment he had gone, Gen slumped on the couch, hiding her face in her hands. "Why didn't I just wait for him? Why did I think I could drive us alone?"

"Don't," Jane said. "Any one of us would have done the same. It isn't your fault. Simon's been neglecting his health for years. We all know that." She gave Gen a gentle shake. "*You* know that. Elliot and I will take care of the children. You just worry about keeping Simon comfortable."

And so began a new season of life. Only a few days after the doctor's visit, Simon went to his room to rest, and did not have the strength to get up. Mrs. Leighton wanted to hire a nurse. Gen refused. Never, people would say, had they seen such devotion. And from an *Indian*, others would add with surprise.

"Genevieve."

From where she lay huddled on the rug beside Simon's bed, Gen started awake. She lay with her eyes closed for a moment, thinking perhaps she had been dreaming.

"Genevieve, are you there?"

Turning around, she took Simon's hand. "I'm here, dear. Right beside you."

Simon lay so quiet she thought he had fallen back asleep. She watched him, heartened that his breathing seemed to come more easily. Perhaps his fever had broken. When she laid her open palm across his forehead, it was cool. She thanked God.

"What time is it?"

"I don't know, really. Not dawn, yet."

"Sit beside me."

Gen got up and perched on the edge of the mattress next to her frail husband.

He didn't open his eyes, but he pressed her hand in his as a faint smile brightened his tired face. He took a slow breath and opened his eyes. "Light a lamp so I can see you more clearly."

As Gen lit the lamp at his bedside, she leaned over to peer out the window. "I can see the very first tinges of pink in the sky now," she said softly. "It will be dawn soon."

"You've been asleep on the floor?"

Gen sat down beside him again, nodding. She stretched and grimaced. "And I must say you should hurry and get well because it's a hard night's rest on that rag rug." She was surprised when her attempt to cheer him resulted in tears welling up in his eyes.

He gave the slightest shake of his head. "I don't deserve such devotion." He closed his eyes again as tears trickled out of the corners of his eyes, across his temples and into his hair.

Gen wiped away his tears with the corner of a linen handkerchief.

"Water," he croaked. "Could you get me a glass of water?"

Gen got up and crossed the room to the marble-topped nightstand where Dr. Merrill had left an assortment of powders and medicines alongside the blue-and-white pitcher and bowl.

After a few sips of water, Simon settled back against his pillow and sighed. "I love you, Genevieve. But not—" His voice broke. "Not as much as I have loved myself." He swiped his hand across his forehead before pointing toward the nightstand. "Bottom drawer. A book. Bring it."

Gen recognized the book immediately. Clutching it to her chest, she drew a high-backed oak chair to the bedside and sat down.

He opened his eyes. "Open it," he said. "Behold how selfish a man you married."

Gen opened the book, obediently turning the pages before she looked up at him. "I don't understand. How could your having my father's journal be a testimony to selfishness? I—I thank you for letting me see it."

He lifted his chin and pressed his head back into the pillow, straining to fill his lungs with air. "Help me sit up a little, will you?"

While Simon clung to her arm and raised himself up, Gen added more pillows behind him. Before she could sit back down, he clutched her hand and brought it to his cheek, bathing it with silent tears. "Having you in my life," he gasped, "has been such joy. At times I was nearly afraid to breathe for fear I would waken from the dream." He released her hand, moistening his lips before continuing. "You gave me every happiness I imagined, Gen—and some I never dared hope for." He looked up at the ceiling. "I sound half mad, don't I?" Finally, he looked at her. "I kept you for myself, Gen. He told me to do it, and I convinced myself it was for the best, but now—" He sighed.

"Stop talking like you aren't going to get well, Simon," Gen said, half frightened.

He looked at her, his eyes bright with emotion. "Stop pretending I am, Genevieve. It doesn't help." He began to talk, the words pouring out like water from a broken dam. "I didn't know it then, but Daniel Two Stars did *not* get hanged in Mankato. Elliot and I saw him. Last winter. At Fort Ridgely. He—he gave me this—" Simon touched the diary. "—And he said to forget I had seen him." He stole a glance at Gen before continuing. "I wanted you so badly for myself, Gen. And for the children." He almost whispered, "Mostly for myself." When he began to cry again, Gen held his hand between hers. "Part of me thinks you should hate me for keeping you from him. I—I cannot bear to think of meeting God with this unconfessed." He turned his face away.

The misery in Simon's face sent a raging torrent of sympathetic love tearing through Gen's heart. "Don't—don't," she urged, grasping his hand. He tried to pull away, but she forced him to let her raise it to her lips and then to her cheek where her own tears moistened the paper-thin skin. She laid her open palm against his cheek and made him turn his face back toward her. "Look at me, dear. Look at me," she whispered. When he finally did, she said, "I've known about Daniel all along."

He looked at her, disbelieving.

"When you were so ill in St. Anthony, I went to empty your bags so I could do the laundry. The journal fell out." She looked down at their clasped hands, murmuring, "I knew there was only one way you could have gotten it. I knew it meant something about Two Stars. Elliot told me what happened."

"Elliot? Told you?"

Gen nodded. "He found me looking at it. I made him tell me." She saw the question in his eyes and answered it before he spoke. "Yes," Gen said softly, brushing his hair back from his forehead. "I knew. And yet I married *you*. And I learned to love *you*. And I would marry you again, and love you still more were I given another lifetime to do it in." She kissed his cheeks, his chin, his lips. "You are a good husband, Simon. A good father. A good man." Her voice trembled as she continued. "And I don't want you to leave me. To leave us. Please. Don't."

"Can you ever forgive me?"

"For what?" she said gently. "For wanting to protect me from chaos? For doing what Daniel wanted?" She leaned over and nestled her head against his shoulder. "Two wonderful men have loved me and protected me. There is nothing to forgive. I love you, Simon." When it seemed he was asleep, Gen slipped away from him. Taking the journal, she turned the lamp down and sat beside the window leafing through the journal as dawn light began to illuminate the room.

She must have dozed off, when Simon's mutterings woke her again. This time when she went to him, she could see tiny beads of perspiration along his forehead. Frowning, she dampened a cloth and positioned it on his forehead. "Simon," she said quietly. "Are you sleeping?" To her relief, he muttered, "Just dreaming—resting—so glad." He sighed then fell to sleep.

An hour later, as the morning light poured through the window next to his bed, he woke abruptly and said, "I need Elliot."

Gen stood up, took the cloth off his forehead and dipped it into the china basin at his bedside.

"Don't." He shook his head. His eyes were bright as he looked up at her and repeated, "Elliot." He inhaled sharply, then closed his eyes as if the effort to breathe wearied him. "Alone."

"I'll get him." Her petticoats rustled as she moved toward the door and made her way down the hall. She knocked gently at Elliot and Miss Jane's door, smiling to herself at the realization that although Elliot and Jane had been married for months, Gen continued to think of her friend as *Miss* Jane.

Jane responded quickly to Gen's slight tapping on the bedroom door. Peeping from beneath her nightcap she grabbed Gen's hand. "Oh, no!"

Gen shook her head. "It's not that. He has a slight fever again, but I think he's better. He's asking for Elliot."

"I'll come immediately." Elliot's deep voice sounded from the shadows in the room. True to his word, he stepped out into the hall so quickly Gen wondered if he might have been sleeping in his clothes. Only his shirt, open at the neck, gave an indication he had hurried to get dressed.

"Alone, Genevieve," Simon said almost sternly when the two opened his door.

With a little frown, Gen left the room, hesitating in the hall. If she went downstairs she would have to contend with the servants who seemed to resent it when she made herself at home in their kitchen. She went to the top of the broad staircase and sat down, tipping her head back against the wall to look out the Palladian window and down on the garden. It was barren now, but in spring and summer it was one of the most admired gardens in the village. Mother Leighton prided herself on her talents with roses. She had promised Meg her own corner of the garden this spring.

Gen sighed and rubbed the back of her neck. Elliot exited the room and walked past her on his way downstairs. "We'll be a while," he said gently. "Why don't you take the opportunity to get some sleep?" Without waiting for her reply, he continued downstairs. He came back up again bearing a sheaf of paper, an ink bottle, and a pen.

"Mrs. Dane?" Betsy called from the foot of the stairs. "Is everything all right?"

Gen stretched and started to get up. "I think so. Mr. Leighton is with the reverend." She smiled. "I've been dismissed."

"Can I get you anything?" Betsy asked.

"I'd love some strong coffee," Gen said. "I just didn't want to invade your territory."

Betsy grinned. "Cook guards the kitchen like it was the last stand in a battle. But this is Cook's day off, and *I* certainly don't mind if you make yourself at home in the kitchen."

Simon lifted his head off the pillow and wheezed, "Promise me you will do it, Elliot. On God's Word. Promise."

Elliot looked up from his papers. "You have my word."

Simon peered into his brother-in-law's eyes for a moment before relaxing back against his pillow with a sigh. "Thank you, Elliot. You have been a good brother."

A few days later, Gen sat in the parlor with Jane, waiting for

Dr. Merrill to come down from Simon's room. When he did, his face did not reveal what the women wanted to see. "But only a week ago you said he had survived the worst," Gen said, her voice wavering. Jane put a comforting hand on Gen's arm.

"I know," the doctor said, stroking his beard self-consciously. "I was wrong. We could expect him to throw it off if he had been in better health, but I'm afraid he's let his general constitution become so run down that even the slightest compromise in his lungs can be serious. And this is more than a slight compromise." He sighed. "Perhaps I am wrong. A person's own will can work miracles. I've seen it happen before. But I've also seen strong-willed individuals succumb to lesser cases. Life and death are in God's hands, Mrs. Dane. I will do all I can." He headed for the back door.

Gen went to Simon, who was resting quietly. "What does he say?" he asked without opening his eyes.

"That there is always hope," Gen answered.

After a moment, Simon whispered, "I'm not afraid, Gen. I've lived a good life. God knows the best time to take me home. And if I am to go now, I do not wish to linger long, although I would be glad to stay longer for the children's sake."

"Stay for *me*," Gen begged, sitting down next to him. "Stay for me."

"I'm tired, Gen," he said, and slipped away. She thought at first he was asleep, but soon realized he was nearly unconscious. His skin felt clammy.

Over the next few days, Simon had odd moments of lucidity when he woke and surprised whoever was tending him with a memory of the past or a comment on some biblical concept. Once, he asked Elliot to read hymns aloud. Another time he requested the Psalms. Meg sang to him. Aaron read an essay he had written on the greatness of God. Several times Simon gave Gen suggestions for the future, insisting that she repeat what he had said, eliciting her promise to obey him.

He wanted the children raised in New York, he said. The schools were better. "Where else would we go, dear?" Gen reassured him.

"They love Jane and Elliot, don't they?" he asked once.

"Of course," Gen said. "It's almost as if they have two sets of parents."

Simon complained of feeling dull and stupid. "I can't make my mind think on anything for more than a second," he murmured, "I don't ever remember feeling so tired."

When fever raged, his mind wandered and fastened onto impossible, imaginary things. He tried to get out of bed one night and mount an imaginary horse. "But I have to get to Cloudman's village, Gen—they want me to marry Blue Eyes and Two Stars—they've been waiting—let me go."

It was several moments before Gen could calm him down. When she did, she sat back in her chair, trembling.

One morning, he asked what day it was. "The Sabbath," Gen answered, and commented that the children had walked up the street with Jane and Elliot to attend church.

"Ah," Simon said, smiling happily. "I think He may come for me today, Gen." He sighed. "I hope He does."

That evening, Simon's breathing changed. Dr. Merrill was summoned. He had only stepped into Simon's room when he shook his head. "The battle will be over soon," he said quietly, looking at Gen. "If his children want to see him—"

Meg and Aaron kissed his cheek.

Hope called out, "Pa! Pa!" And strained to climb onto the bed.

Aaron scooped her up and nuzzled her cheek. "Pa's sleeping, Hope."

"Night-night, Pa," Hope said, waving at Simon as Aaron carried her out of the room.

When Gen put her hand on Meg's head and stroked her red

curls, Meg asked in a forced whisper, "Do you think he'll see Mother right away?"

"The minute he's gone from us he will be there—with your mother."

Meg kissed her father on the cheek and whispered, "Tell Mother hello, Father. Tell her we are safe at Grandma's and we are all right."

In the evening, Simon roused enough to swallow a few drops of tea. Gen slipped out of the room and went to say prayers with Meg. When she came back to his side, he was gone.

"He opened his eyes," Jane said, "called out the name Ellen . . . and then took a long, slow breath . . . and that was all."

*That was all.* The phrase echoed in Gen's mind over the next few weeks. Eventually her prayers cried it out to God. *Was that all, Lord? Was that all You had for me? Is my life over now?*

She donned the mourning clothes Mrs. Leighton deemed appropriate and never went out in public with her face unveiled. Sabbath services were her only outing.

Not long after Simon's funeral, Elliot Leighton left for Washington. He sent them a copy of the new agent's report about conditions at Crow Creek. *One bastion of the stockade has no roof. Plastering is needed, fences in poor condition, prairie sod badly broken. Only two cows and seventeen wagons, mostly in poor condition, to serve the population of 1,043 Indians—900 of them women. Of 170 ox-yokes only thirty serviceable. A leaky boiler in the sawmill, and spoiled beef to eat. Potatoes ravaged by grasshoppers and bugs. Many Indians still living in cloth tepees brought from Minnesota two years ago.* His letter concluded with, *I will not have time to return to New York before departing with a commission appointed to assess the situation firsthand. At last Avery has listened to me. Perhaps now something can be done.*

When Jane read the letter aloud at dinner one April morning, Gen felt a sudden stab of jealousy at Elliot's easy departure for the

West. Men had such different lives from women. She looked down at her black dress, smoothing the folds of her skirt. *Lord, make me willing to be content.* She spent hours in the garden working alongside Mrs. Leighton, inhaling the aroma of the damp earth, coaxing the tendrils of a vine onto the latticework gazebo, thinning raspberry bushes, doing a thousand other things to encourage new life.

Every afternoon when Hope napped she walked up the street and into the brick-walled cemetery, perching on the stone bench beside Simon's and Ellen Dane's graves. She could not shake the sensation that she was waiting for something—some new event or announcement that would suddenly give life as a widow new meaning. She told herself this was just grief working its way in her life. Still, she felt as if she were suspended in life like the marionettes she and the children had once seen perform at a county fair.

As soon as the soil could be worked, they began Meg's promised garden. Meg and her grandmother mulled over plans every evening until they decided on an L-shaped plot in one corner of the yard. Meg was thrilled when her grandmother said she might have a small reflecting pool in the middle. "And we're going to have roses," she told Gen one evening over supper. "One bush for each member of the family. What color would you like?"

Gen didn't know. "I don't know very much about roses, Meg. Whatever you and your grandmother decide will be fine."

Aaron dug the new garden with Meg and Hope working at his side picking rocks from the fresh-turned soil and carrying them to the edge of the flower bed where the women used them for edging.

"Grandmother says Mother loved red roses. So we'll have red for Mother and Father. Pink for us children, and yellow for Uncle Elliot and Aunt Jane," she said. From where she knelt in the garden she looked up at Gen. "And white for you and Grandmother, Gen."

"What color for Hope?" Gen asked.

"Meg said pink for the children," Mrs. Leighton said. "She is one of ours now." She tapped Meg's nose. "And you must teach her to call me Grandmother."

Gen squeezed Mrs. Leighton's shoulder. "Thank you," she said, surprised when her eyes filled with tears.

The rosebushes arrived in a special container sent from a private garden. Gen lingered in the garden long after everyone else wandered off to pursue other concerns. From her seat on the swing beneath an oak tree, she gazed at the nine healthy bushes, marveling at the ability to order plants that might bloom the very first year they were planted. She was happy to see her vine obediently climbing the latticework up one side of the gazebo standing against the stone wall on the opposite side of the garden. Mrs. Leighton told her it was honeysuckle and would attract honeybees and hummingbirds to its orange flowers. It reminded Gen of the wild vine Jane had planted and replanted until it grew up and over the teachers' cottage porch back at the mission in Minnesota.

*Minnesota.* Gen closed her eyes, remembering. When she opened them, she looked up at the blue sky and, as she had as a child, began to imagine figures in the clouds; a horse's head, a turtle, a bird. The game brought back sweet memories . . . and one deep hurt. She must never speak of it to anyone. She was a widow, a resident of New York State, mother to three adopted children. She would be content, she told herself. Sighing, she got up and went inside. It would be summer soon. She should be glad she wasn't back in Minnesota where Elliot said drought was making it almost impossible to grow food, where life was chaos. She should be glad. But she was not.

# Twenty-Nine

"For as the heavens are higher than the earth,
so are my ways higher than your ways,
and my thoughts than your thoughts."

—ISAIAH 55:9

*IN THE MATTER OF MY CHILDREN, AARON RIGGS AND Margaret Marie Dane, and my adopted daughter, Hope Ellen Dane, my desire is that they be remanded to the care of Mr. and Mrs. Elliot Stephen Leighton, to become their legal wards and to be educated in New York.*

Gen's dark eyes widened. She looked at Elliot and Jane, but neither of them returned her gaze. Studying their profiles, she could see they were not surprised. Nor was Mrs. Leighton. Even Aaron, who had been allowed to come, would not look at her. He stood behind Elliot, his hands stuffed in his pockets. At least, Gen thought, she caught a glimmer of a tear in his eyes.

The lawyer's voice droned on, but Gen didn't hear anything after the awful sentence that ripped away the center of her world. She looked down at her hands clasped in her lap and bit her lower lip. At least, she thought, she would not break down and sob. She sat, head bowed, while tears coursed down her cheeks and dripped off her jaw and onto her hands. *Why, Simon? What did I do?* She closed her eyes.

The lawyer's voice receded to a background drone. She felt dizzy and realized she was hardly breathing. *I will not faint in a lawyer's office*, she thought, and willed herself to breathe evenly. She must have done something terrible. She searched the past, castigating herself for every failure, every argument. There must be some clue, if only she could remember what she had done to make him do this. He was not mean-spirited. He had a reason. She must know. She must.

Elliot's hand was on her arm. "Gen."

She blinked and looked at him. He was handing her something. She looked stupidly around the room. Everyone had gone. Everyone except Jane and Elliot.

"This is from Simon. I'm sorry it's taken so long but—" He thrust the letter at her and sat down. "You'll understand why it had to be this way. Just read the letter."

*Beloved wife,*

*If you are reading this, it means that Elliot has succeeded in accomplishing the task with which I charged him on that day when I ordered you out of my room so that I could speak with him alone. Would that I could write something poetic, something beautiful that you would remember. Forgive me for not having the energy to say everything on my heart. I love you. You have given me everything a man could wish for. And now, I am giving you the only thing I can think of that will tell you how much I love you.*

*Elliot has found Daniel Two Stars. I want you to go to him and to live a happy life.*

Gen caught her breath. She put one hand over her mouth and blinked back fresh tears. How could he think she would do that? The words of Simon's will came back. This was why he had given the children to Jane. To free her. She would not let him do it. She could not. She frowned and looked up at Jane.

"I know what you are thinking," Jane said. "Keep reading. Don't say anything until you finish reading."

*You cannot be both mother to my children and wife to Daniel. Society would not allow it. They would take their stupid hatreds and prejudices out on the children. Forgive me for the heartache this must cause you. As you read this, know that Elliot and Jane have already spoken to Aaron and Meg. My instructions were that if Aaron and Meg could not part with you willingly, that Elliot was to take the knowledge of Daniel to his grave. Again, the fact that you are reading this letter means they have, as much as they can, agreed that you should go. They will have a good home here in New York. An education and the best of futures. Elliot has promised me they will visit you.*

*I have loved you with all of my heart that did not already belong to Ellen. I believe you loved me in the same way— with all of your heart that did not already belong to Daniel Two Stars. Ellen and I are together again. I want the same for you and Daniel.*

*Someday, dear Genevieve, you will cross over and be rewarded for your unselfish commitment to me. I will be there and my love will not be diminished.*

*Until THAT DAY . . .*
*Simon*

Gen laid the letter in her lap. She was trembling all over. "How—how can this be?" She looked from Jane to Elliot. "I can't. I can't just walk away from the children. I love them."

"Of course you do," Jane broke in. "And they love you. But they don't want to go back to Minnesota. And you belong there. Not here."

Gen rested her chin in the palm of her hand. Then, she got up and crossed the room to peer out the window and up the street toward the churchyard. She shook her head. "This is too— strange." She looked at Elliot, her eyes pleading. "Why did he have you do this Elliot? Really. Why?"

"Is it so difficult to believe that he did it simply for you?" Jane interrupted. "Do you think you are the only one capable of unselfish love?"

"Of course not," Gen said quickly. "That's not what I meant."

"Your emotions are in a muddle," Jane said. "Take a walk. Think about it. We'll be at the house." She tugged on Elliot's coat and reached inside. "While you are thinking, you can open this." She pressed a small package into Gen's hand and fairly shoved her out the door.

It was a beautiful spring day. Gen walked past the Leighton's and up the hill to the churchyard. Sitting down on the now-familiar cement bench beside Ellen's and Simon's graves, she laid the brown-paper package in her lap.

*Oh Lord, show me what to do. This seems impossible. So selfish.*

She untied the package in her lap, and stared in disbelief at a metal cross hanging from a beaded necklace. She closed her eyes. She could still see him, shaggy black hair, a plaid shirt with sleeves rolled up . . . and this very necklace.

The iron cemetery gate creaked. She turned her head just as Aaron stepped through. He came toward her, his hands shoved in his pockets. He sat next to her on the stone bench. After a moment or two of awkward silence he leaned down and picked up a twig, twirling it between his thumb and index finger nervously. "We were waiting for you at the house."

Gen sighed and picked up Two Stars's necklace. "Do you remember this?"

Aaron nodded. "You used to have one just like it. What happened to it?"

"I took it off and put it away when I decided to marry your father," she said. "Eventually I threw it away. To show God I meant to cut all the ties to the past and to be happy here."

"But you aren't happy here," Aaron said softly, looking up at her, his dark brown eyes filled with understanding far beyond his years. "You love us and you want to do what is right. But you aren't happy."

"Neither are you. We are all sad. It's a sad time in our lives."

Aaron shook his head. "I don't mean Father's dying. With you, it's different." He pursed his lips together. "Father always said I grew up a lot when I was with him at Crow Creek. He said I had a gift for understanding other people's problems." He looked down at the grass. "I think maybe Father was right."

Gen put her arm around Aaron's shoulders. "I know he was right. Someday you are going to make him very proud by doing wonderful things for other people."

"Let me start with you." He cleared his throat. Pushing himself away from her motherly embrace, he said, "We want you to go home where you belong. We'll come visit. It's not like we're saying good-bye or anything. I'm going to the military academy next year. Uncle Elliot said he would help me get in. Meg loves her Aunt Jane. She's going to be very happy tending her rose garden and living here with Grandmother. And Hope—"

"Hope would forget me," Gen said, her voice breaking. She swallowed hard. "She's too young to remember."

"We won't let her forget you," Aaron said abruptly. "We'll never let her forget."

Suddenly Aaron grabbed Gen. He hugged her fiercely. "You belong in Minnesota with Two Stars. Father wanted you to go. And *so do we*." When Gen said nothing, he asked to see the necklace Two Stars had sent and quickly slipped it over her head. "You always told me to do what God wants. I think God wants me to become a soldier so I can go west and help as an interpreter. Sometimes it scares me, but I'm going to do it." He looked at her again, his dark eyes shining with courage and honesty far beyond his years. "It seems to me God has gone to a lot of trouble for you and Two Stars. How can you say no?"

When Gen still did not speak, Aaron said, "Will you at least think about it?"

She nodded. "But I don't think I will be able to change my mind."

"He's happy, Gen. He's with Mother. Why shouldn't you be with Two Stars? You aren't abandoning us. We *like* it here in New York. And we want you to be happy." He sighed and ran his hand through his hair.

Gen shook her head slowly and stood up. "Your father used to do that." She rumpled Aaron's hair. "Although he didn't have nearly as much hair to mess up." She smiled. "Walk me back to the house."

"What are you going to do?" he demanded as they opened the iron cemetery gate and stepped onto the road.

"I can't leave."

He pulled the gate closed and offered his arm. "Do you remember telling me about the time you argued with your father about coming to our house to school?"

Gen nodded, slipping her hand beneath his arm, realizing that he was taller than she.

"Do you remember what you yelled at your father?"

She let out a little breath of frustration and looked away. She nodded.

Aaron said it for her. "You said, 'I'm not going and you can't make me!' And you said you finally realized your father knew what was best for you, even though at the time you didn't understand it."

Gen put her hand on Aaron's arm. "All right, Mr. Thirteen-going-on-thirty. I understand what you are trying to say. Now hush and walk me home."

"I can't," Aaron said. "I can't walk you all the way to Minnesota."

Together, they made their way back to Leighton Hall.

He wasn't ready. Brushing away the sweat running down his face with the back of his sleeve, Two Stars squinted toward a farm wagon coming up the road from the direction of Fort Ridgely.

"You expecting company?" Jeb Grant teased, tossing another ear of corn into the back of his wagon and staring toward the newcomer. He clucked his tongue. "Hoo-ee. Neighbors must know some hi-falutin' people. That there's a parasol. I ain't seen one of them since Marjorie's ma carried one to our weddin' back east." He wiped the palms of his hands on his backside and headed back into his stand of corn to refill the burlap bag slung over his shoulder.

At the mention of the East, Daniel almost panicked. What if it was—he glanced down at the sweat staining the front of his shirt, the field dust splashed across his thighs. He brushed his hands through his shaggy black hair. It had grown too long this summer, what with working all day for Jeb and then building two log cabins. Robert and Nancy had insisted on finishing his first. But with all the work, things like haircuts hadn't seemed important.

But as the wagon grew closer and he strained to see the tiny figure holding the white parasol, he nearly panicked. He smelled like a filthy field hand who hadn't had a bath in a couple of days. He should run away, he thought. But the sight of her made him catch his breath, and so instead of disappearing into Jeb's cornfield and buying himself some time to get presentable, he walked around the back of the farm wagon and headed for the road.

The tiny figure perched on the wagon seat lifted her hand to her throat, and then raised it to shield her eyes, as if the parasol didn't even exist. She motioned to the wagon driver and he pulled his team up. Tossing the parasol into the wagon bed behind her, she jumped down from the wagon seat and began to run. He felt as he had in the dream long ago, as if he could not move . . . but he must have managed it, because there she was in his arms, looking up at him with those blue eyes, her eyes brimming with tears as she whispered his name in Dakota.

When she looked up at him, he traced her eyebrows, ran his finger along her hairline and her jaw, touching the dimple in her chin. "Those eyes have followed me everywhere. Just as I said that night when you stood on Miss Jane's porch in the moonlight." He clutched her to him and now it was his turn to cry. Tears of joy welled up in his eyes and overflowed, running down his cheeks, dampening her dark hair. He held her close, looking across the road to the cabins he and Robert had built this summer. They were small—only two rooms. But he had dreams. Not big dreams, like Jeb Grant, who wanted to be the biggest landholder in the county. No, Daniel thought with a smile. His dreams were small compared to Jeb's. He only wanted this woman in his arms . . . and the chance to add another room to the little cabin across the road someday. For a son. Or perhaps a daughter with abundant dark hair and blue eyes.

Daniel looked down at Gen. He pushed her hair back out of

her eyes. He whispered gently in Dakota, *"Wastecidaka . . . I love you . . ."* and when he kissed her it was just as he had dreamed, as if the last three years were nothing, as if they had never been apart.

"Now unto him that is able to do exceeding abundantly above all that we ask or think . . . Unto him be glory in the church by Christ Jesus throughout all ages, world without end. Amen."

—EPHESIANS 3:20–21

# About the Author

Today, Stephanie and her children live in southeast Nebraska where Stephanie pursues a full-time writing ministry from her home studio. She is the author of eight books, including the bestselling Prairie Winds series: *Walks the Fire, Soaring Eagle,* and *Red Bird;* as well as the Keepsake Legacies series: *Sarah's Patchwork, Karyn's Memory Box,* and *Nora's Ribbon of Memories* and the Dakota Moons series: *Valley of the Shadow, Edge of the Wilderness,* and as yet untitled book three that is to be released in the winter of 2001-2002.

Widowed early in 2001, Stephanie is active in her local independent Bible church and accepts a limited number of speaking engagements each year. She can be reached at the following address:

Stephanie Grace Whitson
3800 Old Cheney Road #101-178
Lincoln, NE 68516